Other Books by Joel B Reed

The Jazz Phillips Mystery Series

Murder in the Choir*

Murder by the Board*

Murder in the Kirk*

Murder was a Blast*

Murder by the Queen*

Murder on the Run*

Jazz in the Cross-hair*

Jazz in the Golden Light*

Jazz Plays the Big Easy Blues*

Jazz Draws a Wild Card*

Jazz and the Black Widow*

The Cowboy McKee Intrigue Series

Angels Fight Dirty*

Black Seraph*

Children of Dust*

A Devil on DOS*

Even Angels Cry*

Other Novels

Lakota Spring*

Paul Radford's Private War*

Paul Radford's Alaskan Exile*

Raven Wolf (Journal of Martin Quinn)*

Ashes in the Outhouse*

Ashes of the Dead*

(*Available in print)

Peru 1943

ECUADOR

- Quito

COLOMBIA

JUNGLE

BRAZIL

- Trujillo

ANDES

- Tingo Maria

● Cerro de Pasco

JUNGLE

Lima ●

- Huancayo

Puerto
Maldonado ●

Pisco ●

●Ayacucho

● Cusco

Rancho Lopez ●

ANDES

Puno
●

La Paz
●

COASTAL DESERT

Camana ●

BOLIVIA

|----200 MILES----|

CHILE

This is a work of fiction. Except for historical people and geographic places, nothing written here is intended to represent any actual person, living or dead, or any actual place or event. The exceptions are Victor Haya de la Torre, political leader and statesman from Trujillo, Perú, whom I admire, and the late J. Edgar Hoover, Director of the FBI, whom I have tried to portray accurately and fairly from historical records. To put it simply, none of the stuff in this book ever happened , but it could have.

The quotation on page 44 is from "The Hound of Heaven" by Francis Thompson, first published in 1893. It resides in the common domain.

ISBN: 978-1-933482-17-0

Cover design by Joel B. Reed

White Turtle Books
Canby, Minnesota
WhiteTurtleBooks.com

Paul Radford's

Return to Peru

by

Joel B Reed

White Turtle Books
Canby, Minnesota

And how am I to face the odds
Of man's bedevilment and God's?
I, a stranger and afraid
In a world I never made.

Alfred E. Housman, *Last Poems*

Prologue

Marfa, Texas. The mood was tense as the four men sat around a large table. It was a stark briefing room, one that was often filled with tension. The briefings here could make the difference between who lived and who died.

The briefing room was at the headquarters for the Army airbase and the special group commander's office was just down the hall. The walls of the room were covered with maps designed to roll up like window shades, concealing the information they held, and the door was kept locked when the room was not in use. Yet, there was no guard stationed in the hallway. Security lay in stealth and discreet surveillance of the isolated hallway that led to it. There was only one way in and out, and a guard at the door would draw unwanted attention. The stenciled sign on the door told the world this was SUPPLY ROOM 8.

Even so, there were no supplies in the room except those needed for briefings. Nor were there any windows and the walls were soundproof. It was designed that way for security. Windows could be opened, allowing listeners outside to hear every word spoken. Lives depended on secure briefings. There was a war on and the enemy had ears, even on an Army Air Corps base. So fresh air was pumped in by a swamp cooler in the warm months and routed down a long duct designed to trap and absorb sound. A forced air furnace delivered warmth on cool days though the same ducts. It was needed far less than the huge cooler.

The four men seated around the table were an unusual collection of military officers. They were the command cadre of a special operations group responsible only to the President and to a select group of congressmen. The existence of this Special Action Group, or SAG in military speak, was a closely kept secret. Its leaders were drawn from every branch of the armed services and its mission was to forestall disasters like Pearl Harbor. The first mandate was gathering and assessing intelligence. The second was to plan and carry out covert missions to thwart the enemy at every turn and to twist his plans into disasters against him.

To carry out the second part of the mission, SAG recruited a carefully screened company of officers and enlisted men. Most of these men were from the Marine Corps, but at the moment the command cadre was discussing a Navy lieutenant named Paul Radford. Though the lieutenant had served them well before in Perú, the question was whether they could still rely on him to carry out a tough assignment.

"I don't know," Alex White, the Executive Officer said. "When I talked to him it was like his body is present, but there's no one at home. I don't know exactly what happened to him in Alaska but he sure has changed."

"To be very honest, he worries me," said Eric Rudd, the group commander. "There's something very wrong there. I wonder if we ought to use him at all. He's too damned cold and he keeps it all inside. I'm afraid he might go off the deep end."

Denis Blieu, third in command, nodded. "I know. The last thing we need is a loose canon on the deck in South America. On the other hand, you busted your butt to get him reassigned. What are we going to do with him if we don't send him to keep an eye on Haya and his commies? Who else can we get? We don't have a lot of time."

Rudd looked at Jacques Paul, their intelligence analyst and chief of field operations. He was the only Army officer in the group, on loan from Army Intelligence. "What do you think, Jock? You think you can work with him?"

The other shrugged. "Well, he hasn't done anything to tell me otherwise. He certainly handled himself well in that fire fight in Perú and there is nothing but good marks in his record from Alaska. Not many people would volunteer for the assignments he took while he was up there, and the colonel he was serving under bitched like hell at loosing him. They put Radford up for a Navy Cross and two Silver Stars. I'd guess whatever is eating at him is something very personal. Maybe the change will do him good. I'd say let's go with him."

"What about you, Denis?" Rudd inquired. "It's your call, too. You won't be working with him directly but he could affect your operations if he goes bad."

Blieu shook his head. "I don't know what to say, Eric. The file says nothing but good about him and he's done good work for us before. He's also a personal friend, but I don't know. We wouldn't be doing him any favors dumping him into a mess he can't handle."

"Oh, I can handle it, all right," came a deathly quiet voice from the doorway. Paul Radford stood there watching them, a faintly mocking smile on his lips. "I came back to ask Denis something. Why are you talking about me behind my back?" He asked this as if he were inquiring about the weather. "Why don't you just ask me face to face? I don't lie."

"You've changed, Paul," Blieu said. "We don't understand the change and it worries us."

Radford shrugged. "I've had some personal problems," he told them. "Now they're under control and they haven't affected my work, have they? What's the deal with Victor Haya? What's he done now?"

"You know him?" Jacques Paul asked.

"Not that well," Radford answered. "We argued politics over beer one night in Lima. I didn't agree with him but I respect him. He's very sharp. He's probably very dangerous, too." The sound of his voice as he spoke was as disembodied as an echo. "So if that's who you're thinking of linking me up with, there's rapport. Or, there was."

Radford stopped and looked around the room. "Unless, of course, you think I'm unfit." He shrugged and sat down. "Personally, I don't give a shit either way," he added, lighting a cigarette. There was no defiance in his tone, just a simple statement of fact. "I'd just as soon go back to Alaska. At least I'm wanted there."

There was quiet for a long time. Finally Rudd spoke. "What I need to know, Paul, is very simple. Can I can trust you?"

"I don't know, Commander," Radford answered quietly. "I don't trust many people myself these days. I guess you can trust me to be who I am, what the hell ever that is."

Radford grinned and took a drag on his cigarette. Then he looked at them calmly. "The main thing is, I do know the guy. I respect him, too."

"You wouldn't mind going back to Perú?" Jacques Paul asked.

For a moment there was a passing shadow of something in Radford's eyes, but when he spoke it was in the same quiet tone. Yet there was a hint of interest, too. "No. The heat should be off by now and I can keep a low profile. The way the Senator described it, I'd mostly be in the back country."

There was silence and Radford looked around the room. "Look, Commander," he said, his voice close to normal. "I'm not going to screw things up. What the hell. Winter's coming. Chasing bananas sure beats the hell out of freezing my nuts off in Nome, all right?" A ghost of a smile played around the edges of his mouth, though the smile didn't reach his eyes. Then Radford chuckled. "I kind of like the idea of Uncle Sam paying my bar bill while I pump Haya for what he knows."

The others laughed, the tension broken.

"That's more like it," Rudd said. "That's the guy I used to know. All right then. You're our man. Alex can make some coffee and we'll go over what we have in the files." He glanced at his watch. "Take five for a head call and a smoke and we'll hit it running."

Cerro de Pasco

1 Perú, October 1943. The man's eyes were compelling. They were hard as burnished steel, unyielding as a glacier. They revealed nothing that lay behind them as they locked on his. Nor was there any hiding from them. They cut through the lies and deceptions, laying bare the depths of his soul. There was no doubt this man was dangerous.

Then the man shifted his gaze. His eyes swept the cafe, looking for danger. It was a dingy place, typical for a mining town. The only thing that set it apart was its German bakery. Two sets of windows flanking the door displayed its goods.

The stranger's eyes lingered briefly on two men sitting at a table to one side, who stopped talking and returned his gaze. Then they moved on to three local men standing at the bar. Seeing no danger, the stranger looked back at the man seated alone and walked straight toward him. The way he moved reminded Haya of a jaguar stalking prey, confident, relaxed, and powerful.

There was no doubt in Haya's mind that he was whom the man was seeking. He thought about reaching for his pistol but did not. He sensed neither threat nor malice in the jaguar man and this was good. Haya also knew the man would probably be on him before he could point his weapon. Nor would he hesitate to kill Victor. Haya was certain of that.

The man reached Victor's table, casually laid his hand on the back of a chair. "May I?" he asked. He spoke softly and the voice was familiar, as was the way the man held himself. Yet Victor could not place him. The full beard and the wide brim of the man's hat obscured his features, and his worn khaki pants and dark plaid shirt gave no clue to his identity. The sturdy hiking boots he was wearing were those favored by local mining engineers. They looked like military issue. As did the flapped leather holster hanging from the man's broad leather belt and the brown leather jacket he wore.

"Please do," Victor told him. When the man sat down he removed his hat and laid it on the table. Haya looked at him closely. "Have we met?" he asked. "You seem familiar."

The man chuckled and Victor had a flash of a younger face, clean-shaven. He was shocked at the change. There were deep lines on either side of the man's nose and around his eyes, and his face was weathered as brown as old leather. "Is that you, Paulo?" he asked quietly, not quite sure he was right. "It's been a long time."

"As big as life and twice as ugly." Radford answered with an easy smile, but Haya noticed that the smile didn't reach his eyes. Yet, the voice was familiar, as was the smile. "It's been seven, eight years by my count."

"It was June, 1937," Haya replied. "I remember it was early winter and I was visiting Lima." He smiled back. "I remember because I was home from exile and I met a lovely lady on that trip. It was just after I met you and she and I wrote wonderful love letters for a while."

"So nothing came of it? That's too bad."

Haya shrugged. "She was married and from another city. You know how it is."

Any reply was interrupted by the waiter. Radford ordered coffee and a slice of the strudel displayed in the front window. His Spanish sounded local, yet it carried a slight twang common to the border area east of El Paso del Norte that Radford called home.

When the waiter left Haya looked at Radford. "Why are you here, Paulo?"

"I prefer Pablo," the other replied and Haya nodded. "I'm here because Tio Samuél sent me to see you."

Haya nodded. "Tio Samuél? I suppose you mean Uncle Sam." The English word sounded alien on Haya's lips, like he was saying, "awn-kell," and Radford smiled. "So what does your government want from me?"

Paul shook his head. "Nothing. They want me to find out what you're up to and keep an eye on you."

"Nothing more than that?"

"I think some of them would like me to kill you, but that's their agenda, not mine. I've killed a lot of people, Victor, but I'm not an assassin."

Haya nodded. "I see. So what is your agenda, Pablo?"

Radford chuckled. It was almost a growl. "I'm trying to thaw out, Victor. They had me chasing Nips in Alaska. I damned near froze off my *juevos*." He looked at his fingers. They were white beneath the tan. "I still feel frostbite when it gets cold like it does in the mountains." Once again there was a bitter edge to his voice. "Believe it or not, that's classified information, my being in Alaska. It's been in the newspaper at home but it's still classified. I suppose if you're going to tell someone, you need to cut your throat first."

Victor nodded and gave this some thought. Radford kept quiet while he did, sipping his coffee as he waited. Then Haya nodded again. "Well, I'm not surprised they sent someone," he murmured. The young man knew when to keep his peace. "As you know, Pablo, I make no bones about my politics and a lot of people in Washington hate socialists. Why did they choose you?"

Paul Radford shrugged. "One reason is that I happen to know you. I also know my way around this part of the world. You may remember I was a roving geologist for a mining company in Perú and Bolivia before the war and I know the back country pretty well. I'm also fluent in Quechua and Spanish. Not to mention *chingada Tejano*."

When Paul said this, he smiled and Haya caught a glimpse of the younger man he'd known. He wondered what happened to make the pleasant young man such a hard-case. "I heard rumors about you, Pablo. I believe it was an old friend on the police force who told me some rather odd things."

Radford nodded. "If it was a captain named Molina, it was probably true. How do you know him?"

"He arrested me when I returned from Mexico in 1931," Haya told him. "I had nothing to hide and was quite candid with him during his interrogation. When I was in prison he came to me looking for information on a murder and I was able to help him. Since then we have found it convenient to exchange information from time to time. Of course, these days it has to be indirect. I'm in hiding from the present government. They want to put me in prison again."

Radford nodded and sat quietly. After a long moment, the older man asked him, "Aren't you curious what Molina told me about you?"

Radford shrugged. "I figured you would either tell me or not, Victor. Molina's an honest man, so what he told you would be what he knows to be the truth. On the other hand, he doesn't know the whole truth. He may suspect it but he doesn't know for sure."

"What he told me is that you set off an international incident that embarrassed Germany."

"That's common knowledge," Paul replied. "The Germans actually embarrassed themselves. They violated Peruvian sovereignty and got caught with their pants down."

"Thereby undercutting the political influence of certain German settlers in Perú," Haya pointed out. "After that he believes you were involved in destroying a secret German sub base off the coast near Camana."

"Molina told you that?" Paul asked, surprised.

"No, not directly. That actually came from another source," Victor told him. "A couple of German officials were overheard talking about it in German. They assumed that their native guide was unable to understand what they were saying."

Radford smiled. "I don't suppose the guide was blind in one eye, was he?" Seeing Haya's surprise he chuckled. "No names, Victor. I'm not going to make the same mistake the *boche* made. We have friends in common."

"I'm surprised that you're here in the city so openly," the other answered. "Aren't you a wanted man, too? My friend from the police told me you offended some very powerful people. I'm certain they have not forgotten."

Radford shrugged. "I may be. It really doesn't matter. The worst they can do to me is kill me. It's no great loss if they do. Why? Are you worried that they'll come down on you for talking to me?"

Haya shook his head. "No, not really. I work very hard to make sure they don't catch me. And if they do, I can tell them the truth. We met a number of years ago and you happened to run into me here. I certainly didn't seek you out." He paused. "How did you know where to find me, Pablo? Here at the top of the world."

Radford smiled. "This is not that big a country, Victor. There are not that many people here and prominent people stand out. Very little happens that isn't noticed and talked about, and you're a public figure, even in hiding. The more interesting question is why you're here."

Haya chuckled. "I'm here for the same reason I go to any other place." he said. "I am a politician and it is useful to talk to people and to be seen. My support is among the people, the little people most politicians ignore. I need to know what they're thinking, how they feel and they need to know I care." He paused and took a couple of deep breaths, almost gasping, then shook his head.

"Are you ill?" Radford asked.

Haya shook his head. "It's the altitude. What I forget, living in Lima most of the time, is how difficult it can be to breathe up here. I seem to have to breathe more when I do much talking. I can't seem to move faster than a slow walk, either." He took another deep breath.

Radford nodded. "We're sitting at over 4,200 meters here. There's about forty percent less oxygen here than on the coast. It takes a few days to adjust." Then he smiled. "Not being able to talk much must be a terrible handicap for a politician."

Haya smiled and nodded. "I never thought of it quite that way, but it is. On the other hand, when one is not talking, there is much to learn."

"So you're here building support for your party."

"No, they might look for me more seriously if I did that. APRA was outlawed in 1935. However, I can still carry the message of *aprismo* to the oppressed. That they haven't declared illegal."

"Yet," Paul replied and Haya nodded. "I'm surprised you travel alone, Victor. Unless those two guys at the bar are your guards. I hope no one's seriously after you."

"They're my guards and my driver will be back soon. I don't like to appear as if I need protection."

Radford nodded. "Yes, but they need some training. The way they're sitting, someone where I am could take them both out with no trouble."

"That would leave me behind them with a loaded pistol in my hand," the other answered.

"Sorry, I meant after taking you out," Radford said. "It's good I'm here as a friend."

"Are you, Pablo?"

"Of course. I meant what I said. I'm no assassin. That doesn't mean they won't send someone else. Who knows? They may even send someone after me."

"Who is 'they,' Pablo? Your government?"

"Yeah, that's who I was thinking of, hard line knuckle-heads. Like J. Edgar Hoover. It could be someone else, too. I'm not very popular with the *fascistias* in Perú. Or the Germans. The point is that you seem to have been pretty lucky, so far. As have I. Or maybe it's true that only the good die young." When he said this, there was a brief flicker of something in Radford's eyes. It disappeared too quickly for him to identify, but Haya was left with a sense of profound grief.

Victor shrugged. "Well, I'm forty-eight now. I wonder how I got this far sometimes. That's about fifteen years longer than most men live in Perú. Here in the mining district, it may be much less. The people here live a very hard life from generations of oppression. They barely earn enough to eat, much less pay for medical care. Even worse, they have no chance to learn what they need to make things change. One of the things I do is give them hope that things will be different for their children."

"You really think so?"

Haya nodded. "Things are changing, Pablo. It may be slow, but they are. It's been almost twenty now since we formed the *Alianza Popular Revolucionaria Americana* in Mexico City, APRA."

Haya paused and smiled, shaking his head. "I have to stop for a breath after saying our full name at this elevation. The point is that APRA is stronger than ever, despite the oppression. *Aprismo* has spread from Mexico to Perú and other areas of South America. The oppressors are gradually losing their grip on their countries, and making APRA illegal has worked in our favor. We have become the party of the little people and, as a result, we suffer the same oppression. Our people know it, too."

Haya paused and looked at Radford. "What I don't understand, Pablo, is why those in power in your country hate us the way they do. We are a democratic movement of the people. We don't advocate violence. Quite the contrary. The revolution we advocate is in how people think. We want to win people's hearts and minds."

"The Russian revolution scared the shit out of people in the States," Paul answered. "Or maybe I should say, some of the robber barons, and they own the newspapers. You guys – socialists – were involved in the labor movement, all the way back to the 1800s. You were rightfully seen as a threat to the status quo and you were aligned with the communists."

"Yes, but we socialists separated from the communists after the Second International dissolved. That's been almost twenty years ago."

"That may be true, but what APRA has been talking about from the beginning is redistribution of wealth, particularly property reform. You advocate communal ownership of farms and government control of industry. Put yourself in the shoes of John D. Rockefeller or Andrew Carnegie. Wouldn't this look like communism to them, taking away their property and giving it to everybody else? Isn't that what happened in Russia? Look what happened there ever since. Stalin rose to the top and sided with Hitler."

"Yes, but we never advocated violence. At least, I never did and part of what I do is to keep the hotheads from wrecking everything we've accomplished. We don't need another Banana Massacre."

"I remember my parents talking about that. I never knew what all the excitement was about but I do remember them being very much against the unions. I think they were afraid it was going to happen in America. I know the communists were heavily involved in the labor movement. I also know it became pretty violent in several cases."

"I think if you look at it carefully, you will see that most of the violence was started by strike breakers brought in by the companies. You'll also find that federal troops were brought in on the side of the companies, as well. Many of the casualties were women and children. Look at the Ludlow strike in Colorado. Your National

Guard machine-gunned two women and eleven children who were not armed, and that was not the only instance."

As Haya spoke, he warmed to his task. He cited instance after instance of violence against American workers who were seeking safer working conditions and more than starvation wages. It was a subject he knew well and his passion for what he was saying seemed to override the trouble he had talking.

Victor must have spoken for ten minutes before he realized that Radford's eyes were beginning to glaze. "I beg your pardon, Pablo," he chuckled. "As you can see, I feel passionate about these things. I get.... How is it you Americans put it? All wound up? Enough about politics! How about you? Do you have a family yet?"

Once again something flickered Paul's eyes and this time Haya recognized it. The man was in pain, haunted by something he kept tightly locked away. "No," Paul said lightly. "I had a wife and a daughter. Victor, but this stupid war took them away from me." Radford shrugged, his eyes once more expressionless. "Now I seem to be too busy for that." He looked around. "Not too many candidates out here in the sticks, either, are there? How about yourself?"

"No, nothing seems to have worked out that way for me," the older man said. "In a sense, my family are the people I try to serve." He nodded toward the two men seated at the table. "Those two would die for me," he said. "Yet, I would never ask that of them. They are like sons to me and I treat them like sons. They may be paid but they are not my servants."

Their conversation was interrupted by a good-looking young man coming in the door. He was tall and lanky, his features almost pretty. The dark riding clothes he wore branded him as a city dweller and fit him quite well. They were clearly tailored and his English riding boots looked like the work of an excellent cobbler.

The young man headed for Haya's table. Seeing Radford, he turned and joined the two bodyguards. Neither of the men did more than glance at the young man before turning their attention back to Haya and Radford. When the newcomer spoke to them softly, neither answered. One simply shrugged and shook his head.

"That's my driver," Haya murmured.

"He's quite the dandy," Paul replied.

Victor chuckled. "Yes, I suppose he must be by American standards. Here he is simply seen as the son of a wealthy family, which he is. He's from Argentina and quite a good horseman. He dresses that way because he thinks that's the way a driver is supposed to look. He's also a remarkably good shot with a pistol." He smiled. "His family, of course, are all scandalized by his driving for me. He does it well."

Paul nodded. "That may turn out to be what counts, being a good shot with a pistol."

"Hopefully, things will not come to that. I've been shot at, as have you, and I'd rather not repeat the experience."

Radford chuckled. "We are in total agreement there. Did your friend, the policeman, tell you about the time I was ambushed in the mountains."

"No, but I'm glad you survived it."

"Thank you. It was the first time I was ever shot at. The Germans hired a guide I had fired to ambush me. It turned out he was in their pocket all along, even when he was guiding me." A grim smile crossed his face. "This was before the war, before I repaid their, ah, warm regards."

Paul reached in his shirt and drew out an ancient amulet held up by a leather thong. It was about the size of an American half-dollar and was severely dented to one side. Yet, the image engraved was still visible. It was a stick figure of what was clearly a man, dancing with his arms raised. One hand brandished a spear and the other held up the severed head of an enemy.

"Oh, my," Haya murmured. "I'm surprised the bullet didn't go all the way through."

"I was carrying an ironwood walking stick. It was hit first and took the brunt of the bullet's force."

"You were very lucky, my friend," Victor told him.

"Or surrounded by grace," Paul answered. "That's what a friend of mine claims, but I don't know. Either way, it's not an experience I want to repeat. My chest hurt like hell for a week."

"Do you know what that is?" Victor asked, nodding toward the amulet.

Radford nodded. "Yes, the message is pretty clear. I wear it outside my shirt when I'm on the trail. It's like a passport in certain areas."

"Those certain areas are ones the army likes to avoid, with good reason. May I ask what happened to the crooked guide who betrayed you?"

"You can ask but I don't have much to say about it. The bullet stunned me for a while and when I came to, it was all over. So I know only what others told me. That's their secret, not mine. The point is, you're right. I do know what it's like to be shot at, up close and personal."

Haya looked at the younger man gravely. "What I don't understand is why you are telling me this."

Radford shrugged. "It's a good story and I thought you are someone who would understand. I think I was right."

"What if I passed this along to my friend, the captain?" Victor held up a hand. "I don't intend to, of course, but you couldn't have known that."

Paul chuckled, and for the first time there was a hint of humor in his eyes. "Our mutual friend would tell you it was something he already knew."

Haya smiled and nodded. "Or, he might not, depending on how things were with us at the moment." He thought for a bit. Radford waited quietly. "So you're going to be keeping an eye on me. How is that going to work?"

"Well, I'm not going to be following you around, Victor. I have other things I need to do from time to time. It would help if I knew your travel plans, at least in general." He smiled. "I'd hate to send in a report about your visit to Arequipa when you were being photographed at a conference in Mexico City."

"Yes, I can see that might be a bit embarrassing. I have no problem with letting you know where I'll be, but you do need to keep that to yourself. I do have enemies and I don't want to make it easy for them. I'm afraid that means your bosses in Washington."

"I agree. I'd hate to see you taken down. Too many people I know are dying these days."

"That's true," Haya nodded. "So how do I get in touch with you, Pablo?"

"Well, if it's urgent, you can get word to the one-eyed man. He'll make sure the message gets to me. Other than that, I'll be getting in touch with you once in a while. Or we can come up with something else if that doesn't work. I think it's best to keep things simple."

"Right," Haya agreed dryly. "You lead such a simple life, yourself, Pablo."

"Actually, I do. I just learn whatever I can and try not to get caught. That's what gets a little tricky sometimes."

Haya nodded, studying the younger man intently. Then he made a decision. Leaning forward he said, "You know, Pablo, I could use you. You could become part of my entourage."

"That would certainly tickle the people in Washington," Radford answered. "What would you get out of it, Victor?"

"I can think of three things. One, of course, is a new set of eyes that see things differently. My people are intensely loyal but I could use an intelligent opinion from a different point of view. As I remember it, you are quick to grasp the essence of something and to respond quickly with a course of action."

Radford smiled. "Keep that up and my hat won't fit. What else, Victor?"

"The second thing is that you are honest and not afraid to tell the truth. You could be a good channel of communication with the people in Washington about what is really going on down here."

Radford grimaced. "I don't know about that one. I mean, you're right. I tend to speak my mind when people ask. However, those in power seem to discount what they don't want to hear. That's been my experience, anyway. I'll tell them the truth but I cannot promise that they will listen. What else?"

"The third is personal. I enjoy your company and admire your integrity. You don't seem to be too impressed by power or prestige."

Radford looked at Haya intently. "Victor, you don't know me that well. You've only seen me what, three times before? I think you may be seeing what you want to see. Either that, or you're feeding me a line of *caca de gallo*."

Haya laughed. "Actually, I know you better than you might think. My friend, the captain, thinks very highly of you. So does another friend, an old bandit named Calderón. His opinion carries a lot of weight."

Radford nodded, his face carefully neutral. He thought for a moment. "I can think of a fourth possible reason," he said. "Keep your enemy close so you can watch him."

Haya looked puzzled. "Are you my enemy, Pablo?"

"No, I'm not, Victor. I was thinking of certain men in Washington. They're not likely to send someone else after you if I'm around. On the other hand, they might."

"Do you really think they would do that?"

"You don't understand how scared they are of people like you. They don't understand you. So they think you will do what they would do in your shoes."

Haya shook his head as if to clear it. "I think we need to talk more about this at another time. Do you take my offer?"

"Sure," Radford nodded and extended his right hand. Victor smiled and took it. "I'll tell them I've infiltrated your camp," Paul added. "That will keep them happy for a while."

"And after that?"

"After that we get creative."

Conversations

2   Marfa, Texas. The two men sat at a long table in a conference room. The room was well lit by the October sun streaming in uncovered windows, reflecting off stark white walls. This made it hard to see and both men wore aviator's glasses. The windows had no shades or curtains to draw.

The bright light also revealed a light layer of dust across the conference table. Nor was this from neglect, for the room had been cleaned the night before. Dust was the rule in western Texas, even in wet years, and it was not uncommon to have to cancel air operations at the base because of vast dust storms that raked the area. The Chihuahuan desert was where the brown blizzards that swept through this area were born. Nor was it clear that the Dust Bowl days were done.

"That's interesting news," the naval commander observed. "Is Jock sure about this? It seems pretty quick." The officer to whom he was speaking was Denis Blieu, a Marine Corps major who served as the third in command of the Special Action Group Rudd headed. While Blieu was still in the chain of command, he also served as a roving military attache. His territory covered Latin and South America. What they were discussing was a report from Captain Jacques Paul, an Army officer on detached duty to the SAG from Military Intelligence.

Blieu chuckled. "I had trouble believing it, too, but after Radford infiltrated from Ecuador, he went directly to Cerro de Pasco and braced Haya directly."

Eric Rudd smiled and nodded. "Now that sounds like the Paul Radford we knew from before."

Blieu nodded. "Yeah, he does tend to rush in where angels fear to tread. The thing is, he's now part of Haya's entourage traveling through the back country."

"How the hell did Radford know where to find him?"

"Apparently he's as good a listener now as he ever was," Denis replied. "I asked Jock and he said Radford told him he used his personal network. He seems to be tighter with tribes in the Andes than we knew."

The commander nodded and smiled. "Yeah, that's what Paul calls jackass diplomacy. Our auditors rake me over the coals for how many burros we use up in Perú."

"Well, it works. He keeps tribes in the outback supplied with fresh meat, and they provide him with intelligence. It's a damned good bargain."

"Maybe we should try it in Washington," Rudd suggested.

"That's one way of thinning out Congress."

Rudd smiled. "The point is that we have a direct pipeline to Haya. Do you suppose he knows Radford is working for us?"

"I doubt Haya knows anything about our Special Action Group, but I'm sure Radford told him he's working for the USA. He told me once that the truth is a pretty good way to lie and that's been my experience, too. You know why Jock is so keen on him, don't you?"

Commander Rudd nodded with distaste. "Oh, yeah. Jock hasn't said it in so many words, but I think he wants Paul for an assassin. I think he's whistling Dixie and I've told him so."

Blieu shook his head. "I would have said that about the old Paul Radford. After Alaska, I'm not so sure. When I read the file I took a trip to Alaska and talked to some people there. I thought Castner was going to shoot me for stealing him back from the Alaska Scouts. He said he could always depend on Radford delivering the goods, but he also said he took ungodly risks doing it. Even so, Radford never put others at risk. You know what they called him up there?"

"Dead-eye was what I heard," Rudd answered.

"That was after he shot down the Zero with a rifle. After Attu, they called him Wildman. Apparently he took out a dozen Japs with a samurai sword when they overran the heavy artillery battery. The general commanding it put him in for a medal of honor. Somebody Radford pissed off got it bumped back to a Silver Star."

Rudd nodded. "I heard about that one. It's a damned shame, too.

What apparently pissed them off was his charging the Japs screaming 'banzai.' The troops followed his example and he didn't lose a man."

Denis shook his head. "No, that's not it, Eric. The real reason is that Radford pissed off the admiral commanding the Kiska operation. The admiral didn't want to risk sending in scouts. He made the mistake of allowing Radford to speak freely. Paul told the admiral that not sending in scouts was foolish and would lose lives. He was proved right, too."

Rudd frowned and shook his head. "Do you ever wonder what keeps him going?" he asked. "He always volunteers for the most dangerous assignments."

"I'm no shrink, Eric, but I think he wants to die. The thing is, he's so damned competent that no one has been able to oblige him. Yet. I think that's why Jock wants him for an assassin. Radford considers himself expendable."

Rudd nodded. "I hope we haven't recruited a loose canon, Denis. He could get other people killed."

"That's just it, Eric. He always puts other people first. When he did his thing with the samurai sword, he was protecting his supervisor, a civilian engineer."

"You think he would do that for Haya?"

Blieu nodded. "I'm sure of it. I just hope someone from Washington doesn't send someone else after Haya. Radford will take them out or die trying."

Lima, Perú. A similar conversation was going on between two men six thousand kilometers to the southeast. The location was the German embassy and the place was the office of the military attache. The light was dim even though the year was approaching the winter solstice and the southern hemisphere was enjoying it's summer. The only electric light on in the room was a small lamp on the side table between the leather chairs where the men sat. Nor did the lamp do much more than accentuate the shadows that draped the massive German furniture.

"Are you sure about this, Jergen?" The short man in black livery asked. He was smoking one of the small, vile cigars he favored. His name was Rott, Helmut Rott, and he was carried on the official embassy list as the driver for Jergen Schwartz, the other man. Unofficially, Rott was known as the military attaché's hatchet man. He rarely smiled, and when he did, it was far more frightening than his glower.

The other man, dressed in well cut mufti, could have been mistaken for a university professor. This is exactly what he had been, a professor of linguistics. Seeing the writing on the wall early in Hitler's rise to power, Jergen Schwartz had joined the Nazi party and called in a number of markers to get himself sent to officer's school. From there he wangled his way into military intelligence and rose to the rank of colonel. He then garnered enough favors to be posted as the military attaché to the embassy in Lima.

Despite being directly responsible for the loss of the submarine base off the southern coast of Perú, as well as a covert inland operation, Schwartz managed to survive the embassy shake-up following these disasters. Thanks to the covert efforts of his driver, who destroyed vital evidence, the colonel was able to shift blame onto the ambassador. That faithful servant of the Reich quickly found himself recalled to Berlin. No word of his fate had filtered back to Lima.

Schwartz thought a moment before answering Rott. "Yes," he finally said. "Our source is reliable and it makes sense. Radford knows Perú and he speaks the languages. He seems to be on good terms with the wild tribes in the Andes. This makes him the best man to send if the Americans are planning something."

"How did your source in Colombia recognize him?" Rott wanted to know. His tone was more of a command than a question.

"Oh," the professor said, blinking. "I beg your pardon, Helmut. I thought I told you about all this. You do remember Johann Weiss, don't you?"

"Of course, I do!" Rott almost snapped. "I recruited him and I trained him." Of all the people in the embassy, he was the only one not worried about offending Schwartz. The two had been together for many years and the scholar knew that his Rottweiler, as he affectionately called his companion, had as much dirt on him as he had on Rott. He knew that if his driver went down, he would make sure to take the colonel with him.

"No need to be snippy, Helmut," Schwartz chided gently. It pleased him to no end when he was able to get under the other's skin. "I thought you knew that Weiss had been sent to Ecuador."

Rott shook his head impatiently and the *oberst* continued. "Well, he was. When Johann was on an official trip to Colombia, he spotted Radford in Bogotá. At first, Weiss didn't recognize the man, but Johann had a camera along and took a few pictures. Later one of his sources in Cuenca spotted an American who fit Radford's description. The American was arranging a trip into the Andes."

Schwartz rummaged around his desk and produced a couple of black and white snapshots. He handed them to Rott, who examined them closely. "These are the pictures he sent me," he continued. "As you can see, Radford looks much older now. Yet, our sources tell us he was involved in combat in the Aleutian Islands. That could be what it is. What do you think?"

"Oh, it's him, all right," Rott growled. "He's lost some weight and that fresh university choirboy look, but it's him. Did Weiss find out what Radford was doing in Colombia and Ecuador?"

"It seems rather obvious," Schwartz pointed out. "Cuenca is not that far from the border. It's apparent that the man was infiltrating Perú."

Rott ignored Schawartz's sarcasm and responded as if he was talking to a child. "Yes, that is rather obvious, Jergen. What I was asking was what else he was up to in Colombia and Ecuador. Do you have any idea if he was simply traveling through or if he was in Botoga and Quito for some other reason?"

Though he was piqued by Rott's tone, Schwartz answered evenly. His style became very pedantic, which he knew Rott hated. "Weiss told me that seeing Radford on the street was the first time he had become aware of his presence. He asked our embassy staff in Bogotá about him, but they had no idea who the man was. They were able to tell Weiss that there was no Paul Radford on the diplomatic roster of the American embassy there. Nor did they recognize his picture. When he queried the embassy in Quito, they told him the same."

Rott nodded. "So we have no idea what the man is up to here in Perú." He thought a moment. "I think we need to keep an eye out for him in Lima, though he may never show up here. The fact he sneaked into the country tells me he's on a covert mission, but what's his target? We don't have any other operations going on like the ones down south." Then he looked directly at Schwartz. "Or do we? Is there something else you haven't been telling me, Jergen?"

Schwartz shook his head. "No, but there may be things the new ambassador is not telling me. His attitude indicates that his predecessor poisoned the well against us. So there's no way of knowing."

Rott chuckled. "Right. As if we couldn't find out for ourselves. But I haven't seen or heard anything suspicious. How about you?"

"Not the least whisper," his companion answered. "Not from Berlin, either," he added. Rott knew he was referring to the coding officer who the two had securely in their camp. The officer was the head of the coding department. He knew he could easily end up on the eastern front for passing along everything that came across his desk to the professor. Yet, he also knew that Schwartz had dirt on him that could result in his being sent to the eastern front in disgrace, if not shot.

"So what do you think we need to do about Radford?" Rott asked. Of the two, Schwartz was the better strategist. His driver excelled in the execution of black operations. As far as Rott was concerned, the dirtier, the better. Nor did he use a pistol or a knife if a garrote or his bare hands would serve.

"I've given it some thought," Schwartz replied. "The simplest thing would be to inform the national police."

"Why not just kill him in the back country?"

"There's too much risk. You would need to take a guide and some other help. Word would get out."

"I would only need a single native guide. Then I could kill him, too."

"Which would raise questions when you returned and he did not," the colonel pointed out.

"I could do it without a guide. I could take a couple of men from the embassy. One of the cook's assistants is a block head, but he's Gestapo and the file says he's well trained. You couldn't prove it by me, but I suspect he won't have qualms about doing whatever must be done." His smile was chilling. "Or he better not."

"That's an even better argument to let the national police arrest Radford," the linguist replied. "It would be easy to arrange for him to be killed in prison or even attempting to escape once he's been taken captive."

Schwartz could see that his driver didn't like this and he knew why. Rott preferred direct intervention and he liked getting his hands dirty. What the linguist proposed would put the outcome too much in the hands of others. "It's too risky," Rott told replied, shaking his head.

"Nonetheless, that's the way it must be done." Schwartz's tone left no room for further debate. "Get word to one of your sources and tell them to pass it along."

"Then it will have to be someone besides Molina," Rott growled. "According to my sources, he cannot be bribed. Nor can his sergeant."

The linguist nodded. "Yes, you're absolutely right, Helmut. So use one of your regular sources and make sure he keeps his mouth shut."

"Oh, he'll keep it to himself," Rott smiled. "He knows what will happen to him if he doesn't." He started to get up, then, seeing the expression on the scholar's face, sat back down. "What?" he demanded.

Schwartz ignored his driver's impatience. "You know, it occurs to me that Radford might be here because the Americans found out about our coca leaf project. That would explain why Radford infiltrated from Colombia and Ecuador. He may have been sent to investigate."

"Pep pills?" Rott asked. "So what? That whole project is just another pipe dream. The Reich would be far better off having its scientists developing better weapons. The cocaine project is bullshit."

"Not if it improves the endurance of our troops. You told me you had tried coca leaves yourself when you were trying to run down Radford in the Andes. You told me it kept you going."

"Yes, and it knocked me on my ass for days afterward. You told me I slept for twenty-seven hours straight when I first got back. I felt like hammered shit when I woke up."

"I didn't notice any effect on your performance," Schwartz

responded with a smile. "You were a little more grouchy than usual, but that was about it."

Near Huánuco, Perú. A week later, Radford was the subject of yet another conversation. This one took place early in the morning at a cantina in Tingo Maria, some three hundred kilometers northeast of Lima. The doors of the place were still barred and eight men were gathered around a table eating a simple meal of beans, flat bread, and strong coffee. Nor was this the beginning of the day for these men. Except for the owner of the place, they had been up for hours and had many kilometers behind them.

"Who is this gringo with Haya?" one of the travelers asked. It was clear that he was the leader of the group. He was taller than the others and much darker. His face was hard, even for a native of the Andes, and his eyes seemed to burn with zeal.

The owner shook his head. "I don't know. Haya showed up here a few days ago and the new man was with him. He acted like he was part of his party. He rode in the back seat with Haya."

"Where were his bodyguards? Weren't they with him?"

"One of them sat up in the front seat with the driver. The other sat on a jump seat in back. He didn't look too happy about it, either."

The leader chuckled dryly. "For a socialist, Haya likes his big touring cars. Nothing but the best for the leader." He looked at his companions. "Not like us, eh, *hermanos*? We go by foot."

"We don't have to worry about flats, either," one of the men pointed out and the others smiled. The speaker was the leader's lieutenant. Unlike the leader, he was short and built like a bulldozer, compact and powerful.

"Just flat feet," the leader answered. "What did Haya do while he was here?"

The owner shrugged. "He made the rounds. He mostly talked to people in their homes. The driver and the guards stood around outside. The new man went inside with him."

"Did they ever come in here?" the leader asked.

The owner nodded. "They took most of their meals here. The guards and the driver sat at one table and kept watch. Haya and the yanqui sat at another and talked. None of them drank much, *cerveza* except for the American. He always drank coffee."

"Were you able to hear what they were saying?"

"Yes, they talked mostly of politics." He smiled. "Haya did most of the talking, mostly about *aprismo*."

"*Aprismo!*" The leader spat the word out like a foul taste. "That's Haya's personal self-serving *caca*! He uses it to pander to the dim-witted. It's nothing but dung, self-serving counter-revolutionary *caca de perro*. He needs to be stopped!"

The other men looked at one another, uncomfortable. The leader might have been trained in Russia, but Victor Haya had widespread support among the ordinary people. Yet none of them dared to object. Unlike Haya, who was opposed to violent tactics, the Russians didn't mind breaking a few heads to make an omelet. They were painfully aware their leader had been trained in Moscow.

Even so, the leader was no fool. He saw the uneasy looks that passed among his men. It was time to distract them from what lay ahead. "We need women," he told the owner of the cantina, and that got the men's attention. "Bring us three, but two will do if you can't find more. We'll also need food to carry with us."

The leader handed the owner a small pouch of coins. "This is not much, but it's all we have for now. There will be more later. Be sure the women are clean. And not a word that we're in town."

After the owner left, the leader sat quietly, smoking a hand made cigarette and thinking. There was a lot on his mind, but mostly he thought of how he could take out Victor Haya without setting off a mutiny among his men. The masters in Moscow had been very explicit in their instructions for what needed to happen. At the very least, the man must die, but they didn't want to create a martyr. So he first needed to be disgraced.

Then the leader smiled, remembering something he had seen in Columbia, and a plan began to come together in his mind. Though the chewing of coca leaves was a common practice in the Andes, and generally overlooked, the refined product known as cocaine was highly illegal. What if a large quantity was discovered hidden in Haya's car after he had been shot? How could his supporters refute the charge that the man had been funding his political activities by the illegal sale of large quantities of refined cocaine?

Seeing their leader smile, the men relaxed. They were well fed and women were on the way. Who would not smile at that prospect, even their fearsome leader?

Lima, Perú. Sergeant Juan Gomez waited patiently for his captain. It was a warm day and he could hear insects buzzing around the flower garden outside the open window of the waiting room of the central police station. The high ceilings and thick walls of the building kept it pleasantly cool, even on the warmest days. It was one of the few benefits of working at headquarters.

Now it was the hour most businesses closed for a long mid day siesta and Gomez had eaten early. After the wonderful meal Rosario had sent with him, the stillness of the early afternoon made his eyes droop. Even so, he struggled to remain alert. Unlike many public officials, Captain Molina was always quite punctual, and he expected the same of his sergeant. Thinking about this, Gomez decided that something urgent must have come up to make his captain late. He wondered what it was. Lost in that thought, his eyes closed and he drifted off into a pleasant nap.

"You must have a clear conscience, Juan" The quiet voice cut through the dream and Gomez awakened. He was looking into the amused eyes of his captain.

"I beg your pardon, sir!" The sergeant jumped to his feet, still half asleep.

"That's what the Germans say," Molina informed him. "Haven't you hear that one? *Ein gutes Gewissen ist ein sanftes Ruhekissen.* A good conscience is a soft pillow."

Gomez nodded, not knowing what to say. "That's who I've just been talking to, the Peruvian driver from the German embassy," the captain added, frowning. "That's why I was late. I thought I was going to have to turn him over to some of our colleagues to get him to talk."

Gomez was surprised. Molina abhorred torture and had said more than once that any information gleaned from it was unreliable. Seeing the confusion in his sergeant's eyes, Molina shook his head.

"No, I haven't changed my mind about torture, Juan. Just the threat was enough. Our colleagues have a reputation for enjoying their work and our countryman sang like a song bird. So the Americans say."

"I imagine he did, sir. I would hate to be in Garcia's hands, myself."

"I wonder, though," Molina mused. "Lico seemed to give in too easily."

"You mean like he was told to do so, sir?"

"Yes. I think the Germans told him to pass along some information they wanted us have, but to so reluctantly. So Lico fed me a little bit at a time. He made me dig. Nor did he seem that concerned until I mentioned Garcia and his men." The captain smiled, shaking his head. "Then he almost fouled his pants. He was talking so fast I could hardly keep up."

The sergeant frowned. "Who initiated the conversation, sir, you or Lico?"

"That's just it. He called me. He said he had information I might want. He insisted we meet in an out of the way place, too, and when I got there, he was very reluctant to talk. Still, I had the impression he was not that worried. Do you see what I mean, Juan?"

"Yes, sir. You think it was an act."

"Exactly, so I played along. I pretended to be impatient. Then, after a bit, I didn't have to pretend." Molina smiled when he said this. "That's when I mentioned Garcia."

"And Lico almost crapped his pants." The sergeant was having trouble not laughing. "So why did the Germans go to all this trouble?"

Molina shook his head. "Well, if it is Rott and Schwartz who are behind this, it makes sense. I don't think either of them is capable of doing anything simply and they love drama and intrigue. They think themselves so much smarter than the rest of us. They don't seem to realize that we see right through them. Which is a good thing."

"So what are they trying to accomplish, sir?"

"What else? I think they want to embarrass the Americans. That submarine base fiasco really hurt their political position here. The

Americans came out of it looking very good except among our German population. Now the Germans would like nothing better than to get even."

"What did they expect? They violated our good will."

"Along with our national sovereignty," Molina agreed, nodding. "One would think they would realize they brought it on themselves."

"If you don't mind my asking, what was the information Lico wanted to tell you, sir?"

Captain Molina looked at his sergeant. There was a great deal of concern in his eyes. "He wanted to tell me that Paul Radford is back in Perú."

Gomez nodded. "I see. Do you know why he's here?"

"No, I don't. I don't think the Germans do, either. I think they're afraid of him and want us to do their dirty work."

"Afraid?" the sergeant asked. "I can see why they would be angry with him. He was the one who discovered what they were up to, but why are they afraid? Do they have some other secret operation going on?"

"No, I don't think so. We've been keeping a close eye on them every since then and they know it. They seem to have scaled back their operations since the last ambassador left. All their efforts seem to be directed toward competing with the Americans for our minerals." Molina smiled. "They are useful to us to keep the price up."

"So what are they afraid of? He's only one man."

"Yes, but he is very well connected in the outlying areas. All the wild tribes consider him a friend. So he can go places where even our army is afraid to travel. I think the Germans are afraid of his power in the Andes. He could make a lot of trouble for them if he chose."

The sergeant nodded and looked at his captain. "That makes sense. Yet, that's not your only concern, is it, sir?"

"No, my primary concern is for you and your family."

"I don't think Radford will make trouble for us, sir. That's not my sense of him as a man."

"No? From his point of view, you stole his woman and are raising his child."

"I didn't exactly steal her, sir. He abandoned her and their child. I know he was forced to but he still abandoned them. Rosario would never have married me if she thought he was coming back. She didn't even know if he was still alive."

Molina nodded. "I know all this, Juan. I know he must be aware that it was the war that forced him to leave. Yet, as you well know, these things aren't rational. I don't have to tell you how many times we have seen good men killing each other over a woman. I don't want to have to bury you or him. He's a good man, as are you."

Gomez nodded. "Thank you, sir. I think we should be safe enough here in Lima. The only risk might be when I have to go other places. My family will look after Rosario and Azúl then and I will take special care when I travel. I think that if he comes after someone, it will be me. I don't think he would hurt Azúl or Rosario."

Molina sighed. "You're probably right. He doesn't seem like that kind of man to me, either." Then he added, gruffly, "Even so, take care, Juan. I would have a devil of a time replacing you."

Gomez was not fooled for a moment. He and his captain had been together a long time and were closer than most brothers. He knew Molina cared.

First Attack

3 Near San Martín, Perú. Paul Radford came awake suddenly and lay still for a long moment, listening. The crude hut was quiet except for the soft snoring of one of the bodyguards and he could hear nothing from outside. Yet his sense of danger was urgent and he quickly slipped in to his trousers and boots. Then he grabbed his backpack, taking out a the silenced pistol he managed to liberate from the Alaska Scouts. Then he quietly woke Haya. "Victor!" he whispered urgently. "Wake up! We need to go."

The older man came to his feet quickly. Seeing the drawn pistol in Radford's hand, he quickly drew his own. So did Timo, who had been asleep next to Victor. "What is it, Pablo?" Haya whispered back.

"I don't know, but we've got to get out of here, now. Wake the others, quietly. I'll take a look." The younger man slipped away in the darkness, carefully lowering himself to his belly before he slowly opened the back door of the hut. He looked outside for several moments before silently crawling through the open door. Once outside, he lay quietly, listening to the darkness, every sense on high alert.

Radford could feel a slight breeze against his face and he caught a whiff of cigarette smoke. Then he saw something move slightly, a dark shadow dimly visible next to a tree in the dim starlight. He began to circle around toward the shadow, watching for other figures in the darkness.

Radford smelled the second man long before he caught sight of him. Once again, it was the stench of cheap tobacco, much stronger than before, that alerted him. He moved forward silently until he could dimly see the outline of the second watcher. The man was holding a rifle pointed toward the hut and Radford wondered why the man had not seen him. Then he heard the slow steady sound of the man's breathing and realized the watcher was almost asleep. He was on the man like a cat, striking the back of the sleeper's head once with the ball of his clenched fist. The man's head bounced against the ground and he lay still.

"Carlos?" came an urgent whisper from the watcher Radford had spotted first. The attack had made little noise, but the first watcher had heard something.

"Shh!" Radford whispered back urgently. Examining the man he'd knocked out, he was relieved to discover he was not a policeman or soldier. At least, he wore no uniform and he was shod in badly worn sandals. This meant he was probably a bandit, and for a moment, Radford considered killing him where he lay. He decided this might create more problems than it solved and he began his second stalk.

This time his quarry was alert and Radford was only able to get within five feet before the man was aware of him. "Carlos?" he whispered again, then began to swing his rifle around when Radford didn't answer. Yet, Radford caught the man's chin with the heel of his hand and he slumped back, dropping his rifle. Fortunately, it made no noise as it hit the ground.

Radford listened for a long two minutes before slipping back to the rear door of the hut. "It's Pablo," he whispered quietly before he got there. "Don't shoot! Come this way! Quickly!"

The other four men followed Radford quietly across the clearing and into the brush behind the hut. Then one of the guards bringing up the rear stumbled over a large rock at the edge of the clearing and fell, dropping the pistol he was carrying. It was cocked to fire and when it hit the ground, the weapon went off, sounding like a clap of thunder in the dead of night.

Fortunately, the barrel was pointed toward the ground and no one was hit. Yet, someone behind them shouted and shots rang out from both sides. Paul could hear the bullets striking tree branches above them. "Follow me!" he said quietly, running down the slope in a crouch. He could hear Victor's labored breathing close behind him and the footsteps of the others. More shots rang out, but one of the bodyguards fired back at a rifle flash and someone cried out. The attackers answered with a fusillade that Paul could hear going over their heads, and he picked up speed.

Then Radford heard Haya stumble and go down. "Victor!" he called urgently, turning around and running back. "Are you hit?"

"No, I fell down," the older man said, gasping for breath. "I have to stop."

The other men came running up just then. "Spread out," Radford told them. "Victor can't go any farther. We have to make a stand here."

Surprised, Timo and the bodyguards looked at one another. "Do as he says!" Victor told them and they quickly obeyed. When they did so, Radford could see they needed training. They moved into cover, but he could see positions closer by that offered a better field of fire.

"What do you think?" Haya asked quietly, his voice laced with fear.

"We need to let them get close," Radford replied. "They have rifles and all we have is pistols." He scurried away to tell the scattered men. In less than a minute, he was back. "I told them not to fire until you gave the order. I'll advise you when, but wait until I do."

Haya looked at the Radford oddly. "Trust me, Victor," Paul said. "I'm combat hardened." Haya could see a flash of white teeth as Radford grinned. "I'm not about to let these stupid *pendejos* take us."

Despite the gravity of the situation, Haya found himself smiling at Paul's use of the crude expression. Then he realized this was exactly what Radford intended and his opinion the younger man went up. He found himself much calmer. I've been given a great gift in this one, he told himself.

They didn't have long to wait for their pursuers. Whoever was leading them knew what he was doing. Not hearing his prey crashing headlong through the woods, he had slowed his men down and was advancing cautiously. Seeing how close their pursuers were getting, Haya grew anxious again. He was about to shout out the order to fire when he felt the light touch of Paul's hand on his arm. Looking at his companion, he saw Radford had a hand raised, signaling him to stop. It was all he could do to keep quiet, and the pursuers were about to step on their prey when Radford hissed, "Now!"

Hay shouted and the simultaneous roar of six pistols broke the dead silence of the night. Victor saw four bodies flung backwards by the hail of bullets. Four flashes answered fire and he heard the spit of Radford's silenced pistol. Then Radford was gone and Victor could see him scurrying forward on his belly. When he disappeared into the darkness, Haya ordered his guards to stop firing.

The next ten minutes were an eternity. Haya thought he heard the soft cough of Paul's pistol twice, and there was a cry of pain the second time. There was silence until a shot rang out and Victor heard the pistol cough twice more. Then there was nothing and Haya was about to order his men to pull out when he became aware of the younger man beside him.

"How did you get there?" Haya said, surprised.

Once again there was a brief flash of teeth. "I told you, Victor. I was well trained. There were at least eight of them. You saw four go down and I took out two more. Two got away. I think the leader was killed, but maybe not. It's hard to tell who's in charge when they aren't wearing uniforms and are dead. What I'm going on is what they had in their pockets, and didn't have. The jeffe was leading from the rear but I think I got him."

"That was wise, if not heroic," Haya said dryly. "I think we better move out of here. I don't suppose we can use our car."

"I wouldn't advise it," Radford said. "They probably had someone watching it and they may have wired it to explode."

Haya's head snapped around toward Radford. "You think so? That sounds pretty sophisticated."

"We don't know who we're up against," Radford pointed out. "Or do we? Is someone after you, Victor?"

"Other than General Benevides?" Haya chuckled. "Let's see. How about the communists? Or your government, or even elements of my own party. After tonight, we can add our friend, Captain Molina."

"We were the ones who were attacked," Paul pointed out.

"It doesn't matter. We will be considered responsible for the violence. After all, six of our attackers are dead."

"Yes, because they weren't properly trained. Experienced troops would have wiped us out."

Haya shook his head. "Not to argue, but I doubt it. We had you with us. That made all the difference."

Radford smiled. "Just remember that the next time you're upset with me." Then he sobered. "Seriously, Victor, your men need some training. The next time it may not be a bunch of bozos coming after you and I may not be there."

"You're not leaving us, are you?"

"No, of course not. I do need to be away from time to time. That's what I'm worried about. Someone's out to do you some serious harm. I don't think these guys were taking prisoners. Your men need to be ready."

Radford hesitated. "What?" Haya asked.

"The man I think was the leader was carrying cocaine, Victor," Paul told him. "The package he had on him weighs about half a kilo, maybe more. I don't understand why they came after us. Maybe they're drug dealers and thought we were the police."

"Those *cabrones*!" Haya declared. "You don't know why they had it?" Radford shook his head and the older man answered with a growl. "I know exactly why! They were going to kill us and leave it on us to be discovered. They wanted to disgrace me as well as murder me, Pablo."

"Well, I brought everything they had in their pockets, except for the cocaine. We can figure out who they are later today. We need to get out of here."

Pisco, Perú. News of the attack took a long time getting to the police headquarters in Lima. It came by a circuitous route through the Andes and south to Pisco. It was only when Sergeant Juan Gomez visited his old friend Juan Emiliano Calderón, the parish priest in Pisco, that he learned of the fire fight several hundred kilometers to the north.

The purpose of the sergeant's visit was to let Fr. Juan know that Paul Radford was back in Perú. Yet, it took a while for the conversation to get around to this. The two men were good friends and the first thing the padre asked about was Rosario and Azúl, the sergeant's wife and adopted daughter. Gomez took great delight in telling the padre of his child's latest antics and added that there was a sibling on the way. The old man was delighted with the news.

After that, there was a substantial mid day meal. It was prepared by Alicia Hernandez, one of Gomez's cousins who had taken Rosario's place as the padre's cook and housekeeper. She was a widow and, while it was clear the two older people got on well, Gomez knew Juan Calderón missed Rosario terribly. Over the years that she had kept house for the padre, they had become quite close. Now the old priest considered her his daughter. Gomez knew there was nothing Juan Calderón would not do for her or for her child.

It was only when the two men were having coffee in the enclosed patio of the rectory that the subject of Radford came up. "Something tells me this is not completely a social visit, Juan," the padre said. "Is there anything you need to tell me?"

The sergeant nodded and sighed. "Yes, padre, I have some troubling news."

Gomez paused and Juan Calderón nodded. "It wouldn't have anything to do with Pablo being back in Perú, would it?"

"How did you know?" the sergeant asked, surprised.

"Well, I have some news about him for you," the older man said, nodding. "It's disturbing news, as well. Why don't you go first, Juan."

The sergeant shrugged and held up his hands. "My news is just that he's back. He's been seen in the north, near Rioja. The information we have is that he came in through Ecuador and headed for the Andes."

"May I ask where you got your information?"

Gomez looked troubled. "The captain didn't instruct me not to tell you, padre, but it's better if the information didn't come to you through us."

Juan Calderón had to fight down his impatience. Aside from his vocation as a priest, he was not known as one who revealed everything he knew. Quite the contrary. Even so, no sign of his feelings reached his face. "Yes, of course," he said. "I will treat where it came from as confessional."

Juan Gomez nodded gratefully. "Thank you, padre. You know how it is."

"I do, indeed," the padre answered dryly. "So where did you hear about this, Juan?"

"It came to us indirectly from the Germans."

Juan Calderón chuckled. "Let me guess, Juan. Schwartz and Rott were overheard talking about it."

"How did you know?" the sergeant asked, dumbfounded.

"It's no great mystery," the padre answered. That's how they operate. They always have and I suspect they always will. They think no one is on to them. Did they pass along any useful details?"

"Only that Pablo came in through Cuenca. He was seen there arranging for a trip into the Andes." The sergeant held up a hand. "No, let me correct that. A *norteamericano* was seen there who fit his description."

"So they have no idea why he's back?"

"We didn't get any information about that. Only that he was seen in Cuenca."

The old priest thought about this. "Are they sure it's him?" he asked.

Gomez shrugged. "Who knows? Someone unknown left us some photos on the step of the police station. They were in a plain envelope addressed to Captain Molina. It was American manufacture." The sergeant reached in a pocket and produced a plain craft envelope with six black and white photos. He handed these to the padre.

Juan Calderón looked at the photos carefully. As happy as he was to see the face of a close friend, he was cut to the heart by what he saw there. He had seen the same thing in the faces of battle hardened recruits in the Mexican revolution, young men who were forced to grow up far too quickly.

The padre nodded. "It's him, all right. It looks like he's been to war. No idea where these pictures came from?"

Gomez shook his head. "We think probably the Germans. No one else would have a reason." He looked at the priest. "You said you had news for me, too. From the north."

Calderón nodded. "Yes, he was apparently with a group of people who were attacked by communist bandits. Six of them were killed in the fight that took place, the leader and five of his followers. Two of them got away."

Gomez thought about this. "What else do you know?"

"Only that no one in the party Radford was with was hurt. Not even a scratch, if my information is right."

"How do you know all this?"

Calderón shrugged. "I know a lot of indios in the Andes. They let me know when strange things like this happen. Their information is always very accurate."

"You think they saw it happen?"

The padre shook his head. "No, but these people can read the wild places like I can read a paper. Better, probably. I imagine they took a good look at where it happened. They wouldn't like a gun fight going on in their territory."

"So it took place in the jungle?"

Calderón nodded. "Yes, somewhere between Moyobamba and Juanjui. The party Paul was with was apparently taking a back road, I imagine to avoid the attention of the army."

"Who was he with?" Gomez asked.

"I was only given a description. Our names are useless to the people who sent the information. They only knew the attackers were communists because one of them had Russian coins in his pocket. I imagine this was the leader." He reached into his cassock and pulled out a small leather purse. Taking a coin out, he handed it to the policeman. A hammer and sickle was clearly visible on one side above a legend that read CCCP. On the reverse was the number 10. "They brought me this. It's yours to keep. The only other information I was given that might help is that there were four other men in the party Pablo was with. One of them was older and heavier than the others and Pablo's boot tracks were different. They were also traveling in a large touring car. I would say a Mercedes from the drawing I was shown."

"You think Radford was traveling with Germans?" Gomez was surprised.

"No, not at all. One doesn't have to be German to drive a Mercedes. I imagine there are lots of Germans in Lima who have them, and I expect a number of government people in Lima do, too." Gomez nodded when he said this, and the older man continued. "What it tells me, Juan, is that Paul is traveling with people with money, important people."

Gomez frowned. "That's a change. From what I knew before, Paul Radford preferred the common people."

Calderón nodded. "Yes, he did. I imagine he still does. He didn't have too much use for the embassy people, or even his bosses. He was very much a man of the people when I saw him last."

"Is there anything else you can tell me?" Gomez asked.

The padre shook his head. "No, not about Pablo. Have you told Rosario?"

Gomez shook his head. "No, it didn't seem wise."

"You may want to. It would be better if she heard the news from you rather than running into him on the street."

"I doubt he will come to Lima," the sergeant said. "He has too many enemies there. Why? Do you think he wants to see Rosario?" Gomez looked worried.

Juan Calderón shrugged. "He may or may not want to see Rosario. I am pretty sure he will want to see Azúl, sooner or later. After all, she is his daughter." He looked at Gomez and added. "It might be better if you made this possible."

"How, padre? The order is out to arrest Pablo on sight. I am honor bound to do that."

"Perhaps you could arrange to be absent when the meeting takes place," Calderón observed dryly. "You're not responsible for what you don't see."

"I don't know. I need to talk to Rosario first and see how she feels. If she says 'no' then I won't do it."

The old priest rewarded Juan with a wry grin. "That's very wise, my friend. Always do exactly what your wife says. Just like I did when she was my housekeeper."

"Ha!" Gomez said, smiling. "That's not the way she tells it, padre." He shrugged. "I don't always do so, either."

"Good. That way she won't get spoiled."

"Right, just like you never spoiled her," the good sergeant riposted and the conversation moved on to other things.

The day after Gomez came to visit, Juan Calderón sent word to Pico that he needed to see him. When she got back from this errand, his housekeeper told him that the one-eyed guide was still in the back country and was not expected to arrive until late that afternoon, or the next day, maybe. Since there was nothing he could do but wait, the padre sat down and began to carefully compose a letter to his young friend. He was very careful to avoid using names or anything else that could identify himself or the recipient.

My dearest friend,

How it pleases me to learn you are back in God's country! Not a day has gone by since your departure that I have not held you in my heart and in my conversations with the One who holds us all in his hand. I have missed your razor sharp wit and your wonderful company and I hope that if there is any rancor you hold from my decisions that you have by now forgiven this old fool.

I write because you need to know those who stole your notebooks are aware of your homecoming. I am sure they have not forgiven you for thwarting their plans, and I suspect they intend to do you ill. I know for a fact that they have made certain officials aware of your current sojourn. I doubt these worthy souls will initiate any action but you need to stay clear of crossing paths with them. You know who they are, so I don't need to tell you.

I would also like to see you at your convenience if you will agree. Our mutual friend, the jaguar man, can bring you to me. I would love to meet you in the high places but these days my legs are telling me they have made their last journey there. So the mountain will have to come to Mohammed this time. I cannot stress strongly enough how good it would be to see you and hear your voice, so, please, forgive this old fool any hurt he has done you.

My sources also tell me you are traveling by motor car these days, which surprises me. You always preferred to walk the high, lonely places and through the deep forests where even the soldiers fear to go. Perhaps your motor car can bring you close by or carry me to meet you somewhere it is safe to meet. The whole world seems to be at arms these days, even in the remote places, so take even greater care than you normally do.

There is so much I want to say to you, my friend. My heart is full of joy knowing you have come through all your travails, and I hope you find peace. That was the hardest thing for me when I finally laid down my arms and became who I am now. Yet through the tender mercy given through a lovely soul we both know, and through your friendship, too, I have been given the grace of a deep and abiding sense that the world is in the hands of the One who made it and that all is well.

It is my fervent hope that the same happens for you, my beloved friend, though I cannot recommend the path I have followed. I don't think the clothes would fit you but I might be wrong. It is, after all, ultimately up to the Hound of Heaven sent to bring us home.

I know you are not a believer, my brother in spirit, but let me share a bit of that long poem with you. I think you will understand me even better than you do if you read the whole thing. Yet, the beginning is enough, perhaps, to pique your interest. It was written by Francis Thompson, a brilliant young Englishman who grew up in comfort. He lived a short, hard life of poverty and died far too young. He was about the age you are now when he wrote The Hound of Heaven.

> *I fled Him, down the nights and down the days;*
> *I fled Him, down the arches of the years;*
> *I fled Him, down the labyrinthine ways*
> *Of my own mind; and in the mist of tears*
> *I hid from Him, and under running laughter.*

It's strange, isn't it, how we use both joy and grief to resist the One who loves us more than all others? But please forgive this old fool for pushing in where he is not invited.

With all my love for you,

J

On the Run

4 Near San Martín, Perú. Paul Radford looked around. It was a good place to put all he had taught Victor's men into practice. They were traveling along a forest trail in the eastern foothills of the Andes and were halfway up a low hill. From where he stood, he could see the trail they stretching out a hundred yards behind them.

Radford turned around and said, "Quickly. An enemy is coming up fast behind us. Take cover to ambush. Pick your targets left to right. Do not fire until I do. Let them get close."

The men began to get into position and Paul walked back the way they had come. At fifty paces he turned around and began to walk back toward where the men were hidden. He was pleased by what he saw. None of Haya's men could be seen from the path. He was ten yards from the closest man before he could make him out and only then did he raise his hand, pointing to the man he could see with his hand cocked like a pistol. When he did, the four men said, "Pow!" in unison.

"Very good," Radford told them. "These drills are paying off. What do you think, Victor?"

"I think you're very lucky we weren't using real bullets," the older man said and the others laughed quietly. "You're making us into real *guerrillas*, Pablo."

Radford looked at him gravely. "I hope it never comes to that, Victor. On the other hand, it pays to be prepared. We lucked out back at the hut."

Haya nodded. "You never talk about the war you fought, Pablo," he replied. "Yet, I know it is always with you."

Radford shrugged. "Not much I can do about it, is there? We better keep moving if we're going to find shelter. I think it's going to rain tonight."

"It always rains at night," Haya grumped. "How far until we get back to civilization? I'd like to sleep in a real bed with a good roof over me."

"And a señorita to keep you warm?" Radford smiled.

Haya smiled and shrugged. "At the moment, a bed and roof would do. Something good to eat, too." He got to his feet. "All right, Pablo. Lead on."

The others rose and lined up in the order they had followed since leaving the car. All but Haya were carrying Mauser carbines they had salvaged from the ambush, and Radford wondered how these had gotten into the hands of the ambushers. They used the same shells as the Peruvian army and were stamped with the crest of Argentina. They were also well kept.

Radford led with Mateo, one of the bodyguards, behind him. Timo, the driver brought up the rear, watching their back trail, with Diego, the other bodyguard just ahead of him. Victor stayed in the middle, not far behind Mateo. This was the safest place for him to be if they walked into an ambush, and it was Paul's job to make sure this didn't happen.

After traveling so much in the touring car, Radford found it a relief to be traveling by foot again. As a geologist for an American oil company, he had walked most of the northern Andes from one end to the other. Normally he would keep to higher trails through the mountains, but there were few places to hide near the crest, and little water. Only when one dropped over onto the eastern side of the mountains did the jungle begin, and while there were more people around, there was also more cover. Nor was water an issue.

Lower down, there were also small villages where they could buy food. Radford was amazed how warm a welcome Haya always found there, despite the fact he had never been to any of these places. Yet his face was well known throughout the nation, and he was seen as the champion of the little people.

Aside from bandits, the problem was avoiding the police and the military. Ever since the July war with Ecuador in 1941, the Peruvian army maintained garrisons in the northern area of the country and every town of any size also had a police force. Since Victor Haya was a wanted man, this meant his entourage could not stay long in any one place.

Paul Radford was also sure his presence as part of Haya's entourage increased the danger to Victor. They talked about it one day while they were resting from their march. "I think the police know I'm in the country, Victor," he said.

Haya nodded. "It would be very surprising if they didn't, Pablo. I think they may well know that you are part of my entourage, too."

"Doesn't that bother you?" Radford asked.

"Why should it?" Haya chuckled. "I'm a fugitive, myself."

"I really made some powerful people here angry," Radford told him. "Do you remember the German bases scandal? We talked about it."

"Yes, there were two bases in the extreme south. Both were mysteriously destroyed. Are you telling me that you really were involved with both?"

"Yes, I was the one who discovered the secret bases," Paul told him. "I was also along with Captain Molina when the first one was destroyed. I don't suppose he told you about that, did he?"

Haya shook his head and looked at Radford with new interest. "No, he didn't. Not in so many words. No wonder he hasn't been anxious to catch you. You did our nation a real service."

Paul nodded and continued. "That's how I see it. Yet, those same incidents made some very powerful people in the German community in Lima very angry. Since I was the only one without diplomatic status, they came after me. I was holed up in the American embassy for months until some of our people smuggled me out of the country. I was not allowed to communicate with anyone I knew here. That included my wife to be and my daughter. It was too dangerous for them."

Haya nodded. "Yes, it would be. I think I see what you mean. These powerful people have long memories and they would like to get revenge. However, I'm not quite sure I understand what that has to do with me."

"Well, I am in the country illegally and you could be accused of aiding and abetting a foreign spy. I could be shot and I imagine you could be, too. My country would not come to my aid. Or yours, either, Victor."

Haya shook his head. "It might happen but it's very unlikely, Pablo. They don't want to make me a martyr." He smiled. "I am in complete agreement with them on that point. To arrest me for assisting a foreign agent would be a mistake, too. All that would do is give them one more reason to put me in prison again and every time they do, APRA grows stronger. They would not want an open trial, either."

"Well, I needed to know you understood that," Paul said. "If you're all right with it, I am, too."

Haya looked at him gravely. "My friend, I meant it when I told you how important personal loyalty is to me. You have put your life on the line for us and I will not forget it."

Radford nodded. "Well, I won't worry about it, then. We better get on the move. It's going to be dark early and we need to find a decent place to camp." He grinned at the older man. "One with beds and hot water. And sweet señoritas to turn down our sheets."

Haya smiled. "Well, you can have the señoritas. At my age a hot bath and a soft bed are more appealing."

"I know what you mean," Radford answered softly, almost as if he was talking to himself. "The señoritas are a lot of trouble, aren't they?" Turning to resume their journey, Paul never saw the odd look Haya gave him. Timo did, however, and felt a sharp pang of jealousy.

Lima, Perú. "So you think it was him?" It was the man in black who asked and his companion nodded. They were seated at a back table in a deserted German food restaurant not far from the embassy. It was a favorite dining place for the German staff, and the food was quite excellent.

It was also a safe place for them to talk. While Rott was diligent looking for hidden microphones in Schwartz's office, it was not safe to assume no one had succeeded putting one there. Here, there was little cause to worry. Rott had found the owner's weakness and let him know he knew about it. It was young boys, very young, and Rott had managed to get photos of the man committing illicit acts with them. Given the strict views of those in power, punishment would be swift and brutal.

"Yes, Helmut, I do. Who else do you think could be that lucky? Twice, now."

Rott had his doubts. "I think you may be underestimating him, Jergen," he said. "It's hard to believe what I hear from my sources, but he's not the young man we knew two years ago. He's survived arctic combat and won three heroic medals doing it. That's not a matter of luck. It's skill."

"Then why is he here in this God-forsaken place?" the linguist demanded. "I'm sure he's not here on his own."

"No, if he had deserted, my sources would know. Nor has he been released from service as an invalid. It's clear to me he was sent here by his superiors. What we need to find out is why they sent him. I'm sure it's something they consider quite important. Otherwise, they would have left him where he was. He's apparently a very good construction geologist. He was working for their combat engineers. They rival our own and they didn't want to let him go."

Schwartz looked at his companion with interest. "You seem to be getting first class intelligence, Helmut. Are you sure of your sources?"

Rott nodded and rewarded his companion with a ghastly smile. "Not even Gehlen has better, I assure you. I own my sources."

"I don't suppose you would care to share who it is, would you?" Schwartz asked.

Rott answered with a snort, but his companion pressed. "Come, now, Helmut. Your secrets are safe with me. What if something happens to you? We would lose not only your services, but also invaluable sources."

Rott answered with a raised eyebrow. "Suppose I told you, Jergen. Then you decide that you don't need me any longer. Where would I be then? This way you have every reason to make sure I stay alive, don't you?"

"I already have every reason I need, Helmut. You are the most valuable asset our cause has here. Besides, we are friends, are we not? One does not abandon long time friends."

"Right," Rott answered dryly. "Now, what do you propose we do with Radford? I doubt we'll see much effort by the national police to catch him."

Schwartz nodded. "Not if Molina has anything to do with it. I don't suppose there's anything we can do about him. Not Molina, Radford."

"No, not without damaging our political position in Perú," Rott assured him. "With the new ambassador in place, we have to be very careful."

"How about their army? The Fatherland has a lot of support among their officers and they have the manpower."

"Normally, that might be a good idea," Rott answered. Now, I don't think so. I don't think you realize how much the situation changed with the discovery of our secret bases. The Peruvian army is still stinging from the insult of that. We pulled it off right under their noses. The general seems to be bending over backwards to cooperate with the Americans these days."

Schwartz nodded. "I still want the man taken out, Helmut. He's dangerous, especially if what I hear from my sources is correct."

Rott waited patiently. He knew the linguist wanted him to ask what Schwartz's sources had to say. Yet, Rott already knew the information his boss had. What the linguist didn't know was that his driver had something on every source the professor had. Even so, he wanted to keep Schwartz in the dark about this until the right moment. This was not it, so he waited patiently.

"Don't you want to know what my sources have to say?" Schwartz asked, peevish.

Rott shrugged. "You always tell me what I need to know, Jergen. Or do you want me to coax it out of you?"

Schwartz felt his face growing warm. "You border on the brink of insolence sometimes, Helmut."

"I beg your pardon, Jergen. I was simply waiting for you to inform me. No offense was intended."

Schwartz knew he was being mocked but there was little he could do about it. Rott was necessary to his plans for surviving the war, regardless who won. After the collapse of the invasion of Russia, it was clear to a lot of people that the Allies might actually prevail. Exact figures were not known but the estimates Schwartz heard amounted to half a million casualties. While it was not safe to talk about this openly, it was clear to many that the little corporal in Berlin had bitten off more than he could chew.

"Apology accepted," Schwartz said stiffly, taking delight in seeing Rott's jaw tighten. "What my sources tell me is that Radford is traveling with Victor Haya, the communist."

"Haya's not a communist, Jergen. The communists all disavow him as a counter-revolutionary socialist," the driver answered. "My information is that they're trying to kill him, too. That would be a mistake on their part."

Schwartz nodded. "I agree, unless it is done right. What must happen is that his reputation must be destroyed first."

"Or he must die under disgraceful circumstances," Rott replied. "Those can be arranged but if word gets out that he was set up, it could be worse than the secret bases fiasco."

"Well, that wasn't all my fault!" Schwartz declared.

"No? As I recall, it was you who provided our enemies with a map of our operations." He and Schwartz glared at one another until the linguist dropped his gaze.

"This is fruitless, Helmut. What's done is done. What we need to focus on is how we can attack our enemies. Radford is at the top of the list, and Haya is right up there with him."

"I agree with your assessment. One place we could go after Haya is his lack of a wife and family. I suspect your sources have told you the same as mine have me. There are rumors that the man is a sodomite. It would be damning if we could link Radford to him sexually."

Schwartz smiled. "Yes, wouldn't it, now? That would be elegant if we could do it." Then he frowned. "The problem is Radford's woman and child. It is known in Pisco that he sired the child the housekeeper had. I am sure Molina is aware of it, too. How do we get around that?"

"We call it a fraud," Rott replied. "After all, he abandoned his wife and daughter and has not been in touch with them as far as we know. I would have heard if he had. I kept watch on the priest until the housekeeper married and moved to Lima." Seeing his companion's sharp look, he added. "I didn't keep watch, myself, Jergen. I had others keeping watch for me. There was never a hint of

Radford's presence in, or around, Pisco. After it was clear he was out of the country, I called them off."

"Perhaps you need to have them start again. Perhaps our young fool will try to get in touch with Calderón again."

"That's been done. Once I knew Radford was back, I restored surveillance of the old priest. I'm certain Radford will try to contact him."

The linguist nodded. "Well, give all this some thought, Helmut. I'll do the same. Just don't do anything without talking to me first."

"The same goes for you," Rott responded. "Another mess like the last one and we'll be lucky to be sent to the eastern front. Most likely, we'll be shot."

Schwartz glared at his driver but made no response. He got up and stalked out of the cafe, where he waited at the car. Rott, left with the check, watched him leave and grinned. The waiter, seeing Rott grin, shuddered and crossed himself. He hoped he was never in the other man's shoes.

Huallaga Valley, Perú. Paul Radford rose from where he sat overlooking the river and stretched. He'd been there since first light, watching the mist gather and drift, playing with the morning light across the heights. Now the others would be up and they would wonder where he was.

As he made his way down the slope to the place they had camped near the river, he caught the sharp smell of wood smoke and the aroma of fresh coffee. Then he saw Victor sitting by the fire, reading from a thin black leather-bound book Paul had seen him consult before. He was so intent on what he was reading that he didn't notice Paul until Radford helped himself to a cup of coffee from the pot by the fire.

"Good morning, Pablo," Haya greeted him. "I wondered where you were."

"Watching the river flow," Paul answered, smiling. "The light on the mist in the heights is incredible." He nodded toward the little black book in the older man's hand. "I hope I didn't interrupt you."

"No, I was just reading something I've read many times before. It always moves me." He handed the little black book to Paul. Opening it, he read, "*NUEVEO TESTAMENTO Y LOS SALMOS.*"

"I didn't know you were a religious man, Victor," Paul said, surprised.

"I'm not, Pablo, at least not in the conventional way" the statesman replied. Yet I draw a lot of wisdom and solace from that. I have for a long time. Did you know I taught at the *Colegio Anglo-Peruano* in Lima? The man who started the place was Reverend John Mackay. He was a missionary of the Free Church of Scotland and I learned a great deal from him. He made the Scriptures come alive for me. I have a great respect for him and his wife. They were very progressive."

"Yet, you didn't become a Presbyterian?"

Haya smiled. "No, that apparently was not predestined. Yet I did find a deep spiritual well from which to draw."

"So you stayed with the Roman church?"

Haya shook his head sadly. "No, even though I was given a good religious education by French priests as the San Carlos seminary in Trujillo, where I was born. It became apparent to me quite early that the Roman Catholic Church was a large part of the problem in Latin America. The bishops aligned themselves with the oppressors, not the people. What they seemed to value was material, and not spiritual, wealth. So I could not in good conscience be part of that."

"Yet you read the New Testament."

"Oh, yes. I have no quarrel with the Nazarine. I consider him a good friend. His teachings are the soul of justice and wisdom. It's with some of those who claim to be his followers that I have trouble. They seem to put themselves in his place."

Radford chuckled. "No kidding. Yet, there are exceptions. You said you have met Father Juan Calderón."

Haya chuckled. "Yes, that old bandit. I have great respect for him. If most of the priests in the Roman Catholic Church were like him, I would gladly come home. Unfortunately, he is the exception, indeed." He looked at Paul intently. "How about you, Pablo? What do you think?"

Paul shrugged. "To be honest, Victor, I think Napoleon was right. I guess that makes me a hypocrite because I would go to mass every time Father Juan says it if I could. Somehow it means something when he is at the altar."

"I imagine it does but I don't understand the reference to Napoleon."

"He said that God is on the side of the heaviest artillery."

Haya chuckled. "So is the Catholic Church in Perú. Did you know I first met Father Juan in Mexico? He wasn't yet a priest. He was a revolutionary who rode with Pancho Villa."

"That's what he told me. I didn't have a bit of trouble believing him, either. He still carries his old cavalry pistol if he thinks he might need it."

Haya laughed. "That, I didn't know but it doesn't surprise me. Not a bit."

Lima, Perú. Captain Carlos Molina was busy reading a report when the officer at the front desk interrupted him. "Pardon, sir. You have a visitor. He's an American."

Molina glanced at the clock on the wall and smiled. The man from the embassy was ten minutes early, a sign of respect. "Tell him I will be with him momentarily," the captain replied. Setting aside the report he was reading, he quickly cleared his desk and strode down the hall leading to the waiting room.

The man Molina was meeting was sitting quietly, smoking a cigarette. The captain noticed that he had taken the best seat in the room for defensive action. A solid wall was at his back and there was a heavy table that could be used for cover if he was attacked. Nor did the captain think this was deliberate. It was probably a habit.

The tall American rose to his feet in one fluid motion as the captain came out of the hallway and headed his way. He was dressed in a dark gray suit that hung as if tailored for him and a British regimental tie was knotted neatly below the starched white collar of his shirt. There was also a slight bulge under his left arm, so slight that anyone less observant would never have seen it. Yet it was the steady eyes and relaxed stance of a gutter fighter that told Molina this was a dangerous man.

"Thank you for coming here, señor," Molina told him as they

walked down the hall. He knew the man's name was Jacques Paul and that he was a captain in the US Army. The two had met before a couple of years earlier during the secret German base operation. Yet, Jacques Paul was listed as an civilian security officer on the embassy staff and Molina knew he was a spy for the American government. Or a spy-master, perhaps. He carried an air of authority that Molina thought belied his rank as a simple army captain.

"Of course, Captain," the other answered. After they entered the office and had sat down, he added. "This is much more discreet than your coming our way. Just to get our stories straight, what's the official reason for my visit?"

Molina shrugged. "As I said over the phone, we need to talk about the security arrangements for your Christmas party. However, that can wait until later. What concerns me is the presence of Paul Radford in the St. Martin Region up north. As far as I can determine, he is not in the country legally."

Jacques Paul nodded. "I understand your concern. Suppose he had entered legally, say, as a member of our embassy staff. What do you think would have been your government's response to that?"

Molina answered without hesitation. "I think his official credentials would have been refused."

"That was our assessment, too. The result would have been official embarrassment on both sides. What about if he had entered as a simple visitor? What would have happened then?"

"He would probably have been arrested. There have not been any orders given yet, but I am sure there would be once it was known he was in the country."

When Jock nodded. When he spoke again, his tone was soft and very courteous. "I have no intention of being difficult, Captain, or denying what we both know is true, so please bear with me for a moment. What I would like to know is if there is any legal proof his enemies could use to substantiate the charge that he was here illegally? His passport is valid and shows an entry visa but no exit visa. Who is to say he was not here all the time, wandering around in the wilderness?"

Molina frowned. "Like Moses, I suppose. You Americans play very fast and loose with the law, señor."

"Aside from irregular entry, Radford has not committed a crime that I am aware of. Or am I wrong?"

"We have reports of a gun fight not far from Moyobamba. Six men were killed, two of them from a distinctly American weapon. This was a .22 caliber pistol or rifle. Another was shot in the arm by a .22."

"How accurate is your source of information?"

"Quite accurate. I sent my very best sergeant. He is not a man who can be bought."

"Did he report anything else?"

Molina looked at his companion for a long moment before nodding. "All right, I'll tell you, but I need answers, too."

"Of course," Jock replied. "However, it may be that your information is more current than mine."

"My sergeant reported that there was a gun fight not far from Moyobamba. Six men were killed and their weapons taken. My sergeant established that they were communists from Ecuador. Their leader was known to us and he was one of the ones killed. They attacked a place where Haya was staying and pursued Haya's party into the woods. Haya's party ambushed them and did not return to the hut to get the car they were driving. They abandoned it and have not been seen since, which puzzles me. I asked the police in the area to check on this and they did. No one will admit to seeing or hearing of them."

"Was there any evidence that tied Radford to the attack, Captain?"

"No, but we have a report of a bearded American traveling with Haya. From what my sergeant observed, the ambush of the attackers was done with military precision. Haya's men are not trained soldiers."

Molina stopped and gave Jaques Paul a stern look. "Now it's your turn, señor. What is Radford doing here?"

"He's keeping an eye on Victor Haya and the communists. He was sent in because he knows the country and is fluent in Spanish and Quechua. And because some powerful people in our government are very worried about communists in South America."

"Yes, your J. Edgar Hoover comes to mind."

"I can assure you, he may or may not be the President's man but he's certainly not mine."

"That may be, but he has great influence. Still, Victor Haya is no communist and his party, APRA, has no ties to communism. I know this because I checked quite carefully. Even so, Haya is a wanted man. So if Radford is helping him, then he is an accomplice."

"Yes, but it's my understanding that Haya wanted for political reasons, not civil crimes. Any information we get about civil crimes will be passed onto you immediately."

"I am a policeman, señor, not a judge or a politician. When my government declares that someone is a criminal, no matter what kind, it is my duty to arrest them."

Jaques Paul nodded. "I understand, Captain. I am a soldier and I must follow orders, too. I will try to make sure that Paul Radford doesn't cross your path."

Molina nodded. "I am glad we understand one another on that. I personally like the man. Now, what about the security arrangements for your Christmas party? We will have men in the street and can make sure your embassy employees get home safely. We will, however, need you to reimburse our government for their time and expenses. I hope you understand."

"We could pay you directly and let you take care of your men," the American replied.

Molina shook his head. "No, that could be construed as bribery. Señor Radford is not the only one with enemies in our government."

Messenger

5 Vicinity of Huánuco. Paul Radford looked at the one-eyed man with affection. As far as he could see, the last two years had not changed the guide at all. The only difference he could see is that his friend now wore a glass eye. In stark contrast to his dark natural eye, the prosthetic was blue. The result was startling, particularly with the clear scars of a jaguar's claws crossing the blue eye. "It's good to see you, Pico," he told the guide. Nor did he need to ask how Pico had found him. The jungle telegraph is almost as fast as one in a small town and the people who lived there kept watch without being seen.

"It's good to see you, Pablo. The padre gave me a letter to give you." He offered an envelope to the younger man. Nor did his remaining eye fail to notice the change in Radford. He looked much older now, like the padre looked when first he met Pico many years before.

Radford looked at letter like it was a poison snake. "I don't know, Pico. The last letter he sent me was full of bad news."

The guide nodded. "He really would like you to forgive him, Pablo. He did only what he had to do and he was very reluctant, even then. He loves you like a son."

"I have forgiven him, Pico. I don't blame him or Rosario, either. Who I blame are the political *pendejos* who started this *chingada* war."

"The padre will be glad to hear this. He really misses you, Pablo. He told me what he wrote in the letter. It's not bad news but it says some things you need to know."

Radford nodded, casually putting the letter in a pocket. Then he grinned. "What I want to know, Pico, is what's with that blue eye?"

The guide laughed. "There was a man I worked for who died, a

German. He was very old and very kind to me. He lost an eye in the last war and he had an extra glass one. So he gave it to me. When I'm in the mountains, I take it out and set it beside me when I sleep. The children think I can still watch them, even if I snore!"

"Well, it's quite striking. People are not likely to forget you. What do you do when you want to hide?"

"What do you think?" the older man laughed. "I put on the patch. Then I'm just old one-eyed Pico, the town drunk."

"Too bad it's not made like a jaguar's eye," Paul said.

Pico's smile disappeared and he shook his head. "No, Pablo, that would be very bad. It would scare me every time I saw my reflection. The people in the forest would think I'm a *brujo*, too, a witch. I would, too."

Paul almost started to tease the guide about it but the look on the older man's face stopped him. "Well, it's great just the way it is. So how have you been? And Father Juan?"

"The padre is getting old now, Pablo. The last year he lost a lot of his strength. Not from sickness, but getting old. He has a hard time even walking to the market and back."

Radford shook his head sadly. "I hate to hear that, Pico. He always seemed like the mountains to me, ageless. Do you have any idea how old he is now?"

"He once told me he was old enough to be Pancho Villa's father," the guide replied. "I looked Pancho Villa up and he died more than twenty years ago. He was forty-five years old."

Radford did the math quickly. "Then Father Juan must be over eighty now, maybe eighty-five." The guide nodded. "I had no idea, Pico. He hides his age well."

The guide nodded. "He has to, Pablo. He has many friends but he has many enemies, too. They are afraid of him, but if they knew how weak he was...." Pico shrugged.

"All he has to be is strong enough to pull the trigger of that old .45 Colt of his," Radford replied. "Hopefully, his enemies know how good a shot he is."

Pico nodded. "They still talk about him killing the attacker the night...his housekeeper was kidnapped."

"You can call Rosario by her name, Pico," Radford said. He'd heard the slight pause when Pico almost said her name. "You don't have to worry about my feelings. What's done is done and there isn't any use hanging on to it."

"Why don't you read the padre's letter and tell me if you want to write one back? I'm not in a hurry but I don't like to be gone too long."

The way the guide said this caused Radford to smile. "Do you have a girlfriend or something, Pico?" he asked.

The guide answered casually, too casually. "The padre's new housekeeper is a very good cook. Not as good as Rosario, of course, but better than me." Seeing Radford's knowing look he shrugged. "She's a widow. We like to talk."

"I bet it's the blue eye," Paul said. "Or does she make you wear the patch when you're in the house?" The guide kept silent and Radford relented. "All right. Let me read the letter and I'll dash off a quick reply. Then you can be on your way. While you're waiting, why don't you fix us all some supper? The others are all tired of my cooking. As a matter of fact, I am, too."

The next morning Paul was up early. After feeding the others, he left them sitting around the fire and made his way to a high place where he could study the lie of the land ahead. He was about to turn around and rejoin the group when he heard Haya walk up behind him.

"That was an interesting visitor you had last night," Victor said, looking out over the jungle below. "I thought he would be here this morning. I wanted to talk to him. He's a remarkable cook."

"He left very early, Victor," Paul told him. "He wanted to get back to his family. He has a long way to go."

"I see," the older man said. "If I remember right, he lives somewhere down south."

"From where we stand, I'd say that describes most of Perú," Radford said, grinning. "Fortunately, it's summer time. He said something about Bolivia and I remember how cold it can get there."

"Do you mind my asking why he came to you?"

The younger man shook his head. He wondered why Haya was

being so inquisitive. "No, not at all. It was a personal matter. An old friend of mine is not doing so well. Father Juan. I'm going to need to get away for a few days and see him at some point. Why do you ask, Victor?"

"A thousand pardons, Pablo. I'm used to having to take care of my people, all my people, so I ask a lot of questions. I just wondered."

Radford nodded. "I'd be curious in your shoes, too. One thing he did tell me does affect you. The Germans are now aware I am traveling with you. That could cause some problems if they decide to come after me."

Haya chuckled dryly. "From what I've seen of you, that could cause them some big problems. They are not exactly my admirers, either."

"Don't sell them short. They can be very efficient when they put their minds to it. Helmut Rott is not someone you want to mess around with. I wouldn't trust his boss as far as I could throw him, either, but Rott is downright evil. So if you or one of your men get a shot at him, I suggest you take it."

"That seems rather cold blooded, Pablo."

Radford shrugged. "Well, we're dealing with cold blooded men, Victor. It's not a good idea to allow a green tree viper to strike first. These people don't care who they hurt, or how."

"I can understand them seeing you as an enemy. You are at war with them. I don't see the point of coming after you."

Radford sighed. "I know. I don't, either, but these guys are not rational. I'm sure they think I'm up to something no good. They want to know what it is, and even if they don't find out, they want to put me out of business, anyway. You know what I mean. That's how it is with you and your government, isn't it?"

The older man nodded. "Yes, unfortunately. They don't seem to understand that we can accomplish more if we work together."

"You're assuming they want to accomplish anything but staying in power. So they make trouble for you and anyone else they see as a threat, on general principles."

Haya looked at Paul Radford, frowning. "You were not such a cynic when I knew you before, Pablo," he said.

"That's true. I hadn't seen good men blown to bits because of some stupid admiral's stiff necked pride," the younger man answered bitterly. "Or some stupid general," he added. He held up his hands. "Victor, we need to talk about something else. I can't allow myself to dwell on this. It's too painful."

"Forgive me, Pablo. I didn't intend to intrude." Radford nodded, though he wondered what else Haya intended. There was nothing inadvertent about his questions.

"What I wanted to talk to you about was getting another car. Or getting back the one we left behind. All this walking is wasting time and killing my feet. I'm not a young man any more, Pablo, and there are people I need to see."

"You would do better investing in a good pair of boots, Victor," Radford answered. "Or maybe some burros. You're too vulnerable on the roads. After that attack, the police will be on their guard. And with the Germans stirring things up the way they will...." He shrugged.

"We're not sure they are. Or that the authorities will pay them any attention if they do."

Radford shook his head. "Riding around in a fancy touring car would be like waving a red cape at a bull. You would be daring the police to act and they would see it as an act of defiance. What would you expect them to do, Victor, give you a hug and a pat on the back? Where do you need to go in such a hurry, anyway?"

"I don't do it for the police, but for the common people. They expect their leaders to travel in a certain style."

"You're a better judge of that than I am," Radford allowed. "I would have thought they would respect you for being like they are, traveling on foot or by burro."

"No, as the wise old Greek pointed out, familiarity breeds contempt. They want so see me as being a man of the people, but different from them in an important way, too."

"Because you're the *jeffe*," Radford said dryly.

"Exactly! They don't want me to be too much like them. If I were, then I would have no power."

"And power is what politics is all about. Tell me, Victor, how do you expect things to be different if you do them the same tired old way?"

Haya started to answer but stopped and shook his head. "You don't understand," he muttered. "It's the way things are. It's human nature."

"I'm afraid I do understand, and that's the problem," Radford replied with a wry smile. "And you call me cynical?"

Haya glared at the younger man but said nothing. "Maybe we need to get back to the subject," Paul said. "Traveling by car is unsafe, so if you want wheels, I suggest a truck. It could be a good ruse, something the police would not expect from a politician."

Haya nodded curtly and Radford sighed. "Look, Victor, I know I'm being a pain in the ass. My mission right now is to keep you alive. That means poking holes in wishful thinking, among other things. You can fire me any time you want."

The older man glanced back where the others were sitting. It was clear they were uneasy. They knew a disagreement was brewing even though they were too far away to hear what was being said. They might accept Paul's leadership when it came to fighting, but Victor was the patriarch, *el patrón*.

Then Haya smiled and shook his head, patting Paul on the shoulder. "No, you're right. I did ask for a fresh point of view and we owe you our lives. I may not like it, but I need someone who will tell me when I'm full of *caca del torro*. Yet I am right about the people, Pablo. Unfortunately, they see the man in the touring car as the leader."

"You know better than I. You don't suppose we could liberate a tank, could we?"

"That might be a bit conspicuous," Victor said, smiling. From where they stood, Paul could see the others relaxing but he knew Haya had not given in. He needed Paul and he had merely kept things agreeable.

"Do you need to be traveling all the time?" Paul asked.

"No, but I do need to be seen from time to time. There are places I can 'hole up' for a while, as you Americans say. I try not to use the same place all the time."

"That's good. Maybe it's time to hole up for a while, give things time to settle down."

"I agree. You mentioned Bolivia. There is a place close to the border, but still in Perú. It's been a long time since I used it. We could go there until after Christmas. How do you propose we travel?"

"Well, if you don't want to ride an ass, we could get horses. That would make you *el caballero* in the eyes of the people, the man on the horse."

"Right," Haya answered dryly. "All I'd need is a sword." Yet Paul could tell that Victor liked the image. While Radford preferred to walk, they could cover a lot more ground on horses. The Victor looked at him and grinned. "For you, we get a mule!"

Near Puno. It was three weeks after the disagreement between Paul and Victor that their party arrived at a large ranch near the border with Bolivia. The ranch was owned by the widow of a powerful friend of Victor, and after so many days in the saddle, Radford was glad to be there. The summer weather was much more pleasant on the high plateau, and the widow had given him a comfortable room with a large, soft bed.

The widow was a handsome middle aged woman named Gloria Lopez and she and Radford hit it off right away. She seemed to be disappointed the second evening they were there when Paul mentioned he needed to head south the next day to visit a sick friend on the coast. Later that evening, after everyone had turned in, she paid a visit to Paul's room and stayed until dawn.

"Are you sure you want to leave today?" Gloria asked. She was snuggled close against Paul and her voice sounded like a purr. "You didn't get much sleep last night."

Paul chuckled. "Neither of us did, did we? Perhaps I could leave tomorrow morning, instead."

"Wonderful. You can take a nice, long siesta after we have our midday meal. Now give me a nice kiss and I'll be gone. I don't want the servants to catch us." Yet, the brief kiss quickly got serious and it was almost an hour later before she slipped out of Paul's bed.

As it turned out, it was two days later before Paul was able to tear himself away. "I really do need to see my friend soon," he told Gloria the night before he left. "He's very old and not doing well."

"I don't suppose it's someone I know," Gloria said.

"His name is Juan Calderón. He's been the priest in Pisco for many, many years."

"Father Juan from Pisco? He and my husband were very good friends. He came and stayed with us several times until Miguel died. He's a delightful man. How do you know him?"

So it was that Paul found himself telling Gloria about his time in Perú before the war. Somehow her presence made it easy to talk about Rosario and Juan Calderón, and of the baby whom he had never seen. Yet the telling took it's toll. By the time he finished, his cheeks were wet with tears he was not aware were flowing, and he felt empty.

"Oh, Pablo, how awful!" Gloria said when he was done.

"Please, Gloria," he said, choking for the first time since he started. "I can't handle sympathy."

"Of course, you can't, you *macho* man," she said gently. "Tears are for women and children. Yet I respect you for them." Then she pinched him, and, seeing the pique in his eyes, said, "There! That will give you something else to think about."

When Radford tried to pinch her back, a struggle ensued and he found himself on top of her, eye to eye, holding her hands down above her head. Then she opened her legs and they began to make love fiercely, as if there would be no tomorrow. When they were done, Paul wept like a child in her arms. Nor was he aware of her leaving their bed at dawn.

"You slept in this morning," Victor observed when Paul came into the kitchen for a cup of coffee. Gloria was seated at a small table with him and she smiled warmly when Radford joined them.

Paul could see Victor was amused by the way the two of them avoided giving the impression of anything but a casual relationship. He started to say something about it, but, seeing alarm in Gloria's eyes, said, "Yes, that's a wonderful bed. I haven't felt this rested in a long time. What's the hour?"

Victor looked at his watch. "Half past ten. Did you have pleasant dreams?" He was looking at Gloria when he asked.

Radford a yawn behind his hand. "Pardon me. I think I'm still waking up. I meant to be up long before this. I better be getting ready."

"Surely, not before breakfast, Pablo," Gloria said. "We've got fresh sweetbread the cook made this morning, *chorizo* and eggs, if you want them."

"That sounds too good to turn down," Radford answered and Gloria left to tell the cook.

Haya looked at the younger man gravely. "Be careful with Gloria, Pablo," he said. "She is a good friend and I would hate to see her mistreated."

"I would, too, Victor. She's good people. I gather there's not any history between the two of you?"

Haya shook his head. "Nothing romantic. Now if you'll excuse me, I think I'll go write a couple of letters and allow you love birds some time alone." He smiled and patted Paul on the shoulder as he left the room.

Washington, DC. The little fat man looked out the window of the conference room. He could see the street below decorated for Christmas, and the mood in the capitol was festive. The Allies had won the war in North Africa under the leadership of General George Patton, who had then captured Sicily. Though Patton had been censured for slapping two soldiers with battle fatigue, and relieved of his command for it, the Allies had the initiative and Americans saw victory on the horizon. Despite the shortages of the war, the public was ready to celebrate.

Even so, the Director was in no mood to be festive. He didn't like the man he was about to see, but such people were useful. Glancing at his watch, he saw that the man was ten minutes late which did nothing to dispel his ill humor. He expected his agents to be prompt, if not early, when they came to see him.

As if on cue, he heard the sound of the door opening and turned around, frowning. What he saw did nothing to soothe his pique. Two special agents walked in escorting someone who looked much more like a suspect than an agent. The man looked like he had slept in his suit and he was carrying a top coat that had clearly seen better days. He smelled like stale beer and cigarette smoke, and it was clear it had been a good while since he stood close to a razor.

"I beg your pardon, sir," one of the escorts said. This man looked like a Special Agent. His dark blue suit was clean and unwrinkled, his shoes were spit polished, and he was well groomed. "This man claims he is supposed to see you."

"He is, Williams. That will be all." The little man's voice sounded like the staccato of rapid machine gun fire.

The agent was clearly surprised. "Don't you want us to stay, sir?" He looked at the man he was escorting. Had it been up to him, the man would be in cuffs.

"No," the little man said curtly. "That won't be necessary." Seeing the agents hesitate, he added, "That will be all."

"Yes, sir." The agent nodded and followed his companion out the door. When he nodded, it almost looked like he was bowing.

"Well, John, it's been a while, hasn't it?" the newcomer drawled. His voice held a broad western twang and there was no hint of his being subservient.

"Yes," the Director answered. "We have a problem we need you to resolve. It will take someone of your talents."

"I see," the other answered. The man, a former Marine Corps sniper, didn't seem surprised. "It's so urgent you can't even greet your shirt-tail cousin properly?"

"There's a war on, in case you haven't noticed," the fat man snapped.

"Oh, I have. There's been a good bit of freelance work, even for us buffalo soldiers. You seem to have been busy, too, John, from what I read in the papers."

"Don't you want to know what I want?"

The visitor shrugged. "You'll tell me when you're good and ready. You always do. How's your love life?"

The Director flushed. The man always found a way of getting under his skin. "That's not germane."

"No? I knew a lady named that once. Only she spelled it with two 'i's and no 'e' tacked on the end."

The Director forced himself to stifle the rebuke on his lips. "We have a problem in South America. We have a rogue agent. He's mixed up with the communists down there and we need him disciplined. We also need the communists he's in cahoots with to be rendered harmless."

"You want me to kill them, in other words."

"I didn't say that!"

"No, but I bet you won't deny it." He looked at the small man with a raised eyebrow. The Director made no response and the rumpled man went on. "You realize this is going to be quite expensive, don't you? Killing always is."

"Standard rates!" the Director snapped.

"Tell me something, cousin. Why did you rat me out with the Marines? I had a good, honest thing going there and now you could have had my services for free."

"You're a Negro!" the Director replied. "Our military is segregated. That's the law."

"We have a common ancestor and I'm lighter complected than you. I can pass for white anywhere in the South. You're the darkie in this woodpile, John."

The Director flushed. There was no question that he had a dark complexion, and there had been rumors about his origin. "My birth certificate says I'm white!"

The other gave him a wry smile and nodded. "Well, it would, wouldn't it, John? Even if the original didn't. You've got a whole department making bogus papers."

The Director didn't bother arguing. "Why do you always have to be so difficult?" he snarled. "Do you want the job or not?"

"That depends on who it is you want killed and what you're paying. What part of South America? I charge more for jungle work."

"This is in the Andes, Perú, in fact. Here's the file." The Director handed his companion a manila folder. Nor did he invite the other to sit down, even though he had to look up to talk to the man.

The rumpled man nodded and walked across the office. He took a seat in a comfortable chair to one side of the Director's desk. "You have an ash tray, John?" he asked, reaching inside his coat and pulling out a half filled pack of cigarettes.

"I don't want you to smoke in here," the Director snapped as sat down behind his desk. It was on an unseen platform six inches higher than the floor, and his chair added another four inches.

The man in the crumpled suit nodded and put away his cigarettes. Nor did it take him long to read through the four pages in the file. Looking up, he smiled, though he didn't share the reason behind it. He wondered if the little fat man knew he looked like a small frog on a large toadstool when he sat behind his enormous desk.

"This is going to cost you, John," the man said. "One of the guys is a war hero and the other is a major politician down there. I've read about them both in the papers."

"That's why I need an outside contractor!" the little man snapped back. What's your fee?"

The rumpled man was thoughtful. "It's going to be difficult. I'd think ten thousand dollars...."

"Agreed!" the Director replied, interrupting the assassin.

"What I was going to say before you cut me off was ten thousand each, plus expenses."

"That's outrageous!" the Director declared.

"So is assassinating a war hero," the other responded calmly. "Not to mention a major player in Latin American politics."

"Ten thousand for both, plus up to two more for expenses. Take it or leave it."

"Only if it's in advance," the rumpled man agreed. "One other thing, John. If I look at it and don't like it for any reason, I can abort and keep the fee. I wouldn't charge you for expenses in that case."

The Director shook his head. "No, I can hire someone else for less. I'll advance you five thousand and pay five more when the job is done. Plus two more for expenses."

The other man thought about this for a few moments. Then he nodded and smiled. "All right, since we're kinfolk, John. Only I'm serious about the right of refusal. The first five is for taking a good look at the situation. The second five is if I decide to do it. I need both in cash."

"Very well." The Director opened a drawer of his desk and took out an envelope. He tossed it across the desk and his companion rose and retrieved it.

Opening the envelope, the man looked inside and sat down again, counting the money. "What's the matter, Mike? Don't you trust me?" he asked with a droll smile.

The other man nodded. "Sure, I do, John. I trust you to be exactly who you are." Then he laughed. "You're very sure of yourself, cousin. I'm not going to ask where you got fifty crisp hundred dollar bills. I bet they're marked, too." He put the bills back in the envelope and tossed it back across the desk. "What I need is fives and tens, all well used." He shrugged. "Nice try, though."

The Director nodded. "It was worth a shot," he said. He reached under his desk and pulled out a battered brief case. "Take a look at this. Five thousand in small bills, all of it used and none of it marked."

The rumpled man looked inside the brief case and nodded. "Good enough," he said, closing the brief case.

"Aren't you going to count it?" the director asked, trying hard to not show his surprise.

"Of course, I am," the other replied. "Just not here. I'll do it when I get back to where I'm staying. If the count is wrong, the advance doubles."

The rumpled man turned and walked to the door. Turning around, he said, "Did I ever tell you I turned down doing a job on you, John? Twice, as a matter of fact."

"Are you threatening me, Mike?" The Director's words were as hard and cold as glacial ice.

"No, of course not," the assassin answered. "I was just passing along information. I don't do kinfolk, John. Besides, you know better than to try and cheat me."

"So who was it?" the Director asked.

The rumpled man grinned and walked to the door. "Now, John, you know better than that, too. I don't kiss and tell. Not even to a shirt-tail cousin."

Strange Visitors

6 Washington, DC. The day was still young when he left the FBI headquarters. Michael O'Leary bought a bagel and an apple for breakfast from a street vendor near the park. Walking to a bench he took a seat and slowly consumed his lunch, going back for a cup of hot coffee when he was done. Seeing a phone booth near by, he took out a little black address book and looked up a number. Then he dropped a nickel into the slot an dialed.

He was in luck. The clerk who answered the phone at the Pentagon patched him directly through to the man he needed. "Hello, Bunt," he said when the clerk came on the line. "Long time no see. I ran into a mutual friend of ours, a Navy lieutenant named Paul Radford. He suggested we get together for dinner tonight."

There was silence on the other end of the line and O'Leary added, "You remember Paul, don't you? He said he had run into you at BUPERS."

"Actually, I do, He's quite a fellow but I don't know if I can do this, Bagger."

"Come on, I'm flush and I'm buying. I've got reservations for three at Risso's at eight."

"I don't know, Bagger. Things are pretty tight around here these days. I don't know if I can get away. There's a war on, you know."

"All the more reason to make it. Look, I'm shipping out tomorrow and God knows when I'll be back. Need me to make it a little later?"

"All right, make it a half hour later. I'll see what I can do to get away but don't take it personally if I don't show."

"Well, I hope you can. I've got a new Ford and I need someone to keep it for a few weeks while I'm gone."

"Nobody has a new Ford these days."

"New to me. I lucked out and got it for two bills."

"Yeah, you did. He could have got twice that. Look, I've got to go. I'll see you if I can make it."

When he hung up, Michael O'Leary smiled. Bunt always worried too much and had to be coaxed. Even so, he would come through. He always did because he was always short of cash. Four hundred dollars would play a lot of ponies. He also liked the food where they were meeting and would be early.

Sure enough, at ten minutes before six Bunt walked in the fancy door at Clancy's Pub. He made his way back to the table where O'Leary was seated and smoothly pocketed the money Michael palmed him when they shook hands. When the waiter came, he ordered the popular stew Clancy made and a Guinness to go with it.

By unspoken agreement, the two men did not discuss the business at hand until they were done eating. "Too bad Paul couldn't make it," Bunt observed dryly when it was time for them to talk. "War heros have a tough schedule these days."

"You know how low key he is," O'Leary replied. "Bring me up to date on what he's been up to."

"I hear he's up for a Medal of Honor," Bunt said. "Lots of brass looking over his file. Congressmen, too. Were you aware he already holds a Navy Cross and two Silver Stars? Not to mention a Purple Heart."

"That sand-bagger," Michael laughed. "That's just like him, playing things down. What did he do, kick Tojo in the balls?"

"So to speak. The Medal of Honor will be for taking out eleven Japanese Marines single-handed with a samurai sword. He was defending an artillery battery and the general in charge saw him do it."

"Sounds like a tough hombre," O'Leary murmured. "A lot tougher than I thought."

"The point is that he's a war hero, Bagger. Don't mess with him. The FBI was the latest agency to request his file."

O'Leary nodded. "That figures. I don't suppose you know what he's up to down south, do you? Way south."

"No," said Bunt, getting up. Michael was surprised when Bunt offered him his hand. He was even more surprised when the man palmed the four hundred dollar bills back. "This is it, Bagger," he said. "Don't call me again. I only came because I really respect the guy. Don't screw him over. He's worth ten of you and me."

Pisco, Perú. Father Juan Calderón was locking the sacristy door when he felt the presence of someone behind him. As he turned to see who it was, he slipped his hand into the pocket of his cassock and grasped the pistol there. There had been several daylight robberies lately and the ornate chalice and paten for the mass were pure silver. They were worth far more than most people in the city made in several years, and there were many who would kill for them.

There was a quiet chuckle from the figure in the shadows. "You won't need the hand cannon, padre," a quiet voice said. "You're lucky I'm not some bandito. I'm surprised you let me get this close."

"Pablo!" the old man declared. He started to give Radford an abrazo but stopped. He sensed a deep reserve had replaced the easy intimacy they once knew. Yet, there was no holding back his delight. "Thank you for coming to see this old fool. I hoped you might. Come into the house. You're just in time for supper."

Radford nodded. "Thank you, Juan Calderón. I'm hungry enough to eat boiled lizard."

The reference cut the old man to the heart. That's what he told Paul Radford they were eating the first time the young man came to dinner. Yet there was no sign of malice in Paul's eyes. There was, in fact, no sign of anything but a wry smile that didn't reach his eyes. Those showed nothing and this worried the padre. It was what he had seen in the photograph, the same look young men had when they'd seen too much combat in the Mexican revolution. He mourned the loss in Paul. "Oh, I think we can do better than that," Calderón replied, smiling, forcing himself to be cheerful. "Someone brought us some *cabrito* and Alicia has prepared us a feast."

"Better *cabrito* than *cabrón*," Radford answered. That, too brought back memories of a far happier time. "Alicia must be your new housekeeper, the one Pico told me about. What's the occasion?"

The old man smiled, relieved that Rosario Gomez, his former housekeeper, had been too close to delivering her latest child to make the trip that year. "It's my birthday, Pablo. Pico and Alicia decided we needed to celebrate."

"Sorry, I didn't remember," Paul replied. "I would have picked up a present. At least a bottle of wine."

"You have given me a wonderful present just being here," the padre assured him. "You have no idea how much I have missed you."

There were tears in the old man's eyes when he said this and Paul was touched in a way he had not been for a long while. Something flickered across his eyes, then disappeared. Paul stepped forward and hugged his friend. "Happy birthday, Juan Calderón," he said. "I'm glad I came...home."

The old man took a deep breath and sighed, relieved. There was hope in the pause before the last word. Paul had once told him how much more at home he felt in the rectory than in his parents' house. "Goodness! Here we are, gabbing like fools when there's good food waiting. Pico's already here."

"Wearing his blue eye, I suppose," Radford said, shaking his head and smiling. "That one surprised me, padre."

"Yes, he's really taken with it, isn't he? Did he take it out and offer to let you hold it?"

"No," Radford chuckled. "He spared me that."

The old priest led the way to the kitchen where Pico stood beside a tall, willowy woman of middle years. There was soft gray hair mingled with the jet black of the rest of her hair, and the simple house dress she word failed to hide her figure. Then she turned and met his gaze with startling gray eyes that reminded him of Lou.

"This is Alicia, who bosses us around," Father Juan said. Then, seeing the look in the younger man's eyes, he asked, "What's wrong, Pablo?"

"Nothing," Paul managed to say. Speaking to Alicia, he said, "I beg your pardon. Your eyes reminded me of someone I knew up north. They are very striking."

"Striking?" Alicia said. "Ugly can be striking."

"Never," Radford smiled, shaking his head, and the padre saw another flicker of life in his eyes. "With you, striking goes far beyond beautiful."

"My goodness," Alicia laughed, speaking to Juan. "This young man could charm the spots off a jaguar." Turning back to Paul she said, "Unfortunately, I am spoken for." Turning to Pico, she scolded, "You didn't warn me how handsome he is!" Yet the warmth of her smile belied her words.

"Careful!" the padre warned her with a smile. "Pablo's hat won't fit."

That set the tone for dinner that night, and Paul found himself telling them about Grigory teaching him how to right a bidarka after capsizing him in it. His description of dancing up and down on the shore trying to get warm had them laughing. This reminded Pico of the time he had seen Paul waving his arms like a "weend-meel," trying to drive off a cloud of biting flies along the trail and hollering "chit!"

Even so, when Alicia asked about the other woman with eyes like her, Paul looked stricken. He shook his head and held up his hands. "I'm sorry," he said. "I still can't talk about her. She died."

Juan Calderón jumped in with a funny story about one of the bishops he had worked for. After that there were funny stories of the goings-on in Pisco and Lima, but the lively spirit of their conversation was gone. Even though Paul laughed politely at the right times, he had withdrawn into himself once again.

When dinner was done, Paul and the padre retired to the courtyard. There they sat quietly, smoking cigarillos and sipping brandy, letting the wonderful meal that Alicia had set before them settle. Pico had remained inside, helping her in the kitchen, sensing that the padre and his guest needed time alone. Nor did a word pass between them once they sat down. A good half hour passed before Juan Calderón cleared his throat and turned to his companion. "I forget how easy you are with silence, Pablo," he said softly. "So, tell me, how is it with you?"

The younger man shrugged. "I don't know, padre," he said. "I don't feel much inside me these days. You know how it is. You've been to war. I keep the memories of that locked away pretty tight. They're still too raw. You saw that tonight. I just couldn't talk about it any more. When I dream about them, I wake up angry or so miserable I want to die."

Juan Calderón nodded. "Yes, I remember when it was like that for me. It took a long time before I could talk about it and even longer before I could lay the memories to rest. Even now I wake up having dreamed about things from then, and I feel very sad. The anger seems to have burned itself out. Or it may be that grace has healed it."

"Are you sure it wasn't just time?"

The padre shook his head. "Yes, quite sure. Time heals nothing. The rage I felt seemed to grow with time. I couldn't get rid of it, no matter how hard I tried."

"So what happened? You are able to talk about it now."

"Something happened I can't really explain. I was cursing the heavens one day in a fit of pique and something touched me. I don't know what else to call it but grace. It was like something reached inside me and took hold of my rage and wrenched it out of me. Yet, it didn't hurt and I found myself filled with joy. To this day I don't know what happened. Or why. Yet I'm grateful it did."

"You never told me about this before." Paul said. "Why not? Why now?"

"I don't know, Pablo. Maybe it was because the right time had not come. I don't remember ever thinking about it when you and I talked before. What's so strange about that is that the memory of this is never far from mind. It's there every time I say the Mass. I don't talk about it much, but I don't hide it." He looked at the younger man. "I didn't hide it from you. It just never came up."

Radford nodded. "I remember your saying the Mass. I always thought there was something very special about it. Is that why you became a priest?"

Calderón nodded. "Yes, but not right away." He smiled. "I was too full of life. Celibacy was a hard pill to swallow and I'm afraid I liked the señoritas a little too much. No, let's be honest. I liked taking them to bed too much. I didn't see how I could ever give that up."

"Yet, here you are?" There was a challenge in Paul's eyes and the old priest was glad to see it. It told him Paul's spirit might be wounded, but it was not dead. There was hope.

Juan Calderón laughed. "Yes, here I am, but I'll tell you a secret, my friend. Long before Rosario came into my life, my housekeeper and I were lovers for more than twenty years. She was several years older than me and when she died, all my desire died with her."

Radford nodded. "I thought mine had, too." Seeing the interest in the padre's eyes, Paul shook his head. "I will tell you more about it, tomorrow, perhaps. There was a woman I loved as much as I did Rosario. The woman with gray eyes. Her name was Lou and we were going to marry after the war. Then she was killed by a plane crash and something inside me died. At least, I thought it had." He stopped talking and was silent for a long while.

Juan Calderón nodded. "Then something happened?"he asked gently. "Just recently?"

Radford looked at him. "This has got to be confessional, padre. I'm not sure whether I have sinned or not, but you know the lady."

"So it needs confessional secrecy," Juan Calderón observed. "Very well. I consider this whole conversation under the seal."

Paul nodded. "Thank you. You're aware I'm traveling with Victor Haya." The padre nodded.

"The reason is that I was sent down here to keep an eye on him and his people. The simplest way to do this was to join his entourage. He's aware of this and he was the one who suggested I do so."

"Keep your friends close but your enemies closer."

"Exactly. He and I have talked about that, too, as well as the possibility I will be ordered to kill him. That's an order I have no intention of carrying out and I told him so. I have taken human life, but I'm not an assassin and I've done everything I can to assure him of that."

"No, that's not who you are," the padre assured him.

"Well, to make a long story short, we went to stay with a friend of his. This friend has a ranch on the Bolivian border and she's a fairly young widow."

The padre smiled. "I know who you're talking about. We don't need to use names."

"Well, we hit it off right away. I was surprised I found her so attractive but I didn't do anything. Then she came to my bed in the night. I was going to leave for here the next day, but I ended up waiting for two more days."

"I can understand why," Juan Calderón said dryly. "She is a very passionate woman. To my way of thinking, this was not a sin.

Widows need comfort and there's really only one way to do so. There are many who would disagree, but they are full of *caca de gallo*."

"I guess I'm lucky to have it back," Paul said. "But it felt a lot safer when I felt nothing."

The padre nodded. "I know. Everything we love, we lose, sooner or later. Yet I am convinced the joy is worth the pain."

The younger man shrugged. "Maybe so, but we don't seem to have much choice about it, do we?" Then he held up his hands. He seemed to be having trouble breathing. "Can we talk about something else? I want to finish this conversation while I'm here, but not right now. It's still too much."

"Of course," Juan Calderón replied. "What do you think of Victor Haya?"

"I think he's in a great deal of danger," Radford replied. "I also think he's not aware just how great the danger is."

"What do you think of him as a man?"

"I think he's a good man, maybe a little full of himself. But, then, what politician isn't? I think his heart's in the right place. He doesn't seem power hungry, either." He smiled. "He and I are very much alike in some ways and very different in others. Have you met him?"

"Yes, but I never had time to spend with him apart from the crowd. He certainly has enough charisma. I could almost touch it. He knows how to work the crowd, too. What are your differences?"

"He's an optimist," Radford replied. "He seems to prefer the company of men, too, though women seem to like him. I could be wrong, but I think he may find men more attractive than women. I haven't seen any sign of this, except that the men he really responds to seem to be a bit light on their feet."

"Agile with their feet?" Juan Calderón asked.

"Sorry, I guess that doesn't translate very well. It comes from male dancers, who are not considered *macho* in some parts of the United States. 'Light on his feet' is a polite term for a *maricón*."

The old man nodded, frowning. "I have heard rumors about this, about Victor, but I discounted them as a malicious attempt at political smear."

"Well, in this case, I think the smoke means fire, too. It's really none of my business, and I really don't care if it's true or not. But you asked what I thought."

The old priest nodded. "Yes, I did. Nor do I see much wrong with this. I have known many *maricónes*, most of them very good people. The love they feel for one another is not too different from the love we feel for certain women. I find it very difficult to see this as evil." He smiled. "Needless to say, there are a lot of things I never discuss with the bishop."

"Who knows? He might grope you," Paul said dryly.

"He might, indeed, knowing how politicians are, but at my age, I would consider it a compliment. Where is the danger to Victor Haya coming from?"

"That's just it. It might be easier to say where it isn't coming from. Take your pick. The Peruvian president is after him, and so are the communists. Then, too, there are the leaders of my country, who consider a socialist as bad as a hard core communist. One of the reasons I'm traveling with Haya is to protect him in case some stupid ass in Washington decides to send an assassin. There are also mining companies, too, not to mention the Germans."

"Yet, the man has a lot of friends in Latin America," Juan Calderón pointed out. "That's how he's managed to survive."

The old priest thought for a moment. "Pico must have told you the Germans are after you. I alluded to it in my letter. Has there been any sign of them?"

"No, the only attack has been from what we think was a bunch of communists. At least, that's what the little evidence we found told us. The Huns haven't paid their respects yet. Do you have any new information on them?"

Juan Calderón smiled at the irony Paul spun in the way he referred to the Germans. "Not a word. I'm told they are keeping a low profile. You speak of the communists in the past tense. You surely don't think they've given up."

Radford chuckled dryly. "No, not for a moment. I used the past tense because only two men from the group who attacked us got away. They weren't very well trained."

"That doesn't surprise me," Calderón replied. "The only training I got in Mexico was on the job. That was true of most of us. We didn't have enough ammunition to spare for training. I wasn't able to get my guns to work until after my first fire fight. I didn't know how to work the safety, but the rifle worked pretty well as a club." He chuckled at the memory. "It took me a while to figure out you had to cock the pistols we had to get them to shoot. I almost shot myself in the foot learning that."

"No Toes Calderón, fastest shot in Mexico."

"You laugh, Pablo, but the first time I tried to draw my pistol, I shot through the side of my holster. Fortunately for me, I was lying on my back and shot the soldier who was about to bayonet me in the knee."

"Well, that was apparently good enough," Radford said dryly. "You're here to tell about it." He yawned and stretched. "Tell you what, why don't we continue this tomorrow? I came a long way today."

Juan Calderón looked at his pocket watch and chuckled. "You mean yesterday. It's after midnight." Then he frowned and looked at his watch closely, and lifted it to his ear. "Or maybe not," he added. "It stopped."

"It helps to wind them, padre," Paul observed. "Where can I bunk down?"

Lima, Perú. The customs official carefully examined the tall, lanky man's passport before looking up at him and speaking in Spanish. His tone was correct, but polite. "Good afternoon, Mr. Lynch," he said. "Do you speak Spanish?"

"Yes, I do, officer," the visitor replied.

"Good, that will simplify things," the official replied. "What is the purpose of your visit to our country?"

"I am a scholar. I am here to collect material for a book on the geography and people of Perú. The equipment in the big black case is for that purpose. The other bag is my clothes and personal affects."

"You travel very light for an American," the official observed.

"I find it easier to buy what I need when I get where I'm going," the American responded, smiling. "With my wife along, it would take two taxis to carry the luggage." The truth was that he had no wife, was never married. Lynch had learned to travel very light early on. Marriage and his trade didn't mix.

The officer nodded and smiled. "How long do you intend to be in our country, Mr. Lynch?"

"I would estimate between two and three months, perhaps longer. It depends on how the local people respond to me. It takes a while to earn trust."

The official nodded again. The man was friendly enough and knew how things worked. There had been a folded fifty dollar bill tucked into the back of his passport. Thumbing through the passport, the officer deftly removed the bill. Then he nodded, using an official stamp to mark one of the back pages. "I am putting down three months," he told Lynch. "You will need to notify us if you need to stay longer. It is a formality, but it must be observed. Have a pleasant visit, Mr. Lynch."

"Thank you," the tall man said. "I'm sure I will. Can you suggest where I might hire a guide and purchase maps?"

"Certainly," the official told him. He took a scrap of paper and wrote the name and address of a local company. "These people will be able to assist you with both. You can tell them that I sent you and they will give you a special price. My name is written below the address."

Right, thought the tall man, smiling pleasantly. It will notify them there's a sucker ripe for the plucking and earn you a kickback. "Thank you, Officer Mendoza. You've been very helpful. I appreciate it." The official didn't bother to tell the man his name was Martinez. Mendoza, whose name appeared on the placard, was on the earlier shift. All he had written on the note was his first name and an initial.

Once he was in a cab, the tall man gave the driver the name of a modest hotel. He might prefer more elegant surroundings, and could easily afford them, but he wanted to be remembered as a penny-pinching scholar. Once he was in the back country, the image of a poor scholar could evolve into that of a seedy prospector. Then he would make sure word could filtered back to Lima that Simon Lynch had suffered a fatal accident. A drowning, he thought. The body would not be recovered and it would be too far from civilization for the body to be returned, anyway.

The hotel where Lynch was staying that night was not far from the address given him by the customs official. Discarding the dark horn rim glasses he used to hide his features, the tall man put the Lynch passport away in a hidden pocket of his valise and changed into the practical clothes that mining engineers wear the world over. Then he removed the dark wig he had been wearing, revealing a crop of light brown hair clipped close to the scalp. Next, he shaved off the mustache he normally wore, now dyed dark brown. Putting on a battered felt hat that had seen better days, he slipped out the back door of the hotel, a different man. There was nothing to tie him to the man who had checked in except for his room key. Even his assumed slouch was gone. Standing almost three inches taller in the well used boots he now wore, his posture was almost military.

It didn't take long to make the purchases the taller man needed. The emporium recommended by the customs official turned out to be a general outfitter and he bought what was necessary to spend several weeks in the back country. This included a good set of maps, waterproof matches and candles, a light weight mess kit, some survival gear, and good supply of halazone tablets to purify his drinking water.

As an afterthought, Lynch added a bottle of quinine tablets and a large canteen. Even though he didn't anticipate being in the jungle, his quarry might lead him there or into arid areas where water might be hard to find. He had experienced malaria and traumatic thirst and wanted to avoid both.

The last three items the tall man purchased were a good pack frame to carry his supplies, a dark green nylon bag to hold these, and a tightly woven wool blanket. The blanket would serve as a serape to preserve body heat and to turn mist and light rain. The pack frame would lighten his load over a long mountain trek.

Packing all of his purchases into the strong, lightweight bag, Lynch tied it to the pack frame with nylon parachute cord he would blacken with shoe dye. He was pleased when he was done. Picking up the pack, he knew his total load would add up to less than thirty-five pounds. This would make all the difference over the hundreds of kilometers he might have to cover on foot.

Walking back to the hotel, Lynch entered by the rear entrance and secured his purchases in his room, planting tell-tale signs to let him know if the room was searched. Then he walked to a bus stop two blocks away. Ten minutes later he was at a cantina the store clerk had told him was favored by guides. The clerk said the best was one named Marino.

There were a number of men standing at the bar when Lynch settled onto a stool. The ones who caught his attention, however, were a group of rough looking men at a table near the rear. Four of them were playing cards while two others watched.

One of the watchers was intently caught up in the game, watching each play carefully. The other only showed casual interest. As the tall man watched, this man constantly swept the room with his eyes, and the tall man noticed he sat with his back to the wall. It was clear to him this was the man he wanted, cautious and alert. He stared at him until he caught the man's eye. When he did, he nodded slightly and signaled with an almost imperceptible turn of his head.

However, the man he wanted gave no sign he had caught the signal. He turned his attention to the game and it was several moments before he looked around. Once again the tall man caught his eye. This time the other nodded, his head moving up and down no more than three millimeters. The tall man responded in kind and turned back to the bar, watching the table in the cracked mirror behind the bar.

Ten minutes later the man Lynch was watching held up his beer bottle and shook it. Setting it down, he got up and made his way to the bar ending up two feet from Lynch. Giving his order to the barkeep, he waited patiently until it came. Then he took a sip and casually looked around the room. No one seemed to be watching.

"You must be Marino," Lynch said softly, intently studying his drink on the bar.

"Who is asking?" Marino answered, yawning and turning back to the bar. He took a drink of his beer

"My name is Lynch. You are supposed to be the best."

Marino chuckled quietly. "Depends on who you ask. The lady I see thinks so. What do you need?"

"I need a very discrete guide who works only for me and knows how to keep his mouth shut."

"Perhaps we should talk about this more," Marino murmured.

"Not here. Buy me dinner at Delgado's. Back table. It's across the plaza. Red door. Flowers in boxes next to it." Lurching up, he belched loudly and made his way back to the card game.

A few minutes later Lynch asked the barkeep where he could relieve himself. The man nodded toward the back door. "Use the alley near the drain."

When Lynch came back inside, Marino was not at the table. Nodding to the bartender, Lynch left a tip and made his way out the door. Then he began to stroll across the plaza, taking his time and looking around. Taking a seat on a wrought iron bench, he rolled himself a cigarette. Leaning back, he lit it watched the traffic around the plaza. There was very little at that hour and after a while, he tossed away the cigarette butt. From where he sat there was nothing that fit Marino's description of Delgado's and he got to his feet and resumed his walk.

Connections

7 Marfa, Texas. Commander Eric Rudd got up and looked out his office window at the fresh snow that covered the airfield. "It's hard to believe, isn't it?" he asked, yawning and stretching his lanky frame. It was just past eight and the briefing had lasted more than an hour. "Six months from now it will be so hot you can fry eggs on the runway."

Turning back to Alex White, his executive officer, he said, "You were lucky you got in when you did. I'd hate to try a night landing in this snow."

White had flown in late in the evening before, landing just as the snow began to fall. Now there was ten inches of heavy, wet slush on the runways and air operations were suspended until they could be cleared. Crews were out with road graders, trying to push the snow aside without tearing up the tarmac underneath.

"You don't know how glad I was to see the landing lights," White replied. "I was too low on fuel to divert and it was hard to make out what was below. I didn't want to hit a high line or plow into the side of a mountain, and the landing lights on the plane weren't much help. They reflected off the snow so bad it washed out everything else."

Rudd nodded, emptying his coffee cup and lighting a bent cigarette. "Well, I'm glad you made it. This place goes to hell in a hand-basket when you're gone."

"It's good to know I'm needed," Alex replied dryly. "Too bad you can't give me a raise." He had been gone less than a week and he knew his desk would be buried in paper. It was always that way when he was gone. There was a war on.

The commander chuckled and took a seat behind his desk. "Too bad I can't give us all one. With double time for pushing paper. You have anything else?"

"There was one other item we may want to look at. I was talking to a friend of ours who keeps an eye on the drug trade, the illegal drug trade. He picked up a rumor that the price of cocaine has been going up steadily for the last six months. When he checked it out with some of his contacts in the trade, it was true. Somebody is buying up high quality coca leaves, so much that it's affecting the supply of cocaine in the States."

"That sounds like good news," the commander replied, "Why would we need to look at it?"

"Normally, we wouldn't, but it might affect our operations in South America. The word going around the street trade is that it's the Germans who are buying up the leaves."

"The Germans? What in the world do they want with it?"

"That's what I wondered, so I did a little research. That's why I was two days late getting back. I talked to a scientist I know in the drug industry, the clean drug trade. According to him, cocaine is a powerful stimulant, one the native people in South America have used for hundreds of years. They claim it increases a man's strength and endurance. They take it in by chewing up coca leaves, but when it's refined, it's apparently much more effective."

Rudd nodded. "Yeah, I remember hearing about it now you mention it. They made it into pep pills, didn't they?"

"They did. One brand was called Forced March and was used by polar explorers and mountain climbers. Back then, it was considered non-addictive. There are still places where you can buy it over the counter."

"So why are the Germans buying up leaves?"

"I asked the drug scientist the same thing and he told me there has been a lot of research done on cocaine in Germany. His guess is that they are either issuing it as pep pills to their combat troops or are considering it."

"Is it that effective?"

"Apparently so. I talked to a couple of people who use it all the time. These weren't street bums or thugs, either. They work in one of the ship yards and they tell me that when they use it, a double shift doesn't phase them. They don't get tired and they remain alert.

One of them said it was ten times more effective than strong coffee. He also said a lot of workers are using it. It's illegal but they claim it makes a big difference in their productivity."

Eric Rudd thought about this for a moment. "Well, it's obvious to me why the Germans are interested. All they'd have to do to produce an army of supermen is give them pills. I can see how that would appeal to them. There's got to be a downside. There's some reason it's illegal in the States."

Alex White nodded. "I had the same thought. So I asked a medical expert. What he told me made me glad I never tried the stuff. It can cause heart attacks, strokes, seizures, kidney failure, ulcers, high blood pressure, and sudden death. To put it a nutshell, it's poison. Any benefits are insignificant compared to the damage it can do."

"Then, maybe we need to encourage the Germans to go for it," Eric Rudd suggested. "I still don't see how it effects us."

"It may not, but I think we need to talk to Denis before we write it off. The hot spots for the cocaine trade in South America are Perú and Bolivia. Or, so I'm told. That got me to thinking about that phony German mining operation we blew up in southern Perú. We always assumed it was some kind of military base. What if it was a processing plant for coca leaves? We could really hurt the Germans in Perú if we could prove that."

The commander thought about this. Then he shook his head. "I don't know, Alex. Perú seems to be pretty much in our camp these days. We've got other, more pressing things to think about."

White nodded. "That's pretty much what I think, too, but I needed to run it by you. It does raise a potential problem we need to look at and I think we need Denis in the loop on this. With Radford back in the country, the Germans in Perú may think he's been sent there to sabotage their coca leaf project. I think we need to alert Paul to what they're up to and warn him to keep away from it."

"I don't know," the commander replied. You know how he is these days. He might get it into his head to take the krauts on head first. That could cause us a lot of grief. We need to talk to Denis before we make a decision. Right now Paul's mission with Haya needs to take priority. The communists are our greatest threat. Look what they did to Russia."

Lima, Perú. Delgado's place was hard to spot and Simon Lynch almost passed it by. There was no sign he could see outside or anything that looked like a cafe around the plaza. He was about to give up and go back to the bar when he spotted a red door with two green flower boxes flanking it. These were down a narrow side street, almost an alley, off the plaza and he wondered if he was being set up for a robbery. Yet, when he drew near, he saw a menu posted in a small display case. The menu was written in an elegant hand on a yellowing sheet of paper. It told the world this was Taqueria Delgado and it was clear to Lynch that this was a place that catered mostly to local people who knew exactly where it was.

Since it was well past the noon hour and too early for the dinner crowd, the dining room was empty when Lynch entered. He wondered if he was at the right place, but he went to the back of the dining area and took a seat at the table farthest from the door. A moment later the guide appeared through the kitchen. A beautiful woman in her middle years followed him, bringing napkins and silverware.

"I took the liberty of ordering for us," Marino told Lynch. "Everything on the menu is good if you like native food. What I ordered is very tasty but if you want something else...." He shrugged.

"Good," Lynch told him. "You know better than I do. I prefer to talk business after the food. I also require complete discretion. Agreed?"

The guide nodded and took a seat. Switching to Quechua, Lynch asked, "How well do you speak the native language?"

Marino looked at him, surprised. "I speak it quite well, both Quechua and a couple of other tribal tongues. Will you be going into the jungle?"

Lynch smiled and answered in Spanish. "You need to repeat that in Spanish, Marino. My understanding of Quechua is very limited. I simply wanted to know if you spoke it. The way you answered tells me you must be very fluent, even if I don't know exactly what you said."

The guide nodded. "So what do I call you? I am Marino Delgado."

"You can call me Lynch, Simon Lynch. I gather this is your place."

Marino smiled. "No, my sister owns it. She feeds me and lets me wash the dishes."

Lynch smiled back. "I see why you wanted me to buy our dinner. I would like *cerveza* with my meal."

The other nodded. "Elena will bring it with the food. What she serves is much better than that slop you were drinking at the cantina."

"It wasn't that bad."

"Wait until you taste what Elena serves. It's what keeps her in business, that and the food. People come from all over Lima to eat here."

Their food arrived just then with beer served in a glass. The two men began to eat and Lynch was surprised to find the food much better than he expected. The beer was, too, and Marino told him his sister brewed it herself. "Everyone wants the recipe," the guide said. "Elena claims she got it from an old German *biermeister* who liked her food. She tells them he made her promise not to tell his secrets." He shrugged. "I think she made the story up, herself, but what do I know? I'm only her brother." Lynch smiled and nodded.

The two men talked about other things as they ate. Lynch had never been to Perú before and was curious about the wildlife in the mountains and in the jungle. He was particularly interested in llamas and their cousins, the alpaca and guanaco.

Lynch was surprised to learn that all three Andean animals were related to camels. Marino knew a lot about them and apparently had a lot of experience with the beasts. "At high altitudes, they are better than a burro, but not in the jungle," he said. "There are those who would disagree, but both animals have their uses." He grinned. "A fat burro is better eating."

Marino looked pointedly at their empty dishes and sighed. "Even so, that's not what you came here to discuss is it, Mr. Simon Lynch?"

"Just call me Lynch," the tall man instructed. "What I am after may take two to three months, and maybe more. Are you available that long?"

The guide nodded and Lynch continued. "I need to talk to two men. I believe they are traveling together with a small party. They have both information I need, things of interest to those I work for."

"Do these men have names?"

Lynch shrugged. "We need to reach an agreement before I tell you names. I'm sure you understand."

The guide nodded and Lynch continued. "The man I need to talk to most is someone you will never have heard of, an American oil company geologist. The other is a well known politician in Perú. It would be useful for me to get in touch with him, too."

"May I ask your business with the politician?"

"You may ask but I can't tell you. It's a business secret."

"Business or political? I am not interested in anything that is illegal or political, Mr. Lynch. I want no trouble with the police. I need their good will. Surely, you understand why."

"I will not ask you to do anything that will get you in trouble with the police. However, as far as anyone else needs to know, I am a scholar collecting information about the local people for a book. One of the things I will need you to do is to find out if any other Americans are in the area we travel."

"And if I don't take the job?"

"We go our separate ways and I find another guide."

"Aren't you afraid I may go to the police with what I know already? They are known to pay for information."

Lynch shook his head. "It doesn't matter. I'm not up to anything illegal. My only concern is with the local Germans. My country is at war with Germany and they may try to do me harm. There may be bandits, too, in the areas we may have to travel. I would expect you to help defend us against them. Is that acceptable to you?"

The guide nodded. "That's a fact of life in some areas. Why would the men you seek be in places like that?"

"I expect because they wish to avoid the police. As you said, it's a matter of politics. Theirs, not mine. All I am after is information."

"I want nothing to do with the communists," Marino told him, shaking his head. "They do nothing but make trouble."

Lynch was beginning to wonder if he was talking to the right man. "Well, if you don't want the job, who would you recommend?" he asked. "I pay well and am not tight about expenses. When I leave the country, whoever guides me will keep the equipment. That's a bonus. I can also assure you I am not after any communists. I would rather avoid them."

The guide looked at Lynch for a long moment. "You sound too good to be true," he said. "I think there is something you are not telling me."

"There's a lot I'm not telling you," Lynch said. "You don't need to know my employer's business. I don't know all of it, myself. I can assure you that my employer is legitimate, but you have no reason to believe me. All you've got is your judgment of character. That's all I have, too." He shrugged.

Lynch saw the man come to a decision. "All right, then. I'll guide you. One month minimum, standard rates. When you go home I keep the equipment and any animals we buy to carry it. I prefer to be paid the first month in advance."

"Very good," Lynch replied. He reached inside his shirt and pulled out an envelope. "Here is two hundred dollars, American. I will need a high quality rifle, preferably a Mauser. I need some soft nose ammunition for it, too, two boxes. You can buy whatever supplies we will need for a month and a burro to carry them. Will this be enough?"

"Yes, but you haven't agreed to a price for my services."

"Half again more than you're normally paid. That buys your complete discretion, too." Seeing the surprise in the other man's eyes, Lynch added, "You're said to be the best, Marino, and quality is not cheap. Besides, you're washing dishes for our meal here tomorrow."

"No way!" Marino chuckled. "Now I can afford to eat here, too!"

On the other side of the city Helmut Rott parked the big Mercedes touring car and hurried into the embassy. Walking past the young clerk who served as Schwartz's secretary he walked into the linguist's office. No one was there and he turned to the clerk. "Is the colonel in yet?" he demanded.

The clerk blinked. "Yes, Herr Rott. "Try the canteen. He went to get breakfast a half hour ago."

Rott stumped past the desk and almost collided with the linguist at the door into the hallway. "Good morning, Helmut," Schwartz greeted him. "What's the hurry?"

"I have some information you need," Rott replied. He glanced at the clerk.

"Good," Schwartz replied. "Come into my office. Let me fix us some coffee." Rott waited impatiently while the scholar set a percolator on a hot plate and measured out the coffee and water. "That's one of the nice benefits of being posted in South America, isn't it, Helmut? We get the best coffee."

Rott growled an answer and Schwartz chuckled. "What's eating at you on such a beautiful morning, Helmut? Life is better when we stop and enjoy the small things like good coffee."

"We're at war, in case you hadn't noticed," Rott replied. "I have news on Radford. Our watchers in Pisco spotted a young American going into the Catholic Church late one afternoon. From his description, it sounds like Radford."

"Excellent," Schwartz smiled. "Is he still there?"

"My watcher didn't know. He spotted him and neither he nor his partner saw the man again. He said they didn't realize who it was at first."

"Really? How did that happen?"

"He told me it was almost dark. The man was dressed like an Indian and slipped in the door quickly. There was a lantern by the door and our watcher only got a brief glimpse of his face. The man was clean shaven and not Indian. He looked European."

"So we're not sure it was him, after all, are we? How late did they keep watch?"

"For a couple of hours after they saw him. Then one of them went inside and pretended to pray. He looked around and there was no one there. Everything was locked up but the front door."

"As I remember, there was no back entrance to the church itself, was there?" Rott shook his head and the scholar nodded. "So it could have been him. Excellent, Helmut, but how does this help us?"

"I can go to Pisco and see if I can pick up his trail."

"How long has it been."

"It was four days ago he was spotted. I only got the news this morning."

"Do you really think you have much chance? He has a four day head start. Nor are we sure it was him."

"It's the closest we've come to finding him, but I need to get going."

Schwartz shook his head. "No, I think not. He'll show up again, assuming it was he whom they saw. Let him think we don't know he's in the country. Then, when we spot him, we'll take him at our convenience."

"And just where are we going to spot him?" Rott growled.

"Keep your watchers on duty in Pisco. Give them a small reward for spotting him but tell them they won't get any more until we catch him. Perhaps we need to have someone keep an eye on the woman's place here in Lima, too."

"Her husband's a policeman, as you well know. What if he spots our watchers and arrests them? Then what?"

"Tell them that if they get caught, they're on their own. We can deny any association. You could also eliminate them."

"That is a lot more difficult in the city than in the country," the driver pointed out.

"Yes, but it's not impossible, Helmut. Not for a man of your talents." Rott's answer was a growl.

Marfa, Texas. Captain Jacques Paul, US Army Intelligence, looked more patient than he felt. It was a cold, windy day at the army airfield and he sat near the gas space heater that warmed the tiny office of the main hangar. A radio played quietly from the top of a dusty filing cabinet and the clerk was busy with something that took him in and out of the office. Even if he had wanted conversation, there was no one to talk with and nothing else he could do. He needed to see his commanding officer, Eric Rudd right away and the plane was late.

Normally, Jaques Paul would have waited for Commander Rudd in the far more comfortable building that housed the Special Action Group's offices. Yet, the news he brought was very sensitive and for command ears only and it required a command decision. The unit's executive officer, Lieutenant Alex White was tied up in a meeting in El Paso and Denis Blieu was off being a diplomat in South America. His absence technically made Captain Paul third in command of the group. Practically, he was rarely present at headquarters and not up to speed on the larger picture. Marfa, a hundred and twenty kilometers from the Mexican border, was as far north as he had been in months.

Jaques Paul thought about the information he had picked up from a reliable source he had run into in Mexico City. Damn the man! He had no business sticking his nose where it didn't belong. It was quite clear to Jacques Paul, and anyone else who crossed the Director's path, that the man was power hungry. His jurisdiction lay within the country, not abroad, and his intrusion could put better people in mortal danger. Not even the President seemed able to control the man. Not that he would intercede. The Director was a fair haired boy as far as the White House was concerned, or so it seemed. Jaques Paul wondered what dirt the Director had on the Chief Executive.

Hearing a twin engine plane approaching the field, Jaques Paul got up and looked out the dusty window. As he watched, the Skytrain settled to the runway gently enough, but a sudden gust of wind caused it to veer to the side just as it touched down. Even so, the pilot was able to keep it from running off the runway and taxied up to the main hangar.

Jacques Paul buttoned the flight jacket he wore and went out to meet the plane. Once the engines were cut, a crew pushed a ladder up to the passenger door and a number of people descended from the aircraft. One of them noticed him waiting and walked over to Jaques Paul.

"You look like you've got a bee in your bonnet, Jock," Rudd told him. "Is it something that can't wait until we get to the office? The heaters went out in the plane and I'm about frozen."

"Let's talk in the car," the captain suggested. "I drove over myself. This is for your ears only. Alec needs to know, too, and word needs to be sent to Denis."

The two men walked to the command sedan parked next to the hangar. Once they had pulled away from the hangar, Jaques Paul looked at Commander Rudd. "It's that little fat toad at the Bureau," the captain said. "I have word from a reliable source that he's sent an assassin to South America. The mission is to take out Victor Haya and Paul Radford, too, if he gets in the way."

Commander Rudd did not respond immediately. "I take it you're sure about this."

"Yes. I ran into our source at the Bureau at the embassy in Mexico City. He told me that Mike O'Leary was brought in to see the Director. I was able to trace O'Leary to Lima. He's going under the alias of Simon Lynch, although he may drop that identity once he gets into the back country. I think we need to get word to Radford."

"Who is O'Leary?" Rudd asked. "I've never heard of him."

"Not many people have. He's a renegade from Boston who returned to the land of his kinfolk and joined the IRA when he was fourteen. When things got hot, he got out of Belfast just ahead of the British police. He escaped to Dublin and then home to Boston, where he met up with other expatriates. He's IRA and the Brits want him for several assassinations. He's also one of the Director's distant cousins, which I think is why he's not been extradited. It's well known that he does the Bureau's dirty work, but nothing has ever been pinned on him."

"Wait a minute. He isn't the guy who did the Orange Pub bombing, is he?"

"One and the same, though there's no proof. What I was able to learn is that he's a Harvard graduate, too. Summa cum laude, class of 1935."

"I wish I could say the same. I got through the Academy 'Thank you, Laudy!' I don't understand why he isn't in the service by now. He sounds like a man who might be useful, particularly with the OSS."

"Well, for one thing, he's legally a negro, but you wouldn't know it. In the pictures I've seen, he looks very Celtic. My information is that he and the Director share a common grandfather."

"I'm not going to ask how you came up with that," Rudd told him. "Am I right in assuming you have those photos?"

"Yes, in the briefcase," Jaques Paul replied, nodding to a worn leather case on the seat between them. Rudd opened it and took out a craft envelope. Inside were several large glossy black and white photos. The images were sharp.

"He and the Director don't look alike," the commander pointed out. "I can't see any family resemblance at all."

"That's what's so stupid. When the man returned home to Boston, he enlisted in the Marine Corps under his mother's name, Wilson, and went through basic training. He was good enough that they sent him on to sniper school. Then his ancestry came to light somehow and he was given the boot."

"This must have been several years before the war. How old is the man now?"

"He's in his thirties, about the same age as Radford. He started quite early, fourteen to sixteen."

"How the hell did he get into Harvard?"

"I really don't know. Is it important?"

Rudd looked at his chief of intelligence. "It could be. Are you sure his credentials are for real?"

The captain shook his head. "What I am passing along is what the Bureau has and one never knows. Sometimes their 'hard' intelligence is made up of smoke and mirrors. I think we need to assume the threat is real. It would be hard to fake the military records."

The commander looked at him with disbelief. "We do it all the time, Jock. The OSS has a whole department set up for nothing but false documents. Are you sure this isn't a Bureau legend."

"It seems a little strange to be invented history," Jaques Paul replied. "The part about being a negro isn't something I would consider including in a legend. It could backfire. The IRA has no love for colored people."

"Nor does the Navy, for that matter. Except for ship cooks, and even then it's touchy. On the other hand, there's Dorie Miller at Pearl Harbor."

Jaques Paul nodded. "Yeah, he should have gotten the Medal of Honor. He would if he wasn't Negro."

"There's nothing wrong with a Navy Cross," Rudd pointed out. "The irony is that the Corps would accept O'Leary now."

"I doubt he wants to be reinstated," the captain replied dryly. "I think we need to get word to Radford."

"Do we even know where he is?" Rudd asked. "How would we find him? Who would we send?"

"Why not send Denis Blieu? Or me, either? It needs to be

someone Radford knows."

"Then it will have to be you. Blieu is tied up with something urgent in Argentina."

"Knowing Blieu, I bet she's lovely," Jaques Paul chuckled. "All right. I don't have anything on my board that can't wait. I'll take off in the morning. I assume I will be traveling with diplomatic credentials. I still have the passport."

"Yes, you will," Rudd nodded. "You'll need local help, too. You think that one-eyed guide is still around? What was his name, Pisco?"

"No, I believe it's Pico. Pisco is the town where Radford met that old priest. I'm sure he'll help us, too, assuming he's still alive. He knows how to keep his mouth shut."

The commander nodded. "It sounds like you need to talk to him yourself, Jock. Anything else you need to talk to me about before you head south?"

"Yes, but let's go to your office. I could use some coffee."

Ojos del Gato

8 Lima, Perú. The bright afternoon sunlight filtered through the thin scrim covering the dusty windows of the professor's office. It reflected off a cloud of dust motes, giving the room the ambiance of a smoky men's club. Schwartz was seated behind his desk, as usual, and Rott was in the comfortable leather chair he preferred. Both men had a snifter a third filled with Napoleon cognac beside them and they were smoking Cuban cigars that Schwartz had persuaded his driver to try. To the linguist's long nose, Rott's normal small black cigars smelled like smoldering rope saturated with tar.

Even so, neither man was concerned with the quality of either the cigars or the cognac, and neither noticed the light. They were discussing the attack on Haya's party and trying to gauge where they might be. There had been no news of either Radford or other any members of the party from any of their sources in several weeks. The last report they had came from near Sapito, three hundred kilometers west of Lima and six hundred south of the ambush.

"I don't understand the attack," Schwartz said. "It must have been on Haya. Didn't you tell me that the police believe it was a party of communist revolutionaries?"

"That's what they told me but I'm not sure how much of it I believe. They claim six men were killed and that they caught a seventh man they think was with them. The man they got is a simple peon who claims he was guiding a hunting party. He also claims they were the ones who were attacked, by bandits. No mention was made of Haya or Radford."

Rott paused and Schwartz waited patiently, taking a sip of his cognac. There was no rushing the man, just as there was no stopping him if he was in a rush. "The story I believe came from another source, a new one," Rott continued. "I talked with him and I believe he was telling me the truth. He had no reason to lie. He trades with the Indians who live in the area. They told him about the attack in great detail." He stopped, frowning, then shook his head.

"Would you care to share what you are thinking, Helmut?" the professor asked.

"I was thinking about the way he told me the story, the new source. I am fairly confident he was not exaggerating but the Indians may have been. They said that eight men were after five men staying in an abandoned hut. Something went wrong for the attackers and the five men were able to escape without injury. Then they turned the tables on the attackers, who were chasing them. Four of the attackers were killed in the ambush and the other four fled. One man from Haya's group went after them and killed two or three more. He told me only two of the attackers got away and one of them was badly wounded. The border guards caught one trying to slip into Ecuador."

Rott stopped and looked at Schwartz. "What I think is that Radford is the man who went after the four who ran. I think he knew the wounded man would die and he let the fourth man go so word would get out. This squares with what I have found out about his time in Alaska. He has become a very dangerous man."

"Though not as dangerous as you, Helmut."

The man in black shook his head. "Maybe even more so in the wild country," he said. "He seems to have some sort of magical reputation with the Indians. When I was looking for him before, another trader told me they talk about him as if he is protected by their gods."

"Are you saying we should give up trying to find him?" The scholar sounded alarmed. He had never seen Rott in awe of any man except the legendary Rommel.

"No, of course not, Jergen. I'm saying we need to be very careful not to underestimate the man. We may need to lure him out of Indian country before we can attack safely."

"How can we do that?" Schwartz asked. "You told me his woman married someone else. I doubt we can use her as a hostage again. Do you?"

"No, but she had his child, a girl. We can use her."

"I don't know," the linguist replied. "If I remember rightly, you told me she married a policeman. We certainly don't want to stir up trouble with them. We'll find ourselves back in Berlin or on the Russian front. Neither of us want that."

"Don't worry, Jergen. I'll be careful. I always am. Aside from the bullet I took pushing you out of the way, I've never been caught, have I?"

Colonel Schwartz shrugged and took another sip of cognac. The reminder of his debt to Rott always stung. Nor did he share the snide thought he had staring into his snifter. Not yet, Helmut. You've not been caught, yet.

Schwartz was so absorbed in this thought that he missed the next thing Rott said. "What? Sorry, Helmut. I didn't catch that. I was thinking about what you said."

Rott smiled knowingly. His reminder had hit the mark as it always did. Schwartz was so easy. "I said that we need to do more than kill Radford. We need to destroy him."

"Oh? What did you have in mind?"

"The Americans are very puritanical when it comes to certain things. So is the government in Perú. What we need to do is set it so Radford ends up in disgrace as well as dead."

"Interesting," the professor replied. "I gather you have an idea how to accomplish just that. What might it be?"

"The common aversion is drugs. What would happen if the police found Radford shot dead with a kilo of cocaine concealed in his backpack? I was thinking of Captain Molina, in particular."

"Very interesting. I doubt that Molina would be inclined to try to cover it up, even if he is Radford's friend."

"We could make sure that one of our friends in the press knew all about it. That would keep him from even trying."

Schwartz smiled. "The General would be outraged by an American spy caught dealing drugs. It might even destroy Victor Haya. Especially if he, too, was found there dead."

"Exactly. No loose ends."

Near Puno. Paul Radford awoke suddenly, aware that he was

being watched. Reaching under his pillow for his pistol, he started to jump out of bed. Then he saw the smiling face of Gloria, her chin resting on an arm and her startled eyes looking into his. For a moment he didn't recognize her, but he relaxed when he did. He left the pistol under his pillow and kissed her beautiful lips.

"Good morning, beautiful," he said but the lady was not to be distracted.

"You scared me, Pablo. For a moment I thought you were going to attack me."

"I am," he said with a broad grin. "Again and again."

"No, Pablo, don't make a joke. The look on your face was awful, wild and crazy."

"I'm sorry, bonita," he said, caressing her cheek. "I must have been having a war dream. I can't remember them but I know when I have them. I wake up all keyed up."

"The look in your eyes," she said. "It reminded me of a jaguar I saw in Lima. It was in a cage, but it still scared me."

Radford nodded seriously. "Victor told me he thought the same when I first saw him this time. It may be what kept me alive in combat. I must have been dreaming about that." He looked around. The room was bright with morning light. "I'm surprised you're still in bed."

Gloria nodded. "I decided I'm tired of sneaking around. I am a widow and this is my house. The rules are different." She touched his cheek. "I'm becoming too fond of you."

Radford smiled. "Well, you looked like you had something in mind when I first woke. Do the rules include making love on such a lovely morning?"

An hour later Paul and Gloria were eating sweetbreads the cook had made early that morning, dipping them into honey and sipping dark Colombian coffee. "Where is everyone?" Paul asked, looking around. The cook was busy in the kitchen but there was no sign of Victor or his men. "Señor Haya is writing in the library," the cook told them. "Timo is with him and Mateo and Diego are out at the corral looking at horses."

"Thank you, Marta," Gloria said. "So what do you want to do

today, Pablo? Would you like to go riding?" She gave him a stern look seeing his wry grin.

"Yes, I would like to see your ranch."

Gloria laughed. "That would take us two weeks!"

"Well, I'm sure there are some special places. How about some of those?"

Gloria nodded. "There is one that is close enough to get to and back before dark." She turned to the cook. "Marta, would you fix us something to take to eat? We may be getting back after supper." Handing Paul a small key ring, she said, "This is to the gun cabinet. Find a rifle you know how to shoot and bring some shells, too. I'll bring the horses."

"What do we need with a rifle?" he asked. "I have a pistol."

"We probably won't but desperadoes sometimes ride across the ranch," she told him. "They are usually well armed. Occasionally we get a jaguar or a big desert cat, too, hunting our stock."

"Well, I don't mind shooting desperadoes, but not a jaguar. They're my kinfolk."

Marta gave Paul a strange look and Gloria shook her head and switched to English. "Don't ever joke about the jaguar like that, Pablo. The people up here are very superstitious. They might think you're a witch."

"I wasn't really joking," he replied in kind. "I feel a great kinship with them, and with grizzly bears, too."

Gloria nodded. "I understand, but it might be better to keep things like that to yourself. Like that amulet you wear around your neck, too."

"It saved my life, Gloria," he told her. "That's how it got so bent. It's what got us safely through the jungle getting here."

"Then I'm glad, but please be careful what you say."

Despite his preference for traveling on foot, Paul Radford found the ride around the ranch very relaxing. The horse Gloria chose for him had a much more easier gait than the mule he'd ridden through the mountains, and the saddle was built for comfort. "My husband was a big man, but very bony," she said, laughing, when Paul commented on how comfortable the saddle was. "He needed lots of padding."

"Well, I'm very grateful for it, too."

The land they were riding through since leaving the hacienda was rough and dry, not unlike the country Paul had seen in far western Texas and in Wyoming. There were very few trees to be seen, and most of these were twisted into large trunks with very few branches. Lumber for building had to be hauled over the Andes from the jungle on the eastern side, which was expensive. So most of the buildings he saw were built from either stacked stone or mud bricks held together with strands of reed and straw. The mud walls were kept from eroding by cement plaster, for those who could afford it. Others used a smooth layer of mud or a mixture of mud and ashes or mud and cement.

The other thing that caught Paul's attention were thatched roofs much like those he'd seen in English photos. "Do those really turn rain?" he asked.

"Quite well," Gloria assured him. "That's what we had at the hacienda before we were able to make tile. It worked quite well. The only real problem was insects living in it and birds trying to nest in it or dig them out."

"I'd think fire would be a problem," Paul said. "You must have to be very careful."

Gloria shook her head. "No, no more than you normally do. Thatch doesn't burn very well, even when it's dry. It's like trying to burn a newspaper without opening the pages. Tile is pretty, but thatch kept us warmer."

Their ride took the two of them through rolling country and Paul was surprised when they approached what looked like a tall hill. As they reached the top, the ground fell away sharply from a long rocky outcrop, and Paul could see a beautiful lake at the foot of the hill. Beyond the lake the land became rolling hills again, stretching perhaps sixty or seventy kilometers to the horizon.

The odd thing was that the lake was not surrounded by trees and brush as it would be most places in the world. Nor was there much vegetation that he could see in the distance and this made the countryside appear more barren than it was. Thinking about this, he realized this high plateau they were on was probably above the tree line. Lake Titicaca near Puno had an elevation of over 3800 meters, right at 12,500 feet. This was the average tree line for the Peruvian Andes and where they stood was a bit higher. Added to the dry climate and strong winds, this kept all but the hardiest and most adaptable natural plants from growing.

"This is amazing," Paul murmured. He was speaking to himself, but Gloria heard him.

"What is so amazing?" Gloria asked.

"This whole country. The people, the wildlife, the Andes, the jungle.... It's amazing how life has adapted to such a harsh environment." He pointed to a herd of llamas in the distance. "Take the llamas, for example. What you have are camels that have adapted to high elevation. They're quite intelligent, far more than sheep or cattle. And look at the native people, the descendents of the Incas. It's incredible how large an empire they built and how sophisticated the engineering technology they developed is, all without a written language. This whole country's like that."

Gloria looked at Paul oddly. "You seem very taken with our part of the world, Pablo. Most Americans seem to see it as a source of personal wealth. You seem to love it."

"I do, far more than anywhere else I've been. When I first came here, it was just a place to work for a while before I was sent home to a better job. Then, after a while, things changed. I think it was while I was in Pisco. I got to know Father Juan and Pico, and through them I got to know the people in the Andes, and the people of the jungle, too. Now, traveling with Victor, it feels like I have come home. And where I thought home was, the place where I grew up, has become a foreign country. Yet it's the land I have sworn to defend. It's all very strange and confusing."

"Well, Pablo, when the war is done, you have a home here if you want it. There is a place for you here at the ranch."

"That's very generous of you, Gloria." Paul was touched by her offer. "I don't know what to say, except thank you."

"I'm not pushing you to decide, Pablo. Take as long as you want. I'm not being generous, either. I'm being selfish. I want you in my life, but I know how it is. We've only known each other a short while. I understand your being cautious."

"I'm not being cautious, Gloria. I'm scared to death. I feel a great deal of affection for you. I believe I could come to love you with all my heart. I knew this from the beginning. Yet, every woman I've loved has been taken away from me."

When he said this, Paul's face was bleak with anguish and Gloria was overwhelmed by a deluge of feelings. One was fear, a dread mixed with joy. Nor was there mistaking the sadness she still felt over losing her husband mixed in with this. Yet oddly enough, the greatest of them all was curiosity. "Tell me, Pablo," she said gently. "Tell me about this and, please, don't leave anything out."

Paul nodded. "All right, Gloria, but not here, not right now." He leaned over and pulled her close, kissing her lightly on the lips. "You're an incredible woman," he told her. "As incredible as this wild, beautiful country."

"I'm glad I have you fooled," she replied. "You make me feel young again."

"You are young, bonita. There are lot of people with fewer years who are a lot older than you."

That evening after they got back to the hacienda, Paul took Gloria into the bathing room and gently washed her from head to foot. Then she did the same for him, and after that they made sweet, poignant love. It was only then that he opened his grief and told her about losing Rosario and their daughter, Azúl, and about the tragic death of Louise Thacker.

"I don't blame Rosario for the choice she made," he said, tears streaming unnoticed down his checks. "Juan Gomez is a good man and I'm sure he will be a wonderful father to Azúl. Rosario had to look out after her and I was kept from seeing her after I became persona non grata. Powerful people in the government, people friendly to the Nazis, were quite embarrassed when the German military base was discovered southeast of Yauca. It was too dangerous to Juan Calderón and Rosario for me to try to see them."

"Military base? The papers said it was a mining operation that exploded."

Radford chuckled. "Right. I suspect those were all papers friendly to the Third Reich. We found proof positive it was not a mine, and the guards opened fire on a clearly identified police patrol."

"So you were involved in that?"

"I'm not supposed to tell anyone I was, but it's common knowledge to the Germans. And to the police here in Perú, too. The point is that I didn't have diplomatic immunity and the Germans wanted to go after me. They still do."

"So that's why you have to slip around quietly," she said. "I know Victor would be arrested if they found him. Yet, he is no threat. He abhors violence."

Paul shrugged. "It depends on how you look at it. I think he's a greater threat than they think. His ideas are changing how the people think, the common people. The military is right to be afraid. Victor stands for everything they don't."

Gloria nodded. "I think you're right, but I didn't think we were going to talk about Victor tonight. What about the other women you mentioned."

Paul's face turned grave. "Actually, there was only one other. I can't tell you what she did but her name was Lou and she was involved in the war effort while I was in Alaska. I think I loved her as much, if not more, than I loved Rosario. We were to be married after the war and then she died when a plane crashed during take-off."

Paul paused and took a deep breath. "After that I didn't want to live. I volunteered for the most dangerous missions I could find, hoping I'd be killed. It obviously didn't work. All I did was pile up a ridiculous number of medals. Then, when I was asked to come back to Perú, I hoped I might die here." He gave Gloria a wry smile. "So far, that hasn't happened. Now I've met this wonderful lady I care for greatly and I'm scared spitless. Not for myself, but for her. Bad things seem to happen to the women I love."

Gloria smiled and touched his cheek. "You may not believe me, but it's worth it, knowing you, Pablo. I loved Roberto, my husband, dearly and we had a good life together. My grief is that I couldn't give him children. Yet, with you it's much different. With you there's so much passion, so much fire."

"I noticed you seemed rather enthusiastic," Paul observed then yelped when Gloria pinched him. He grabbed her and held her close, giving her a kiss that left her breathless. "Let's make fire, *corazón*," he murmured. "Lets make fire!"

Lima, Perú. Colonel Jergen Schwartz was worried. His driver was long overdue back in Lima. Rott had flown out to Bogotá as a diplomatic courier eight days before. The plan was for him to deliver dispatches to the embassy there and to consult with Johannes Weiss where two kilos of cocaine might be had. Not knowing what it would cost, Rott had taken several thousand marks in American currency along and was traveling with the Gestapo agent for a bodyguard.

Remembering how Rott had responded when Schwartz insisted he take the cook's assistant along, the scholar smiled. "I don't have time to baby-sit a ham-fisted Gestapo agent," Rott told him. "I'll wind up guarding the documents and the cocaine, too, mostly from Dieter, if my information is right."

"Oh?" Schwartz asked. Gestapo agents were lower than sewer rats as far as most Germans were concerned, and the professor was no exception. They were accountable to no one but their superiors, who tended to turn a blind eye toward whatever their agents did. Knowing Dieter had a taste for narcotics not only gave his superiors a strong hold over the man, and also a good source of evidence they could plant wherever they wished. Possession of narcotics was sufficient grounds for a one way ticket to a concentration camp. A drug user could be accused of all sorts of unrelated crimes.

What finally convinced Rott to take the Gestapo agent with him was Dieter's uncanny ability to find a source. The man knew of several in Lima, but Rott was hesitant to use local sources. "That could come back to bite us, Jergen," he argued. "We are known here in Lima and if something went wrong, we could find ourselves persona non grata in an instant. The new ambassador would be glad to see us gone."

"Going to Bogotá is much preferable than going home to Berlin, is it not?" the linguist asked. "Dieter can find a source and make the actual purchase, which gives us an added margin of safety. Even though he's Gestapo, we could claim he was acting without our knowledge or consent."

Rott paused and nodded. "And if a Gestapo drug user gets shot buying drugs, no one can blame us. Or will even care. Do we even want to bring him back to Lima?"

Schwartz nodded. "That would be more prudent."

"Then that's what we'll do. Dieter will have custody of the drugs until we arrive back here at the embassy. I'll make sure he doesn't get into them."

That was ten days before and eight days since the two men had flown out. They were scheduled to be back in Lima in four days at most and normally Rott was as reliable as a Swiss watch. Nor had there been any news of a plane going down in the last eight days. Something was wrong and there had been no news from the embassy in Bogotá.

When the phone on his desk rang, Schwartz jumped. Then he snatched up the instrument and was relieved to hear the distinct voice of his driver. "It's me, Colonel. I knew you'd want to know right away. I was successful but there were some complications. I'll tell you when I get there." The line went dead before the professor could respond.

An hour later, Rott was seated in a comfortable chair across from the scholar. "I know you want details but I haven't had a decent meal in a week. Would you mind talking about this over wiener schnitzel?"

"That would be good," Schwartz said affably. It was quite clear they needed complete privacy. Rott had not been there to sweep the office for bugs for over a week. "I haven't eaten since breakfast and Steng's won't be crowded at this hour."

Once they were seated in the German restaurant, Rott didn't waste any time getting down to business. "We got what we went for but Dieter almost got us killed. I swear, if he's any indication, I don't see how the Gestapo gets anything done! He's not only completely corrupt. He's incompetent, to boot. He found a seller right away, someone who was supposed to be a wholesaler, and we met the third day we were in Bogotá. The bastard tried to rob us and I had to shoot our way out. Dieter was no help! He wasn't even armed!"

"Did both of you get out?"

"Yes, unfortunately. Then we had to spend three days in hiding before Weiss could extract us. Fortunately, he knows a police captain who is fond of American greenbacks, but it was touch and go. The irony is that the police captain got most of the money we were going to give the dealer. The day after we got back to the embassy, we flew out. The item we were after is now locked in my personal safe at the embassy. I thought I was going to have to shoot Dieter to keep his hands off it."

"Do you think Dieter is going to be a problem down the line?" Schwartz asked.

Rott nodded. "Yes, I need to keep him close. So I'll take him with me to make delivery. I doubt he will make it back. It's time for him to make the ultimate sacrifice for the glory of the Fatherland. I'm sure you can arrange an Iron Cross."

"That's normally reserved to military service," Schwartz reminded him.

It was all Rott could do to keep from rolling his eyes. "Yes, Jergen, I know. On the other hand, do you know anything that's normal in Berlin these days? Dieter was a nitwit they sent here to limit the damage he could do. The Gestapo will be happy to use him as a safely dead hero."

Change of Plans

9 Near Pasco, Perú. Mike O'Leary, locally known as Simon Lynch, swept the jungle below with his field glasses. He and his guide, Marino, were prone at the top of a high ridge overlooking a river valley below. They were peering over the edge of the ridge at a wide sheer face, and from where they lay, they could see the forest trail for half a mile in either direction.

"See anything?" Lynch asked. Like himself, Marino had binoculars and was surveying the valley below."

The guide shook his head. "Nothing. Who are these men, señor? It's like looking for ghosts, two weeks and no sign of them. No one wants to tell us a thing."

Lynch continued to sweep the forest. "Like I told you, the man I need to see most is a young American soldier. He is traveling with a well known politician and the information I have is that he is acting as a guide."

"An American? Are you sure? Even a stupid politician is not foolish enough to use an American as a guide."

"This man knows the Andes. He spent several years here as a mining company geologist before the war. At least, that's what I was told. My source is known to embellish."

"Is his name Pablo?" Marino asked.

"Yes," Lynch responded, surprised. "Paul Radford. He knows this country from one end to the other."

"I know him," Marino replied. "I worked for him before he moved south. He was very young and inexperienced, but he was a quick learner."

Lynch looked up from his binoculars. "Have you heard of him since then?"

The guide nodded. "What I have heard is hard to believe. He

is said to move like a ghost through the jungle and to have killed many men. He is said to be friends of the Indians there, but it hard to believe it's the same man. He is called Pablo *el gato*, Pablo the cat, and it's said that he sometimes travels with an old priest and the jaguar man." He looked at Lynch gravely. "Are you going to try to kill him?"

Lynch shook his head. "No. I simply need to talk to him. The man he is traveling with has powerful enemies who would like him dead."

"The politician? Most people wouldn't mind seeing a lot of them dead. What is his name?"

Lynch paused, then made a decision. John Edgar might not like it but Lynch was going to refuse the contract. There was no reason to lie to Marino. "His name is Victor Haya. Do you know him?"

"Haya? He's one of the good ones, señor. Are you going to kill him?"

Lynch shook his head. "No, I don't think so. I was hired to do that but I've heard a lot of good things about the man."

"Then why are you trying to find him?"

"I'm not. I'm trying to find Pablo. Only, he seems to be traveling with Haya. He needs to know who's behind this."

Marino thought about all this for a moment. "So you're betraying the man who hired you?" There was no mistaking what he thought of this.

Lynch shook his head. "That's what he might claim, but I'm not. I told him I might decide to refuse the job."

"So you will be giving his money back?"

"No. All I agreed to do was to look at the job and that's all he paid me to do. He knew that from the start. He agreed to pay me more if I decided to do it."

"So why aren't you doing it?"

"The short answer is that it would be wrong, Marino. The long answer is that the man who hired me has gone out of his way to make trouble for me before. He is as treacherous as a green viper. From where I stand, I'm just paying him back."

"Then he will come after you."

Lynch shook his head again. "No, if he ever did he would get hurt and he knows it. Or, he will if he thinks about it. I may need to spell it out for him." He shrugged. "To tell you the truth, I think he's a little crazy. He's hungry for power."

It was evident that Marino was far from convinced. "I don't know, señor. This is bad business. I want no part of killing Victor Haya. Or the man who hired you."

"I'm telling you the truth, Marino," Lynch assured him. "I was to get paid whether I do the deed or not. I'm choosing not to go through with it. Of course, you have no way of knowing if I mean what I say or if I'm telling the truth." He shrugged. "You can walk away, if you want. I won't try to stop you. You can even take your pick of the animals."

The guide said nothing and Lynch looked down at the trail. "I think we're chasing a ghost here, anyway. I think I need to look farther south."

The assassin crawled back from the verge. Then he rose and stretched before walking to the pack animals tied to rocks. Turning back to the guide, he asked, "Well? Are you coming with me, or not?"

Lopez Ranch, Perú. Victor Haya was feeling restless. This was apparent a week before he said anything. When he did, he and his men were at dinner with Gloria and Paul and he approached the subject indirectly. "Your wonderful hospitality is ruining me, Gloria," he told her. My greatest ambition these days is finding out what's for dinner or taking a long nap."

"Why do I doubt that, Victor?" Gloria asked with a smile. "Admit it. You're just getting bored."

"No, not exactly. There are some people I need to see, to talk with. I suppose I could send a letter, but that would lead back here. The last thing I want is to make trouble for you."

"Come on, Victor, this is Gloria. The last thing you want is to wither on the vine here at the end of nowhere." She smiled to let him know she was only half serious. "You need to be in the thick of things. You love it."

Haya looked at Paul and shrugged. "How can I deny it, Pablo?" he asked, shrugging. "There is so much that needs to be done and so little time to do it."

"And you're the one who has to do it all?" Gloria asked.

Haya chuckled. "No, but I don't want them to discover they can do without me."

"Now the truth comes out," she replied. "How soon are you thinking of leaving?"

"Soon. Perhaps the day after tomorrow."

Gloria nodded. "Well, your horses are in good shape." She turned to Paul and smiled. "Your mule is, too."

"I was actually thinking of looking for a car," Victor told her. "I had enough riding horseback when we came south."

"I don't think that's a good idea, Victor," Paul said. "It's far too dangerous. Your movements are too predictable once it's known you're traveling that way. I think that must be how the communists found us up north."

"Pablo's right," Gloria said. "There aren't that many people who have cars."

"You can't eat them, either," Paul volunteered. Seeing the look of horror on Gloria's face, he added. "I was thinking of my mule. I think I'd walk a thousand kilometers rather than ride that damned beast another hundred."

Haya chuckled. "You're assuming it's tender enough to eat, Pablo." Then he frowned. "You are probably right, both of you, but I'm afraid I'm a city dweller now. Traveling by horse is so slow."

"You have somewhere you need to be right away?" Radford asked.

"No, that's not it. On a horse, I have to guide it. In a car, I can relax and let Timo get us where we're going safely."

"I suspect Timo would rather be on a horse if he had the police chasing him," Radford observed dryly. When he looked at Timo, the driver smiled and nodded.

"What about you guys?" Paul asked Diego and Mateo.

"Whatever the *jeffe* wants," Montoya said. Vargas nodded.

Radford looked at Haya. "You know, Victor, it really doesn't make much difference to me if you want to risk your life and mine. Are you willing to risk the lives of three loyal men for your comfort and convenience?"

Gloria looked shocked and Haya flushed. Paul wondered if he

had gone too far. He was surprised when Haya took a deep breath and shook his head. "No, of course not. I had not thought of it that way, Pablo. Thank you for reminding me."

Radford nodded. "I know, Victor. No offense intended. You're a good, honorable man."

Even so, Gloria pinned his ears back when they were by themselves a while later. "That was very discourteous, Pablo!" She declared. "You should be ashamed!"

Radford sighed. "I can't afford to be courteous, *corazón*. Not when lives are at stake. I have seen too many good men sacrificed for someone else's pride. I owe Victor the honest truth as I see it and he relies on that. Even he agreed I was right. I apologize for offending you."

Gloria glared at him a moment longer. Then her eyes filled and she threw herself into Paul's arms. A few moments later she pulled back and looked at him. "You remind me so much of my husband, Pablo. It's uncanny."

"I wish I had known him."

Gloria chuckled. "I'm not so sure. The two of you would have butted heads like young *cabritos*. He was the same way with Father Juan."

Radford smiled, glad to see he was forgiven. "I have a question, *querida*."

"Then ask it, *mi mulallero*."

Paul laughed. "I guess I deserve being called a mule rider."

"You do, but what is your question?"

"Well, I'm going to be leaving soon and I don't know when I'll be able to get back. So why are we spending so much time talking?"

Gloria's answer was a kiss that left him weak in the knees.

Lima. Rosario thought about the news her husband had brought the evening before. He'd returned late from a long visit in the countryside and she was disturbed that he had put off telling her what he apparently had known for some time. Nor was she sure why he had delayed telling her. He'd come home exhausted from his travels, too tired to discuss anything. Even though he promised to talk about it at length once he got home from work the next day, she felt an unusual irritation with Juan. She wondered why he had not waited to give her the news when he had time to answer her questions.

Even so, she was relieved to learn that Paul was alive and well. Despite her marriage to Juan Gomez, her love for Paul had not changed. Nor was she sure how she would respond if she met him face to face. The news of his return had awoken memories she had firmly shut away, and through the day she felt herself becoming excited at the prospect of seeing him once more. It would be hard for her to keep from taking him into her arms and giving him as freely of herself as she had from the first. Yet she wondered how he would respond.

Even so, she was aware how wrong this might be. She was not the only one who would be affected by her decision. Juan Gomez had been a wonderful husband and a competent lover, and she owed him a great debt for giving her and Azúl the home Pablo could not. Now she was carrying Juan's child and there was no doubt Azúl had become Juan's daughter. The two of them took great delight in one another's company, and Juan Gomez was the only father Azúl had ever known.

"What do I do, Angelica?" she asked the cat curled up in a chair. It had come to her as a kitten while she was in captivity, being used by the Germans as a hostage to manipulate Pablo. Nor was there any doubt in Rosario's mind that the kitten had been sent to reassure her that all would be well, a furry messenger from the Most High.

"Mwar," the cat responded softly.

"Now why didn't I think of that?" Rosario laughed. First checking that Azúl was still asleep, she picked up the cat and took it to the bedroom There they both lay down on the big, comfortable bed for a nap. Yet her thoughts returned to Pablo and it was a long time before she could get to sleep.

Lopez ranch, Perú. Even though he acknowledged being in the wrong, Victor was cool toward Paul for a few days after their argument. He was not rude or discourteous, but the easy intimacy the two men shared was gone. It was also obvious the older man was choosing his words carefully whenever they talked. Finally, Radford had enough. The night before they were to leave, he asked for a private word with the older man after supper. Once they were alone, Paul took the bull by the horns.

"Look, Victor. I didn't say what I did to hurt your feelings or insult you. If I did, you have my apologies. I thought you wanted the truth from me, a different point of view."

"I do, Pablo, but you have sharp fangs. How is it you *yanquis* say it? Your bite is worse than your bark?"

Paul smiled. "Actually, it's the other way around but your point is well taken. Please pardon me for not being more polite."

"Of course, Pablo. Perhaps it would help to be a little more diplomatic. You seemed very angry when you said it."

"There are reasons for that, Victor. They have nothing to do with you. They come from my experience with command decisions that ignored the obvious and got people killed."

"What is obvious to you may not be what is obvious to others," Haya pointed out.

"Yes, but let me give you an example. During a joint navy and army operation I was in, the navy was in charge. The army wanted to send in scouts to see if an island was under enemy control. There had been no sign of them for days. It would have been simple to send in a couple of teams of trained scouts to make sure."

Radford shook his head sadly. "I was one of those urging this decision. The admiral refused to let the scouts go in and twenty-eight men were killed in a fire-fight between two American units in the fog. They died for nothing because the enemy had already evacuated the island a week before. Scouts could have verified that."

There was no mistaking the pain in Radford's eyes. "That was just one of several decisions just like it that I witnessed. The anger you saw was from that. I was not angry with you, just impatient."

"Thank you for telling me this, Pablo. I understand now. Let's put it behind us. Perhaps a little more diplomacy, no?"

"Definitely a lot more diplomacy, Victor. Thank you."

Later that evening Paul told Gloria about the conversation. "Thank you, Pablo," she said. "I hated two of my favorite people being upset with each other. Now, there's something else I want to discuss with you."

"What's that, *querida*?"

"I want to make a trade. I want a mule and I am willing to trade a very good horse and a well padded saddle for it."

"You don't have to do that, Gloria. I can't take your husband's saddle."

"Of course, you can, silly man. It's of no use to him now, or even to me. I am padded enough. It would please me very much to know you were riding it."

"I don't know. I'd feel guilty trading that mule for a good horse, even to a crooked trader."

"Then keep the mule and use it to eat," she laughed. "Or give it to the *indios*, like you did the burros you told me about. I want you to have the horse you rode the other day and I want you riding that saddle."

Paul nuzzled her neck. "Actually, *corazón*, there's another saddle I'd rather be riding."

"You're terrible," she murmured. Then she gasped when he touched her and nothing was said for a long while.

Lima. Helmut Rott was beyond agitated. He was livid. It was bad enough having to start their journey in the rain. Nor did he take it kindly when Schwartz suggested he put off his departure for a day or two. Rott had gone to great pains to plan the trip down to the smallest detail, but he had not anticipated rain. This was the dry season and all the rain gear had been carefully packed the night before. It was clear across town and there was no way of getting there without being drenched or attracting unwanted attention.

Then, one by one, all his carefully made arrangements began to fall apart. The first sign of real trouble came when Dieter showed up late without either the pack animals or the guide. Nor did it help when Rott launched into an incendiary diatribe, blaming Dieter for what was clearly beyond his control.

Nor had the assistant cook done anything wrong. Taking the initiative, which Dieter rarely did, he set out to find the guide when the man failed to show. Knowing the guide's weakness for anything containing alcohol, Dieter first checked the guide's quarters. Not finding Chino at home, he began making the rounds of every cantina in town. Yet even after enduring the verbal abuse of the irate bar owners whom he had woken, and carefully searching the alleys behind the bars, the guide was not to be found.

Not knowing what to do next, Dieter made his way to the place they were supposed to meet. Doing so was an act of real courage, for he dreaded bringing the news to Helmut Rott. The little man in black was known for killing the messenger, and when Dieter saw the state Rott was in, he could barely speak. This, of course, only made matters worse.

This being so, it took Rott twice as long as it should to drag the information out of the terrified scullion. This, of course, did nothing to abate Rott's ire. Once he grasped the situation, however, he knew that Dieter had done everything that could reasonably be expected.

At that point, Rott suddenly became icy calm as he began to pace back and forth like a caged tiger, assessing his choices. This was something Dieter had never seen before. He found it even more frightening than the worst of Rott's fiery invective. When Rott suddenly whirled around to speak to Dieter, the poor cook's helper almost shat his pants.

"Did you look in the church?" the driver demanded.

"No, Herr Rott. Why would he be there?"

"To sleep it off, of course," Rott told him. "That's the one place that's never locked. Go search the pews and the choir loft, too. When you find him, bring him here. I don't care if you have to drag him by the hair on his head. Now, go!"

Dieter took off like a scared cat at full throttle. Rott took off at a fast walk for the stable, pacing so fast his limp was scarcely noticeable. It was at that point that Chino, still full of rum, staggered into the plaza and slumped down on a bench near the fountain. "Where the hell is everybody?" he asked, loudly indignant. "The *cabrón* tells me to be here early and he doesn't even show up, himself! The devil take him!"

Having delivered himself of his opinion, Chino stretched out on a bench sheltered from the rain and passed out. That was where Rott found him fifteen minutes later. Dieter, who arrived a moment later, saw Rott grab the guide by the hair and drag him to his feet, cursing him and slapping him sober. For an awful moment, Dieter thought Rott might actually shoot the man or strangle him.

Once the guide was slapped sober, the loading went very quickly. The guide was not much help, but Dieter and Rott managed to get everything secured on the animals. Then they took off for the mountains, the guide walking ahead, prodded by Rott with a pointed walking stick. Dieter followed, leading the burros. As much as he disliked the man, Dieter felt sorry for the guide. Nor did he miss the irony when the rain suddenly stopped as they left town.

Lopez ranch, Perú. The evening before they left Gloria's ranch, Paul sought out Haya to discuss their itinerary. "I'm not sure," the older man told him. There are people I need to see in Lima within the next few weeks, but there are others I need to see in Puerto Maldonado. The problem with both, of course, is that there is a strong police force."

"No kidding," Paul replied. "Puerto Maldonado has a wild reputation. I imagine there must be an army garrison there. Do you really need to go?"

Haya nodded. "Yes. It's been a long time since I was there. I need to renew some acquaintances and to make some new ones." He shrugged. "It's what a politician does."

"Perhaps you need to split it up into two trips. Which is more important, Lima or Puerto Maldonado?"

"Lima is more pressing, but Puerto Maldonado is really the most important. With Lima there are some events coming up for which I need to do some ground work. With Puerto Maldonado, I need to spend some time among the people. As in many other places, they are oppressed by the rubber barons and the mining and lumber interests. They are ripe for what I have to say, for *Aprismo*."

"Mining?" Paul asked. "Puerto Maldonado's in the middle of the jungle. What's worth mining there?"

"Gold. Every year the Madre de Dios and Rio de Piedras wash down large amounts of gold dust that's deposited along the river banks. Dredging operations bring it up off the bottom, too. The people who own the claims get rich and the people who dig the gold are paid almost nothing."

Radford nodded. "What else is new? I don't know, Victor. I'd advise against going either place. We've been out of sight for a couple of months now. Why not give it a little more time? You know, out of sight, out of mind."

Victor chuckled. "What politician is not aware of that, my friend? What that tells me is that I need to be seen before they forget me completely."

"I see your point. Maybe we need to look at how we can limit your vulnerability."

"Now that, I can endorse completely. What do you have in mind?"

"Not to bring up a sore subject, but we need to travel by horse. At least, we do until we get to town. Then we need to stay somewhere neither the police nor your enemies will expect. Do you have any friends you can stay with there?"

"Not like Gloria, no. We will probably need to rent a place. That may be difficult."

"We probably need to rent two, if we can. One can be your known address in town. The other is where we will stay. I think we need to let Mateo and Diego be the...front guys?" Not knowing the right Spanish word, Radford said them in English.

"Front guys? I'm not familiar with that expression, Pablo."

"In this case, it's the people who appear to be renting the two places. It means the people are only apparently in charge. Sometimes it's called a straw-man or figurehead."

"Ah, figurehead I know. The Spanish is *mascarón de proa*. A *mascarón* is someone who wears a big, ugly mask like they use in parades. *Proa* is the front of a ship or airplane."

"Exactly. As far as anyone else needs to know, Diego and Mateo are simply strangers wanting a place to stay. They look enough alike to pass for brothers."

Haya smiled. "That's because they are brothers. They had different fathers." Victor paused, then said, "I don't know. It seems like an unnecessary expense. It would be cheaper to bribe the local police captain." Seeing the look on Radford's face, he added, "Don't be shocked, Pablo. How do you think I have stayed at large so long? I don't like it, but it works."

Paul shrugged. "Only so long as they stay bought, Victor. Who makes the approach?"

"Timo is very good at that. He has the manner."

Radford nodded. "So where do you want to go first?"

"Lima, I think. I have friends who have been working out a rapprochement with the General. I think it's wishful thinking, myself, but I need to be sure. I don't want to poke a peaceful wasp's nest."

"That would make life easier," Radford agreed. "I don't have to tell you to be sure everyone is on board, especially the General."

Haya nodded. "The problem is how he can reverse himself and still save face."

"Blame it on the communists."

Haya chuckled. "At long last I have found out something they are good for." Then he sobered. "The thing is, Pablo, there may be too much history to surmount. The military and I are natural enemies. It has been so since the beginning of my career. I want freedom and they want control."

Radford nodded. "That pretty much sums it up. They are against freedom because they are afraid of it. They think they will lose their power."

Haya nodded. "Who wants to do that?"

"So someone needs to convince them that they will gain more power by reconciling with you. You are probably the only one who can do that."

"Yet, if I go to them directly, they will throw me in prison. I certainly don't like it there and prefer not to go, even if it would give us great opportunity."

Radford grinned. "And if I go on your behalf, they will shoot me. Let me give it some thought."

"Well, if we travel by horseback, you'll have a lot of time for that."

Rough Crossing

10 Pisco. Juan Calderón was worried. Pico had returned from a trip to the capital the evening before and the news the one-eyed guide brought was disturbing. He had heard an amusing story about one of the German embassy drivers from a cousin who ran a small stable. The German had hired a notorious local drunk as a guide and had made the mistake of giving the guide money to hire pack animals. What the guide did was to make a deposit to reserve the animals, promising to pay the balance when he picked them up. Then the guide proceeded to the nearest cantina and drank up the balance of the money the German had given him.

Pico was amused by the story, but when he learned that the driver was Helmut Rott, he became concerned. There was no doubt in his mind that the German was headed into the mountains to hunt down Paul Radford. The party was said to be heavily armed and they were carrying supplies for an extended stay in the back country.

Not waiting to even spend the night, Pico set off for Pisco late in the afternoon. Luck was with him and he caught a ride on a supply truck for most of the 250 kilometer trip down the coast. The truck arrived just before midnight and Pico hurried across town to the rectory. There the padre and Alicia listened while he repeated what he'd heard and the old priest was as concerned as Pico.

"You need to rest," Juan Calderón told him. "We need to get word to Pablo, but there's not much more we can do tonight. Tomorrow we will decide how to reach him." He looked at Alicia. "Not a word of this to anyone. The Germans have ears everywhere."

"That must be who's been watching us," the housekeeper replied. When the two men looked at her in surprise, she said, "One of the neighbors saw them, two local men. They have no business around here and they take turns watching." She gave them two names.

"I saw them, too," the old priest said. "I thought they were after the silver. That's why I've been so careful locking up at night. It never occurred to me they might be after Pablo."

"I haven't heard of any German strangers in town," Alicia told them. "Or any other Europeans."

"All they have to do is inform the local police," the padre pointed out. "I think our local captain is in their pay. Once the police have Pablo, the Germans can get at him."

Then the old priest frowned. "You don't suppose they are waiting for Rosario to pay us a visit, do you? They used her for a hostage once. Surely they know she married Gomez and doesn't live here any more. I don't think they would risk kidnapping her in Lima, not a policeman's wife."

"Maybe it's not Rosario they are after," Pico suggested.

"Then who, me? I'm not much use to them," the padre said. Then his face grew grave when he realized what Pico was saying. "Not Azúl," he murmured. "Dear God, not Azúl!"

Central Perú. Dieter Braun was miserable. The first day out of Lima had been bad enough. After the rain stopped, the intense summer sun turned the trail into a sauna, drenching the three men with sweat. Then the biting bugs descended in swarms. Rott had thought to include mosquito nets that fit over their hats, but they had to keep their sleeves rolled down and wear gloves to protect their hands. The repellent they had brought proved useless.

Despite the heat and humidity, Rott drove them like a fiend. When the poor guide, suffering from the mother of all hangovers, refused to get up after the first short stop for rest, Rott whipped out his Luger and threatened to shoot the man on the spot. It hung in the balance for four eternal seconds before the guide shrugged and struggled to his feet. To keep him from slipping away, Rott forced the guide to travel directly in front of him, with Dieter bringing up the rear with the two pack animals. By the time they stopped to make camp for the night, the guide was exhausted and slumped to the ground and passed out without touching the rations Rott tossed down before him.

Even so, Rott shackled the guide's feet. "That will save us having to run him down if he decides to run away," he told Dieter. "You take the first watch. Wake me at midnight."

Dieter wondered how they could trust a guide they had to shackle, but Rott answered, as if he was reading the young man's mind. "This is just for tonight and perhaps tomorrow night, too. Once we get to the back country, he'll straighten out. He's a good guide when he's not drinking." Then Rott grinned, terrifying the Gestapo agent. "He knows how long it will take him to die if I have to run him down."

The second day on the trail was somewhat better, but it brought it's own challenges. At the higher altitudes it was cooler and far less humid, and the bugs were less voracious. Yet the road they were following grew far steeper and it seemed to Dieter that their climb would never end. As soon as they had reached the apparent summit of one steep slope, there was always another, higher assent beyond it. Quite often they had to descend hundreds of meters, yielding hard earned altitude, before going up the next slope. Even so, they covered forty kilometers before Rott called a halt just before dark.

By the third day, it was clear that the guide was recovering from his spree. He had been able to eat breakfast the second morning and, by the third day, he began to lead them up trails not visible to Dieter's untrained eye. The higher they climbed, the better the guide seemed to feel, but Dieter, used to living at sea level, found it increasingly hard to breathe. Even Rott seemed to suffer from the altitude, and he called stops for rest far more often the higher they went.

Dieter was surprised when Rott called a halt just after noon on their fifth day out. They had reached the summit of a high ridge overlooking a nameless river, and from their perch, they could see higher peaks extending fifty kilometers to the horizon. From there they could also keep watch over several kilometers of a well defined path that followed the river and Dieter guessed this was why Rott chose to set up camp and remain there for three days.

The rest was welcome. Dieter was no stranger to high mountains, growing up near the Swiss border in Austria. Yet the Andes were different, and as they kept watch, he thought about this, feeling homesick. At least he did when he wasn't standing watch with Rott. There was no relaxing then as the two of them stood watching silently, alternating sweeps of the valley with the powerful pair of binoculars Rott had brought along.

It was during one these watches with Dieter that Rott discovered that the young cook's assistant had never been through full Gestapo orientation or even basic military training. "What!" he exclaimed when Dieter admitted he had never been schooled as anything but a cook until the Gestapo recruited him as a snitch. "I thought you were a fully trained agent! That's what your file says!"

"I had nothing to do with my file, Herr Rott," Dieter told him. His face was so pale the driver thought he might faint. "I have no idea what my file says. They told me they wanted me to watch certain people and send them reports. I was with an army unit headed for Italy when they came and talked to me. Then they sent me here."

"Who were you supposed to spy on?" Rott demanded.

"Everyone at the embassy, sir. They to me to pay special attention to the ambassador and Colonel Schwartz."

"What about me?" Rott growled.

"You have done nothing to report," Dieter told him, avoiding the question. "They said nothing about anyone else by name and I didn't ask."

Rott fixed the young man with a steely stare. "You better not be lying to me, Dieter," he growled. "If I ever find you do, you better cut your throat before I get to you. Understand!"

"Yes, sir, Herr Rott!" Dieter stammered, cringing as if he expected to be kicked.

Rott stared at him for six painfully long seconds before he relented. "What about military training?" he asked gruffly. "Why didn't you go to infantry school?"

"I don't know," Dieter replied. "I thought I was going but I was never sent. All they ever trained me to do was to cook until the Gestapo trained me how to send coded messages."

"Odin's balls, man! Do you even know how to use a rifle?" The poor scullion shook his head timidly. "Why did you think I brought you along, Dieter? Why didn't you say something when I gave you a rifle and ammunition?"

"I thought you just wanted me to carry them for you, Herr Rott. I didn't know you meant me to use them. I thought you brought me along to cook."

Rott just shook his head and, with visible effort, forced himself to calm down. "All right, Dieter," he said, almost kindly. "Have you ever used any firearms at all?"

"No, sir, not at all. I wanted to learn but the Gestapo told me it wasn't necessary. They said they needed me here right away. It was a few weeks before the other ambassador was recalled home."

"You must have reported quite a bit about him," Rott said.

"Yes, sir, I did. Colonel Schwartz was very helpful."

"Yes, I imagine he was," Rott said dryly. "How did he find out you were Gestapo?"

"I don't know, Herr Rott. He talked to me the first day I was on duty. He knew I was Gestapo from the beginning, but he didn't know I was told to spy on him. He thought I was there to spy on everyone else. I didn't tell him, either."

"All right, Dieter. You can still use your eyes and ears. Here comes Chino. Not a word about this to him. Understand? I don't think he understands German but watch what you say. Now cook us a good supper. I'll finish the watch by myself."

Dieter hurried away to get supper started and Rott swept the valley with the binoculars while he waited for their guide. "What did you find out?" he asked when Chino drew near.

Chino shrugged. "Not much. Five men passed through here on horseback about four to six weeks ago. No one was certain of exactly when and they didn't have many details. Or maybe they didn't tell me. One of the men looked like an American. They said he was fluent in Spanish but he talked funny, like he was from somewhere else. He also spoke Quechua. There were three other younger men besides the American and one old man. All of them carried rifles and pistols and they had a pack animal."

"Which way were they headed?"

"South. Someone overheard them talking about Machu Picchu and Aquas Calientas. The old man wanted to go there." Chino shrugged. "Of course, they might have allowed themselves to be overheard." He shrugged again.

Rott nodded. "Anything else?"

Chino nodded. "Someone told me the American seemed to know where he was going and they didn't seem to be in a hurry to get there. Their horses were fat and in good shape and they spent two nights in the village. The old man talked to the people there in Spanish, like a politician one man told me, and the American translated into Quechua."

The guide paused and Rott looked at him closely. "What?" the German asked.

"Maybe nothing, señor, but the American said something about going through a certain area on their way south. That was before they got to the village. I have heard of this area. The people who live there are very bad. Not even the army dares go there. Yet the American claimed to pass through the worst part of it."

"Are you sure you got it right?" Rott asked.

The guide nodded. "I thought I was not hearing right, so I asked. They told me that was the place they were talking about. I asked how this was possible but no one was willing to talk. They are afraid of the bad people, the *indios*. They don't like to talk about them."

Rott nodded. "All right, we'll head south first thing in the morning. I don't see much point in staying here any longer. How far to Machu Picchu?"

"Three days, maybe four, if we take the main road. Longer if we follow the trails."

Mexico City. The hour was half past six when Commander Eric Rudd walked up the drive to the American embassy. As he did, he passed a squad of Marine guards in dress uniform and stopped. The American flag was being raised and Rudd joined the Marines in saluting it. The sergeant in charge was someone he knew, and he greeted the man before he walked up the steps to the ornate entrance.

"You're here early, sir," the sergeant observed. "I hope you don't expect to find anybody up at this hour except us."

Rudd chuckled. "As a matter of fact, I'm here to see one of yours. Unless the pencil pushers have softened him up."

"Well, if you're talking about Major Blieu, sir, it hasn't happened.

And I doubt it will."

"Loose lips sink ships, Marine," the commander reminded him gently."

"Yes, and Marines ride those ships," the sergeant agreed. "Not to worry, sir. I'll zip the lip."

"Thanks, sergeant. Any idea where I might find the man?"

"Try the mess hall, sir. It's in a separate wing around the corner to the left. He's usually there about now."

The commander walked around a well tended flower bed that extended around the corner. Someone had done a good job organizing local varieties of native flowers, and it was tempting to stop and look at some of these more carefully. Yet Rudd moved on. "There's a war on, sailor," he murmured, his eyes never leaving the flower bed.

"There is, indeed," said a familiar voice and Rudd looked up and saw Denis Blieu sitting on a bench in front of the mess hall door. He was facing a riot of tulips in all colors and it was obvious he had sat down to take them in. "Even so, one needs to stop and appreciate the flowers once in a while. The ambassador's wife had these put in last year."

"She did a good job," Rudd said. "I didn't think that tulips flowered at this time of year."

"It seems they do. Miriam's surprised a lot of people with what she can do with flowers."

Miriam? Rudd thought, wondering if Blieu had bedded the lady. The man had a reputation for being a nooky hound. No one could figure out how he did it. Denis wasn't exactly homely, but he wasn't handsome, either. "You want to meet here?" he asked the major.

"Outside is more secure," Blieu responded. "But there's a better place." He got up and led the commander across a well tended lawn to a formal garden. There was a gazebo with cast iron benches and a clear field of view in every direction. Rudd smiled when he saw this. There was no way anyone could sneak up to eavesdrop.

"So what can I do for you, Eric?" Blieu asked.

"I'm worried about Paul," the commander told him. "The way we put him into the country still bothers me. It could get him shot."

Blieu shrugged. "He knew that going in, Eric, remember? He

volunteered. We hashed all this through."

Rudd shook his head. "No, he agreed to take the mission on those terms. I think we need to do something to give him more protection."

"What does the Senator say about that?" Blieu asked. "He wasn't too happy with Paul the last time they met."

The commander shrugged. "You know the Senator. He's been known to change his mind. You may not know it, but he asked for the file on Paul. He also talked to people in the field in Alaska when he was up there nosing around. He was so impressed he's pushing for a Medal of Honor for Paul for his record on Attu. The way he put it was, 'He may be a horse's ass, but he's our horse's ass, and he deserves it.' It didn't hurt that J. Edgar Hoover threw a wall-eyed hissy over us sending Paul to Perú in the first place. The Senator knows giving him a Medal of Honor will ruin the Director's whole week."

"It could keep the Director from having Paul shot, too," Blieu told him. His face was grave.

"Do you really think he'd actually do that?"

"Yeah, I do," Denis responded. "The man's not playing with a full deck, Eric. Jock caught wind of a rumor that Hoover was making a move on Haya. So he started digging and found out J. Edgar sent in an outside contractor. The man he sent used to be a Marine sniper, one of the best. Jock is going after him. I'm surprised he didn't brief you."

Rudd shrugged. "He did but there was a flap going on just then and I got called to Washington. I told Jock to do whatever he needed to do to protect Paul. I didn't connect the dots when he asked for John Yellowhawk. I thought it was for something else. John flew to Lima ten days ago as a diplomatic courier."

"Well, it sounds like we have the situation covered," Blieu pointed out. "But that's not what you came to talk about."

"No, I had no idea the assassin was a threat to Paul, but Jock apparently has that in hand. What I'm worried about is what could happen if Paul gets arrested by the police. He's in the country illegally and they could drum up some old charges from when he was there before."

"I don't see what we can do about that."

"The last time I talked to Jock, he had an idea. I mulled it over and I think it might work. He thinks we need to give Paul diplomatic status."

"We talked about that before. The current government will never accept Paul's credentials."

"Not under the name of Radford, no. What if he had his name legally changed for the duration? What if he took his mother's surname? She was a Jones, and what if he became John P. Jones? It's such a common name I doubt anyone would figure it out."

"I assume the middle initial is for Paul." Blieu shook his head. "It's too risky, Eric. We need to avoid the same initials, too. If we do it, I think we need something simple like Walter James Cook or Steven Lee Hill."

"How about Hall? That at least rhymes with Paul. We could give him a fancy name like Ramsey or Quincy, one he never uses."

"Actually, I think it might be best to find someone born the same year and who died before the war began. That way we wouldn't have to invent a background to cover him."

Rudd looked at Blieu and shook his head. "You know, Denis, it occurs to me that we may be getting too creative. Who's going to be asking? As embassy staff, he can refuse to reveal anything that's not on his papers. As far as other embassy personnel go, he will never be around long enough to get acquainted."

"How would he explain his presence in the boondocks?" Denis asked. "He can't just wander around anywhere."

"Unless it's his job. We caught a rumor that the Germans are trying to use cocaine as a stimulant for their troops. It's a mix of stuff called D-IX. We could give Paul a new identity and send him in as a special investigator. We could even offer to share our results with the Peruvian authorities."

Denis frowned. "You know, all this is getting very complicated. Why not just tell the Peruvian government the truth, that we have an investigator we want to send into the back country to keep track of communists. We can offer to share our results, if any."

"I like the cocaine idea better," Eric Rudd replied. "It is an illegal drug in Perú just like it is back home. It's believable and we can even mention the German work on a stimulant."

"Right," Denis replied, dryly. "We could give Paul the name of Charles Oliver Caine." Seeing Rudd's confusion, he added, "Use only the initials for the first two names. Paul could be Dr. C.O. Caine."

Near Ayacucho. Simon Lynch and Marino set out early that morning, just after it got light enough to see where they were stepping. They been on the trail a good three hours before the guide stopped suddenly and held up his hand. "Someone's coming," he whispered to Lynch. "You take that side of the trail."

Quiet as ghosts, the two slipped into the forest on either side of the trail, pulling their pack animal with them. Thirty seconds later Lynch picked up the faint sound of something coming down the trail, and a long minute after that, he saw something moving. Quietly easing off the safety of his rifle he waited to see what it was. Twenty seconds later he could make out the head of a burro walking toward him. It was wearing a packed cargo saddle and trailing a long lead behind.

A strong voice from directly behind him shattered the silence. "Stand down, O'Leary!"

Swinging around, Lynch swung his rifle around but stopped with it pointed straight up. A tall, thin figure in jungle fatigues stood within thirty feet with a rifle leveled at his chest. Nor was it lost on him that the thin man had a large tree between himself and Marino. "Easy does it, Marine!" the voice commanded. "Lay down the rifle and tell your guide to stand down. We've been tracking you for two days."

"Do as he says, Marino," Lynch called out in Spanish. A moment later his guide stepped out onto the trail, followed by another figure in fatigues. This one carried a rifle, too, as well as an automatic pistol in a military holster.

"Now lay aside your side-arm very slowly and move back to the path and sit down," the tall man commanded. We are not here to harm you. We need to talk."

When Simon and Marino were seated, the tall figure picked up Simon's pistol and sat down several feet away, facing the two prisoners. The other man in fatigues stood guard to one side with a tree at his back. Lynch saw quickly that it would be very difficult to attack either of them.

"Nice piece," the tall man said, examining Lynch's pistol. "I haven't seen one of these in a while." He quickly opened the triple-lock cylinder and ejected the shells. Looking at the bottom of one he nodded. "A good round to have in the jungle, 249 grains. Minimal brush deflection."

Setting the shells aside, the tall man looked at Lynch and said, "I don't see any reason to beat around the bush. I'm Captain Jaques Paul, United States Army, and that's Corporal, no, pardon me, newly promoted Sergeant John Yellowhawk, United States Marine Corps. He trained at the same place you did."

"My condolences," O'Leary said to the sergeant and was rewarded with a wry smile.

The captain continued. "To get to the point, we know quite a bit about you, Mike. Among other things, I know you've been sent here by J. Edgar Hoover to assassinate Victor Haya. The Director might not have used those words but that was the mission you were given."

Lynch made no sign of agreement or denial and Jaques Paul continued. "We also know your background. You joined the Marine Corps right after college and did well enough that you were selected for sniper training. You distinguished yourself as a sniper, setting marks that no one has matched since. Shortly after you were promoted to Corporal, the Secretary of the Navy received a copy of your birth certificate and an anonymous letter pointing out that you could not be a Negro and remain a Marine. Despite your excellent record, you were released from the Corps. Your commander hated to lose you but that was the law."

Again, there was no response and the captain nodded. "After that, you worked at menial jobs here and there until someone wanted someone else removed. Both the victim and the target were underworld characters, and the victim was killed in a hunting accident in the northern Catskills. The shooter was never identified and the local coroner ruled it an accident, even though the victim was wearing a red jacket and hat. No one was terribly concerned by one mobster being taken out by another and the case was shelved."

The captain paused and lit a cigarette, tossing the pack and matches over to Lynch, who let them lie. "The interesting thing is that after that, you dropped out of sight for a couple of years. Then someone spotted you in Kenya, working for a safari company. You made the mistake of entering a local shooting contest and won the grand prize of a thousand pounds. Unfortunately, that made the news."

The captain paused again, then continued. "The man who used your services before heard about the contest and needed another favor done. I suspect he was not a man you wanted to turn down. The interesting thing is that he turned up dead, shot by an unknown assailant who took him out at over a thousand yards with a single shot. The bullet was dug out of a tree it hit after going through the target. It was match grade military issue. Then, later, the intended victim died the same way on a golf course. The shot came from the same rifle and the bullet was also match grade. The irony was that the victim was having his best day in years. Does any of this sound familiar?"

"It's a very interesting story," Lynch replied. "I really liked the part about the victim getting hit, too. I wonder who hired that done. Did they ever find out?"

"No, Pearl Harbor happened not long after that and other things seemed more pressing than the murder of two crooks. So that case got put on the shelf, too. I doubt it will ever be opened again, much less solved. It was just another thug to the police. They had other worries. They still do."

"What does this have to do with me?"

"Nothing, I suppose. At least, nothing probable. Whoever made the shots is in the clear."

"Then why did you go to all this trouble? This couldn't have been the easiest place to find me."

"You might be surprised. The point of all this trouble is to bring you a message. Hoover was off base ordering the kill. We want Victor Haya left alone."

Lynch gave the captain a wry smile. It told Jacques Paul the assassin understood the underlying message: he had been tracked down and caught. He could have easily been shot and left to rot in the jungle. "Who's we?" Lynch asked. He didn't expect an answer.

"The governmental entity I work for. The US government, to be clear. We also want you to come to work for us."

"Governmental entity? That's an interesting term. What do you have to offer?"

"A clean slate and the chance to serve your country in an honorable way."

"That sounds sort of vague. What does it mean?"

"Well, to get down to brass tacks, the first item is a full Presidential pardon for anything you may have done since you left the Corps. You had an excellent record up to then."

"That's fine, but what's going to pay the rent?"

"You have a choice there. You can work for us as a civilian specialist or you can have full reinstatement as a Marine. The law has changed. You would then be assigned to us on detached duty. Personally, I think you'd be better off as a civilian. You will be classified as in a critical occupation and won't be drafted."

"I assume you want me for my shooting skills."

The captain smiled. "Well, there is a war on." He reloaded Lynch's pistol and handed it back, butt first. Lynch put back in the holster on his belt. Nor did he consider trying to shoot the captain. The sergeant would have nailed him first.

"Well, just for the record, Captain, I had already decided to abort the mission. Marino can verify that, but then, you have no reason to believe him. The other thing is, I don't have much stomach for the killing."

"We wouldn't want you if you did, Mike," Jacques Paul answered gently. "Hopefully, it won't be required that often. You need some time to think it over?"

Lynch shook his head. "No, it's a good deal. Assuming it's for real."

"It is," the captain assured him. "You think your cousin will be pissed about your turning him down?"

"Yes, I'm sure he will but I doubt if he'll do much. I hired on to look at the job and reserved the right to abort."

"He strikes me as a pretty vindictive soul," Jaques replied. "We can protect you as long as you're on the team. of course, but he may make an end run around us."

"Oh, he is vindictive, but if he had me killed, our common ancestry would come out. I've seen to that and he knows it. He also knows I turned town two contracts on him, but that's not what scares him. Embarrassment is what he fears most and that would do the trick."

"Two contracts? What was he worth?"

"A cool quarter million."

"Who would pay that?"

"Let me put it this way. He's underworld enemy number one. About the offer. Who would I be working for, you?"

"I will be your supervisor at first, but that can change from time to time, just like in the military. Who you would be working for is the United States government as part of a special military unit. Where you would be working is here in South America, at least for the foreseeable future. I know we need someone in Argentina, too. The Nazis are pretty strong there and we need someone to keep an eye on them. Wherever you are, you will be attached to the embassy. You'll have diplomatic status."

Lynch shook his head. "This all seems too good to be true, but what the hell? Let's up the ante. I'm summa cum laude from Harvard, class of 1935. Think you can shake the Corps down for a commission? It's better pay."

Jacques Paul chuckled. "It's possible but I think you'd have to be a Section 8 to accept one."

"You're right," Lynch said with a wry grin. "I'd have to be frigging crazy, now wouldn't I?"

Gẹstapo

11 Lima. Colonel Jergen Schwartz didn't really trust the man sitting across the table from him. His connections in Berlin had warned him that Gunther Berg was a Gestapo agent, one sent to keep an eye on everyone in the embassy. Unlike Dieter Braun, the cook's assistant, whom everyone knew was with the Gestapo, Gunther was not known to be anything but a staff officer in charge of supplies. Nor was it unusual for the Gestapo to assign someone like Dieter to act as a stalking horse, while Gunther was the unseen shooter who brought down the birds.

Even so, Schwartz believed Gunther could be useful if he were approached the right way. The trick would be to get him to commit himself to a course of action and to be an active participant. The colonel had to assume the man was no fool, so it would be necessary to be very careful in his approach. The best course of action would to be to stick as close to the truth as he could without getting caught in a lie.

"I'm glad you were able to come to lunch today. I find it's better to talk about certain things here at Steng's rather than in the office. The ambiance is certainly much more pleasant."

Gunther's nod was ambiguous. "It's certainly very pleasant here. It reminds me of places back home."

"Yes. I suppose it's due to the large German population in the city. There's a wonderful German bakery not far from here, too. I'd put anything they make up against French pastry any day."

"That's very patriotic," Berg answered dryly. "On the other hand, we occupy most of France." He returned to eating.

Schwartz waited patiently, but the Gestapo agent was very attentive to his food and didn't seem the least bit curious. So after a long wait, the linguist continued. "There is a situation here in Perú that needs some attention. Is the name Paul Radford familiar to you?"

Gunther shook his head. "I've come across the name but that's about it." The truth was that Radford was the reason he had been sent to Lima. The former ambassador had powerful friends and Berg had been told to investigate the situation. He was also told to pay particular attention to Colonel Jergen Schwartz and his driver, Helmut Rott.

"Well, Radford was a geologist for an American mining company before the Pearl Harbor attack. He also held a naval commission, and when America came into the war he was activated. Unfortunately, he gained access to some very sensitive documents that put him onto two operations we had almost completed here. One of these was a submarine base off the southern coast of this country, but still inside the twenty-kilometer limit. Another was a hidden ordinance plant that was disguised as a mining operation. Radford's interference was responsible for the destruction of both. It caused the recall of the ambassador who was here."

"So that's why he was called home," Berg nodded. "I wondered. This Paul Radford sounds like a pretty bad enemy."

"He is, which is why something must be done about him. One of my sources reported he was seen entering the country about three months ago. I suspect he is here to interfere with our procurement of coca leaves for our D-IX project."

Berg was surprised to hear that Schwartz was aware of the project. He covered his surprise by asking, "D-IX? What's that, Colonel?"

"I'm surprised you haven't heard of it. It's one of the worst kept secrets of the Reich. I'm no scientist, but I believe there is something in the leaves that will greatly increase our soldiers' endurance. It has to be extracted from the leaves. It apparently cannot be synthesized yet."

"I heard rumors of something like that," the Gestapo agent replied. "I didn't know if they could be taken seriously. One hears so many rumors these days."

"Well, this one is apparently true. The point is, Helmut Rott, my assistant, has taken off into the wilds to hunt the man down. On reflection, I wondered if it might not be far better to bring

Radford to us. We could spend months tracking him down in the mountains."

"Why would he come to us?" Berg asked.

"When he was here before, he had a common law wife, a local basket maker. Our information is that Radford sired a daughter by her and she and her mother live here in the city. It occurred to me that the two of them might make very good hostages."

"Does he even know about the child?" Gunther asked.

"My information is that he does, although he has never seen her. I believe he is also aware that his woman married a local man. That is, lawfully married."

"Then why would he bother to come after his former mistress? She has been disloyal, if not unfaithful."

Schwartz nodded. "Yes, but I believe he is very sentimental and would attempt to rescue his daughter if she were being held hostage."

Berg nodded. "Perhaps. How would you take her hostage? Assuming you did, how would you get word to him after you had her?"

"That's why I wanted to talk with you. Normally, Rott and I would work this out, but he's not available. I understand that you have operational experience in this kind of thing?"

Berg raised an eyebrow. "Where on earth did you get that idea, Colonel?"

"Don't play innocent with me, Herr Berg. Or should I say 'Captain Berg?' I am well aware who you work for, and I knew who you were before you arrived. I have good sources back home."

"Then you will be aware that my superiors would probably not agree to me being part of this so-called operation. It could very easily backfire, especially since I know the woman you are talking about is married to a policeman." He shook his head, as if in wonder. "You apparently are not aware how well known your part in the submarine base fiasco is. I suspect your man, Rott, was who did the dirty work and got rid of any evidence connecting either of you to it. Yet, the former ambassador knew and he was very forthcoming with us before he died."

Schwartz tried not to show the panic he felt. "He seems to have done a very good job maligning us. The fact remains that the evidence points to him, not us."

"Which is why it was he, not you, who was arrested." Berg looked at him coldly. "I would advise you not to pursue this debacle, Colonel. There has been embarrassment enough already." Then he added, "Just hope there is no further embarrassment to the Reich if Rott finds the man you're looking for. If there is, the two of you will be on the next plane to Berlin."

Near Ayanchucho. Paul Radford surveyed the trail behind them carefully. He was lying fully prone just below the crest of a high ridge. A large bush concealed him from below as he peered out the small gap below the branches. Turning his head, he could see the other four men making their way north about two kilometers away. Turning back he could see the trail stretching five or six kilometers to the south. Nothing moved along the path, but what he was watching most closely were the high points along the trail that offered a good overlook. That's were watchers would be. It was also why he had approached this particular spot very carefully.

It was two weeks by his count since they had left Gloria's ranch. They were traveling slowly, taking their time and being careful. The trail was one that saw little use. There were few signs that anyone or anything but wild creatures had been this way for years. None of the faint human tracks he had seen were made by modern shoes or boots.

Even so, Radford knew they were being watched. While he never spotted the watchers, he felt their presence. Yet he had no sense of danger. Those watching were *indios* as wild as the few animals they spotted, and Paul had been careful to leave a burro behind when they broke camp two days before.

Nor did Radford allow any of the men to shoot at game, and he insisted they kept their rifles in the scabbard. "We're here as guests," he told the others. "So long as we don't cause trouble, we won't find it. Game is scarce, and if we take it, the local people will have less to eat."

"Why did we come this way, Pablo?" Diego asked, clearly worried.

"Because no one else dares," Radford told him. "Even the army is very reluctant to come here. These are the people who defeated the Spanish and they allow very few outsiders to even pass through."

"Yet, they allow us to do so freely," Timo pointed out. "Why is that?"

"They know me," Radford told them, touching the silver pendant hanging outside his shirt. "They also know the man who gave me this and they trust him."

"And who is that?" Victor asked.

"A good friend of our hostess," Paul answered. "It's better not to speak names, even here."

Haya looked around uneasily. "There's no one here."

"No one we can see," Paul pointed out gently. "I suspect there are at least three watchers keeping an eye on us, but don't worry. They mean us no harm."

"Do they understand Spanish?" the statesman asked.

"I would be very surprised if they didn't," Paul answered. "At least one of them. It's a matter of survival."

"Would they warn you if someone was following you?" Timo asked.

"Probably not. They would expect me to know it, too."

"Which is why you keep such careful watch," Haya mused. Paul nodded.

Thinking of this, Paul smiled. Then something caught his eye for just a moment. The figure of a man stood out at the top of a ridge several hundred meters away. It was a spot that Radford had considered before choosing the one he did. Nor was the man an Indian. He was wearing dark pants and a green serape that blended into the surrounding forest, and on his head was a traditional gray felt hat worn by villagers.

Carefully turning back to look at his companions, Radford decided that the watcher could not see them from where he stood. They were almost out of sight from Paul's perspective and he slowly turned his binoculars back to where he had spotted the man. There was no one to be seen.

Paul carefully looked at every bush and rock along the ridge. Finally, he spotted what looked like a corner of the serape behind a large bush, and when he looked carefully with the binoculars, he could make out a vague outline of the man. He was standing behind the bush, looking in Paul's direction but not directly at him.

Paul was glad he had selected a blind down from the top of the ridge. He didn't think the man would spot him if he didn't move but that meant he had to stay in place. It also meant he needed to avoid staring directly at the fellow. Like wild game that senses predators, people become aware when they are being watched. This was particularly true when it came to stalkers. So Paul turned his binoculars until the watcher was at the side of his field of view. Then he chose a tree at the other side and focused on that.

Even so, the man looked in his direction a couple of times, but never directly at him. It was only when Paul saw him turn and walk behind a clump of brush that he scurried back over the top of the ridge and began to work his way down to the trail.

It took Paul a couple of hours to catch up with Victor and his men. When he did, he told Haya about the watcher. "We need to pick up the pace for a while," he said. "I think they are traveling faster than we are."

"Who are they?" Victor asked.

"I don't know," Paul replied. "I decided to come and warn you instead of following them and finding out. We need to get off this trail as soon as we can. I think they know we're on it. We haven't been hiding our tracks."

"How do they know the tracks are ours?" Victor asked.

Paul smiled. "To the people who live here, our tracks are as good identification as fingerprints. On the other hand, I don't think the man I saw was an *indio*. I'd guess he's probably a professional guide, and tracking is one of the things they have to know. I don't think he's working for the military, either."

"Why do you think that?" Timo asked.

Radford shook his head. "I don't know, but that's what I think based on what I've seen so far. Maybe it's the way he carried himself. Military scouts are...different."

As he said this, Paul felt an almost overwhelming sense of loss no longer being among the Alaska Scouts. Yet he shut this firmly away. He was in Perú and someone was on his trail, or maybe Haya's. He couldn't afford distractions.

Even so, Haya saw the feeling in Paul's eyes. "What is it, Pablo?"

he asked. "What's wrong?"

Radford shook his head. "Nothing, Victor," he said. "Only a memory." Then he forced himself to grin. "Believe it or not, Victor, I was just then feeling homesick for my old outfit in Alaska, even in the dead of winter. How crazy is that?"

Lima. The capital city was reaching the height of its warm season when the five men quietly arrived. They had stabled their horses with a trusted friend of Victor's in an outlying village and walked the last fifteen kilometers to the estate of another friend who would be their host. It was a beautiful day with temperatures in the low eighties, but after so many months in the Andes, Paul felt like he was swimming through the warm, moist air.

They arrived late in the afternoon. After a wonderful meal, Paul excused himself and went to his room. It felt odd to sleep inside, but he welcomed a good night's rest in a in bed. The next morning he awakened feeling refreshed and ready to explore the city. It was unlikely that anyone in the city would recognize him, aside from Captain Molina and some of the people at the embassy. Yet, he had no intention of going there. He was sure the Germans had people watching to see who came and went, and when. He was certain the Americans did the same at the German embassy, too.

More than anything, Paul simply wanted to get away for a while. He had spent almost four months in the company of Haya and his people. His only respite had been his quick trip to Pisco on their way south and the time he spent alone with Gloria. Even then, Victor's presence overshadowed all else, and Paul suspected that Haya was as weary of his company as he was of Victor's. Here on his own turf, the statesman was safe enough in the company of his men.

"I may be gone for a few days, Victor," he told Haya the next morning. "How long do you need to be in town?"

"A week or ten days, Pablo," the older man replied. Seeing how Paul was dressed, he asked, "Is something wrong?"

"Not as far as I know," Radford answered. "I'm going to hang around some watering holes and listen to the gossip. I want to blend into the background."

Haya nodded. "You look like a miner from Cerro de Pasco or

maybe a laborer here in the city. You need to keep shaved, though, and wear a hat. Your eyes will give you away if you don't. Your accent may, too."

"Yes, I'll avoid long philosophical conversations," Paul replied dryly. Haya chuckled.

Radford spend most of the morning wandering around the city looking for working class cantinas. He ended up at the main city market, a vast collection of small shops and stands where one could buy everything from basic shoes and clothing to household necessities, fresh produce, and leather goods. There were also any number of small food stands scattered around the market, most of them specializing in one kind of food.

Paul was sitting near a food stand, eating the simple meal he had ordered, when he spotted a familiar figure. At first he was sure he was mistaken, but as he watched the young mother shop, he knew it was Rosario. Then he realized who the child she carried in a sling across one shoulder must be. It was his daughter, Azúl, and he found himself suddenly at sea among a number of feelings he was not aware he had.

Paul's first impulse was to turn away and disappear into the crowd, but he could not take his eyes off the child. Then her mother sensed something and turned her head. When she did, her eyes locked with his and he realized she knew exactly who it was she beheld. Then she smiled and Paul found it strangely hard to breathe as all the old, forgotten feelings came to the fore. Unable to move, he watched dumbly as she turned and quickly walked toward him.

"Pablo!" she said, delighted, and Paul felt her arms around his neck. Then he realized that his arms had responded on their own and had wrapped themselves around the mother and her child. It was then he felt the tears pouring down his cheeks and realized that nothing else mattered. They were there, together, as if all the painful months had never been.

Then Rosario looked into his eyes. "You're so thin, Pablo," she said, clearly concerned. Touching the deep lines in his face she asked, "What has happened to you?"

"It's the war," he said, freeing a hand and touching her face. Then, without thinking, he kissed her and pulled her close. "God, it's good to see you."

The two of them stood there for a long time, drinking one another in with their eyes. Then the baby stirred and cried, and Rosario pulled back. "This is your daughter, Azúl," she told him. "She has your eyes."

"Her eyes remind me of her grandmother," Paul replied. Then he chuckled. "I see she got her smile from her mother."

"That's gas," Rosario informed him. "She's about to give us a present." Then she added, "Come to my house, Pablo. I need to feed her and let her nap."

There was no question in Paul's mind what the invitation meant. "Where is your...." he started to ask, but stopped.

"He is down in the south, chasing bandits," she answered simply and took his hand. "Come home with me, Pablo. We have things to say to one another."

Radford found himself nodding and following Rosario as she led him out of the market and down a narrow street. At the end of it she turned right and walked up to a door about half a block down. "I have to keep it locked up, living in the city," she told him, taking out a key and inserting it into the door. A moment later they were in the house and Rosario gave him another kiss. "First Azúl, then love, and then we talk," she told him. Then she laughed. "Unless you need to eat first. I interrupted your meal."

"Food before talk," he said, smiling and feeling himself becoming aroused. "Change her quickly."

Caught up as they were with one another, neither had spotted the watcher at the end of the block.

An hour later, Paul and Rosario were lying in one another's arms, spent from their passion. After the first time they had made love, Rosario began to weep. "I'm so sorry, Pablo," she said. "I should have waited for you."

"No," he told her. "You did what was best for Azúl. Now give me another kiss. It's been too long." This led to other things and it was some time before Paul was able to satisfy his growling stomach.

When Azúl awoke, Rosario brought her into the bedroom. "This is your padre, *chica*," Rosario told her, handing her to Paul. "Padre

Pablo. Give him a kiss."

"No!" Azúl responded, pulling back and reaching for Rosario. Clinging to her mother's neck, she glared at Paul.

"Let me get her settled down and we can talk, Pablo," Rosario said.

"I think we've already said all we need to say. It's pretty clear we feel the same about one another. It's also pretty clear where your duty lies. You're carrying your husband's child, aren't you?" Rosario nodded and Paul continued. "Then there is nothing we can do. Nothing has changed in my situation except that I am back here for now. They could call me away tomorrow and I would have to go."

Rosario looked unhappy, but Paul continued. "You have made some promises you need to keep, Rosario. I don't even know if we should do this again. I don't believe we've done anything wrong and I'm glad we did. Yet, I think it might be wrong to do it again."

"We need to talk," Rosario said. "You are my husband."

Radford sighed and nodded. "You're absolutely right, my love," he told her. "We do need to talk."

El Parajo

12 Central Perú. Helmut Rott was not pleased and he made no effort to hide his displeasure. The mission had been fruitless. They had searched the Andes high and low for three weeks and found no trace of either Paul Radford or Victor Haya. It was like the earth had swallowed the five men whole, leaving no evidence of them having ever walked upon it.

Nor was this from lack of information. Everywhere they went there were vague rumors of a party of men guided by a *norteamericano*, but these were contradictory. Some said the party had been headed south and others said north. The number in the party varied from three to twelve and when asked when they had passed by, the answer ranged from a few days to several months. One old fellow told them he thought they were headed for Bolivia, and his equally ancient friend who overheard said he was sure they were headed for Brazil.

At one point, Rott became convinced they were being fed false information. Yet, there was nothing they could do about it. One man described the men in the party in detail, but then swore it had been at least three years since he had seen them in Trujillo, a coastal town about five hundred kilometers northwest of Lima. Yet it was clear he had stayed too long at the cantina.

It didn't help Rott's humor that the native people seemed far more forthcoming with Dieter and their guide, Chino, than with him. Six hundred years of oppression, first by the Inca royalty, then by the Spanish, and still later by landed aristocracy had inbred a fatalistic countenance that revealed nothing of what went on in the minds of the native people. These people were used to dealing with arbitrary authority and neither intimidation nor bribes seemed to move them anywhere they were not willing to go.

Dieter, with Chino to translate, did far better. The native people seemed to be amused by his obvious delight in chewing coca leaves. They happily joined in when he offered to share the leaves and the best information the Germans got was after everyone was feeling mellow. This irritated Rott to no end but there was no arguing with success. His only outburst came when Dieter offered to share his leaves with Rott, pointing out that it might help the man stay calm.

"What?" Rott demanded, indignant. "What do you think I am, you blockhead? I'm not about to chew that shit!"

Dieter, who was quite stoned by that point, tried to argue. "But, Herr Rott, it will give you more stamina, too."

"I have more stamina in my little finger than you'll ever have!" Rott declared.

Even so, Helmut stopped short of savagely reaming out the scullion. He had noticed that Dieter was far more energetic after he had chewed a few leaves, and far more useful. Rott had also tried the leaves, himself, once. While it was true that they had given him more energy, he had also lost that fierce drive that allowed him to accomplish things others could not. The loss of his sharp edge was simply too high a price to pay for serenity.

It was at this point that the Germans began to search the high slopes of the jungle. After another fruitless fortnight of following endless trails without catching sight of the Indians who lived there, Rott had enough. "We're wasting our time," he told Dieter and Chino. "Tomorrow we head back to Lima."

A week later Rott was sitting comfortably across the table from Jergen Schwartz. They were meeting at the German restaurant near the embassy. Rott had searched the office for hidden microphones, finding two without disabling them. Sure that there were others, Rott looked at Schwartz. "Let's get something to eat at Steng's. Dieter's a good cook but I've had nothing but camp food since we left."

Fifteen minutes later they were seated at an isolated table at the restaurant. "We obviously need to change tactics," Rott told his companion once they had ordered. "The fellow we're looking for knows the country too well."

"We've got to be careful," Schwartz told him. "Gunther Berg is suspicious."

"So what?" Rott asked, puzzled.

"He was told to keep an eye on you and me when he was sent here. He's Gestapo."

Rott nodded. "He makes a lot more sense than Dieter. How do you know?"

Schwartz was surprised. "One of my sources in Berlin got word to me before he came. I'm sure I told you."

Rott looked at his companion severely. "You certainly did not. This is the first I've heard. How do you know he's suspicious?"

"We had lunch together, right here. I talked to him about the problem with Radford. He was most unhelpful."

"You what!" Rott hissed. Had he shouted, his displeasure could not have been more clear. "Without talking to me?"

"You weren't available," Schwartz replied defensively. "He thinks taking Radford's child hostage is a bad idea."

"You told him that!" Rott was almost speechless. "When was this?"

"A few days ago, maybe two weeks. Why?"

"Are you trying to get us killed? He's probably gotten word back to Gestapo headquarters by now. At the very least, we'll be called home. I, for one, don't intend to go."

"You won't have much choice," Schwartz reminded him. "You'll be arrested. Besides, they have no cause to arrest us."

"You stupid fool! Do you really think the Gestapo needs a reason? They can arrest whoever they want."

"I still have powerful connections back home," Schwartz reminded him, stung by Rott's words. "You forget, Helmut, who is the colonel here."

"Remember that when they come for you in the middle of the night. I, for one, will not be easily taken."

Schwartz fought down the panic growing in his belly. "I'm sure you worry needlessly. What's done is done. The best thing we can do now is take care of the Radford problem."

Rott glared at the scholar for a long moment. Then he shrugged. "All right, but we do need to change tactics. I've given it some thought. We need to get word out that there is a five thousand sol reward for information that leads to his capture. Then, when we know where he is, we go after him."

"He'll be gone by the time you get there."

"Not if we move quickly enough. Here's what I have in mind." Quickly, Rott outlined the plan he had developed on the trip back to Lima. As he did, his mind was already at work on another plan to avoid what he believed was their sure and certain arrest.

Yet Rott was not the only one with private thoughts. Schwartz started to tell him that they had heard from their watchers at Rosario's home in Lima, but stopped. Too much time had passed. It had been three weeks since he got the first report and Radford had not been seen there in a week. Schwartz was sure Radford must be long gone. Later he wondered if not telling Rott had been a mistake.

Lima. Three weeks after they arrived in Lima, Victor Haya decided it was time to head for Puerto Maldonado. Paul was reluctant to leave, even though he knew it was better that way. He and Rosario had been together every day for the first two weeks, stopping only when Juan Gomez was expected home. It was like the last two years had never happened and after a couple of visits, Azúl warmed to him.

After Gomez returned home, they met at the markets in different areas of town, and Rosario always brought lunch. When her husband asked how she spent her days, she told him she and Azúl were exploring different areas of the city. She told him she had decided to start weaving baskets again and was looking for a good source of materials.

Nor was this a lie. This is one of the things she and Paul liked to do together, something they had done quite often in Pisco. She was also careful to bring home bundles of reeds and rushes of different colors and textures.

One of the things Paul realized the first time he visited was that Azúl might give them away. So he cautioned Rosario against calling him by his name, suggesting that she call him something else. They had a good time thinking of possible names but it was Azúl who inadvertently suggested the best. To win her over Paul was imitating bird calls he'd heard hiking around the country and the child was fascinated. "*Mas pajaro!*" she demanded, more birds, and Paul complied. The next day when she saw him, she cried, "*Pajaro!*"

"*Si, yo soy el parajo!*" Paul answered and that was who he became to her, The Bird. Rosario reinforced this by calling him that, too, and when Juan Gomez asked about it later when he heard Azúl talking about *el parajo*, she shrugged. "Who knows? She loves the birds she sees when we go to the market. There was a man there who made bird calls."

Gomez nodded, smiling. He wondered why Rosario was lying but said nothing. "Some of my nieces and nephews do that. They fix on a word and use it until they wear it out."

So Paul was just as glad when Victor told him it was time to leave the city. He would miss Rosario and Azúl terribly, but having to sneak around to see them was unsettling. When he said goodbye to Rosario, he wondered if it was their last. Later, when she was grown, Azúl might seek him out if he was still alive. But Rosario, by her own choice, was another man's wife with another child on the way. He doubted they would ever meet again. He was not sure he wanted to, either, which troubled him even more.

"Why are you so quiet tonight, Pablo?" Victor asked over dinner. "You seem very sad."

"I am, Victor. I had to say goodbye to someone I loved."

"A woman, I suppose," Haya said with sympathy and Paul nodded. "I wondered what was taking up so much of your time. I suppose she's married."

Paul nodded. "I'll be glad to get back to Gloria. I would appreciate it if you didn't mention...."

"Of course, Pablo," the older man said, smiling. "No need to hurt her feelings, especially if it was a younger woman."

Mexico City. Alex White was waiting patiently in the foyer of the American embassy when Denis Blieu came to escort him to Blieu's office. Alex was surprised to find him wearing a dress uniform. "What's the deal?" Alex asked. "I've been here before. I know how to get to your office."

"They moved me," Blieu told him. "I thought it would be simpler this way. Besides, we're meeting somewhere else."

The lieutenant commander nodded and followed Blieu into the basement of the embassy. "The belly of the beast," the major quipped. "I thought you'd like to see our torture chamber."

White chuckled. "If you were Jock, I'd believe you." He followed Blieu through some thick stone walls into a room about five meters square. There was no window in the room and the only illumination was a bright florescent fixture in the ceiling high above. Nor was there any furnishing but a round oak table with four captain's chairs around it and six oak bow chairs against the walls.

"This used to be their emergency shelter until some bright soul figured out there is only one way out," Blieu told him. "Now it's used for secure conversations. I gathered that's what you had in mind. As you can see, it would be damned hard to wire for sound, and the door is soundproof. It swings inward and only locks from inside."

Blieu pulled out a chair for White and took one himself. Alex noticed it faced the door. "So what's up?" Denis asked.

"We got a coded message from Jock a couple of weeks ago, just before he took off for the Andes. I hoped he'd be back by now, but he isn't and we need your take on things. Eric and I don't quite know what to make of it. Did Jock talk to you before he left?"

"No, I was in Argentina checking up on the Nazis there. I can tell you there's a shit load of them, but what else is new?"

"Good way of putting it," White nodded. "To get down to brass tacks, Jock is concerned how close Paul has become to Victor Haya. There's no question of his loyalty to the nation, but Jock says Paul has been less than forthcoming in his reports. Those are his words, by the way, not mine."

"Did he give you any specifics?"

"Jock thought he was being a bit evasive with some of the details of what they've been up to. He reported that Victor and his men had holed up for a while at a hideout in the country near Peno, but he was vague when Jock asked him to pinpoint it on a map. Then, when they were in Lima, Paul was vague about how he spent his time in the city. He says he spent it getting the lay of the land, mostly visiting the city markets to pick up whatever intelligence he could. When asked which ones, he said he covered all the major ones and named a few. Yet Jock had the sense he was holding back."

Blieu chuckled when Alex mentioned this. "What's so funny?" he asked.

"Paul doesn't kiss and tell," Denis replied. "Were you aware that his fiancee had married someone else and moved here to Lima?"

"You think he was bird-dogging her?"

Denis shrugged. "You tell me. I happen to know her husband was out of town for several weeks. I got a heads-up from Carlos Molina about an investigation in the south. I'd bet that was while Haya was in the city."

"That's another thing," White said. "Paul didn't let Jock know about the visit until after it was over. He was evasive about exactly where Victor and his men stayed while they were here. He told Jock that normally one of Victor's men rented a place for them to stay. When Jock pinned him down, Paul added that sometimes Victor stays with friends. He says he told Victor not to formally introduce him. He didn't want their names appearing in an official report."

Blieu nodded. "Murphy's law. What can happen, does. He doesn't want their names getting into the wrong hands."

"We have secure files!" Alex snapped. "Doesn't he trust us? We keep any information we get close to the chest."

"Look at it from his perspective, Alex. We are the assholes who pulled him out of Perú before he could get married. We wouldn't let him see anyone while he was in the embassy. He was treated like a prisoner and he damned sure didn't deserve it. Yet, he was the one who turned up those Nazi operations and risked his life doing it."

"He's a US Navy officer," Alex replied. "He took an oath. We couldn't risk him getting caught and spilling the beans."

"Yes, and I was part of that decision. I'm surprised he was willing to come back down here or work with us at all, to tell the truth. A lot of men would have told us to stick it."

"Even if it was a direct order?"

Denis laughed. "Especially if it was a direct order. Paul would ask for it in writing, then put us in a jam for giving him an illegal order. He could have also gone back to Alaska, too. We owe him big, but he's too much of a gentleman to say so." He shook his head. "Besides all that, the last time I checked this was a voluntary outfit."

"Yes, but we can't have him running around like a loose cannon."

"He's not. He is following our orders like a good sailor. The irony is that the man we've assigned to supervise him is the one man among us he distrusts the most. Do you wonder why he's so vague?"

"Are you serious?"

"I'm dead serious, Alex. Jock wants to make him into an assassin. He hinted as much one night when the two of us were killing a bottle of single malt. I think Paul knows it and he's having no part of it."

White sat quietly for several moments. Then he nodded. "That would explain a lot. I've never been that comfortable with Jock, myself, but I never knew why."

"Jock has his own agenda," Blieu replied. Then he grinned. "Besides, he's Army, and Army Intelligence, to boot. What can you expect from a damned dog-face?"

Alex smiled. "Well, there is that."

Lima. Captain Carlos Molina looked up to see his sergeant standing at his office door. "Come in, Juan," he said. "Have a chair. Have you had coffee?"

"Yes, sir, thank you. My apologies for being tardy. I didn't get in until very late last night."

"You're actually early," Molina replied with a smile. "I didn't expect you until this afternoon, at the earliest." He glanced at the clock. It told him it was five minutes past nine. He, himself, had only arrived ten minutes earlier.

"I don't have my report written up either, sir," Gomez replied. "I thought I would do it this morning."

"That will be fine but go ahead and tell me what you have to report now."

"Yes, sir. It looks like your suspicions are correct. The area around Puerto Maldonado is where most of the coca is coming into Perú. A lot of it comes up the Madre Dios river from Bolivia, but a lot of it comes overland from Brazil. Iberia is the entry point for that."

Gomez paused. "There is a strong market for cocaine but I have no idea where it is coming from. A large amount is being produced here in Perú, but I don't understand why it is being imported. A lot of people chew the leaves, but manufactured cocaine is too expensive for them. Even the low quality pasta the farmers make is too expensive. So I don't know where the pasta is going. I did hear there is a refining plant in Puerto Maldonado, but I couldn't find out where it was. I was afraid to ask too many questions or those talking to me would stop. I'm afraid I gave them the impression I was trying to make some money."

Molina nodded. "Excellent. It's never a motive one has to explain. I think a lot of the pasta may be going to the Germans, the foreign ones. You remember that German military operation we blew up down south? It was between Nazca and Camana."

Gomez nodded and Molina went on. "Having a military base there never made sense to me so I went back and took another look a few months later. You weren't with me that time. What I found was evidence that it was also a cocaine refining plant. I think one of the things the Germans intended to do was to refine coca leaves and pasta into pure cocaine and ship it back to Germany by submarine."

Gomez nodded. "So the pasta and leaves would be brought south from Puerto Maldonado. That makes sense. There was very little chance of them being seen. Not many people live out there."

"With good reason," Molina said. "It's hard to see how the people who live there survive."

Gomez frowned. "On second thought, this doesn't make sense, sir. It must be over eight hundred kilometers from Puerto Maldonado to the coast. That's a long way to haul pasta, and too much chance of discovery. They would have to use pack animals. It would be much easier to buy leaves in the Ayachucho area and move them out through Pisco."

Molina nodded. "Yes, except for police presence. There are a lot more police in Pisco."

Gomez shrugged. "Many of whom can be bought."

Molina smiled at the expression on Gomez's face and nodded. "Yes, one would think that would be less expensive. On the other hand, the ways of God and the Germans is incomprehensible."

Gomez grinned. "I thought that was God and women, sir."

"Perhaps, but I find the Germans harder to understand than women." What Molina didn't have to explain was that the particular Germans he had in mind were the ones who had emigrated to Perú.

Lima. Helmut Rott was pleased, something which rarely happened. It was not an emotion he was comfortable having and he tried to hide it. The result was that he came across more gruff and taciturn than usual, and most people at the embassy read this as anger. Needless to say, this amused Rott.

The exception was Jurgen Schwartz. When Rott showed up one morning more gruff than usual, the colonel looked at Rott intently and asked, "What are you so pleased about this morning, Helmut?"

Rott actually smiled. When he did, it looked like his face was broken. Nor was it a pretty picture. "Believe it or not, Jurgen, Dieter may turn out to be useful to us after all."

"How so?" the scholar asked, surprised. The last time they had talked about the scullion, he had been hard pressed to keep Rott from thrashing the man.

"I told you he has not had any military training," Rott said. "He told me he wanted to learn to shoot but the Gestapo was in a hurry to get another snitch in place. He had not had any experience with guns and barely knew which end was dangerous."

The colonel nodded, wishing his driver would get to the point. Yet there was no hurrying the man when he was pleased. Rott was only impatient with others, not himself, and he liked to spin the yarn.

Rott was aware of the colonel's impatience but ignored it. "I thought it might be good to teach him the rudiments of shooting so he didn't accidentally kill someone by accident. So I took him out to the firing range – the police let us use theirs. Anyway, I spent some time explaining how a Mauser works and how to aim and fire one. Then I had Dieter load a full magazine and shoot from a prone position. I was shocked when he brought the target back. At fifty meters, all the bullet holes were inside a five centimeter circle to one side of the target. So I showed him how to adjust the sights and had him fire again. He had the same result, this time just above the exact center of the target."

Schwartz nodded. "So he caught on quickly. That's easy enough from a prone position."

Rott chuckled. It sounded like he was choking. "That's what I thought, too. So I taught him how to make a standing shot. This time all the shots were inside seven centimeters. He had the same results kneeling and better results squatting. Twenty-five shots, Jergen, all inside a tight circle the size of a biscuit."

"How can that be? I remember how long it took us to get that kind of accuracy."

Rott nodded. "I was suspicious myself, especially when the idiot tried to apologize for not getting them in the same hole! Then I realized he honestly thought he'd done wrong. I told him he would improve with practice and not to worry. I also told him he needed to keep quiet about it."

Schwartz nodded. "That is impressive, but that's shooting at a fixed target, Helmut. One that's not shooting back."

"Give me some credit for a little sense, Jurgen," he said. "Two days later I took him out again and he repeated the same results. Then I told him I wanted him to hit a rolling tennis ball. He missed, just barely, when I threw the first ball, but he hit the second squarely. Then I told him I wanted him to keep shooting at the same ball until he was out of shots and threw the third ball as far as I could. He hit it four out of five times. The first shot hit while it was in the air, thirty meters away! I tried it again and he hit every shot."

"I imagine you told him to keep quiet about that, too!" the colonel exclaimed. "What do you have in mind?"

"I'm going to take him with me when I go after Radford again," Helmut replied. "One of us should be able to score."

"When do you plan to go out again?"

"When I get word about his whereabouts. Trying to hunt him in the back country is useless. It didn't work two years ago and it's not working now. So I have my sources on the lookout. When we learn where he's headed, Dieter and I will fly to the nearest airfield ahead of him and set up an ambush. Our equipment is packed for a two-week stay and I have a plane on standby." Seeing the colonel's alarm, Rott shook his head. "It's a civilian plane, Jurgen. The owner owes me a big favor. It cannot be tied to the Reich."

"Excellent!" Schwartz replied. "The word I have from my sources is that Radford and Haya have headed south. He was seen several weeks ago here in Lima but I didn't get word about it until too late.

You were gone at the time, too."

Normally, Rott would be irritated by getting this news so long after the fact. Yet, he didn't show it. "South?" he asked. "That's a big area. The only big cities are Cuzco and Puerto Maldonado. I can't think of any reason for them going to Puno. Maybe Dieter and I need to go to Cuzco. That way we'll be close by when he's spotted."

Vicinity of Urcos. Paul Radford had his horse saddled and the other four in halters before the sun was up. Slipping into the large stone barn where they spent the night, he woke Victor. "I'm on my way," he said quietly. "I'll see you in a couple of weeks. There's coffee by the fire."

"Go with God, Pablo," the older man said. "Thank you for all you have done for us. Give my love to Gloria."

"Hey, Victor, it's not like I won't see you again."

Haya smiled and shrugged. "You know how uncertain life can be, Pablo. At this season of my life, I have lost a lot of friends. I know that each farewell may be the last."

Radford thought about this as he rode south. They had done well on horseback until they came to Cuzco, less than thirty kilometers to the north. There Victor had insisted on traveling to Puerto Maldonado by car. A friend of his had arranged for one to be waiting for them in Cuzco, and nothing Paul said could convince Victor to continue on horses. "We are going to have to follow the road, anyway, Pablo. Horses are no good in the jungle and I need to get there soon. It's much faster by car."

"What are we going to do with the horses?" Paul asked. "I think Gloria would like to have them back."

"Then take them to her," Haya replied, smiling. "I think she will be glad to see you. Take some time there, too. There is little you can do in Puerto Maldonado. I will take Diego or Mateo when I go to visit the people I need to see. It would be awkward to arrive with a stranger."

"Particularly a *gringo*."

"That is not what I meant."

"No, but we both know it's true, Victor. The minute I open my mouth they'll know I'm a *norteamericano*. That could put them off.

How will I find you when I get there?"

"There is a market a few streets south of the Plaza de Armas. Timo will be there every day at noon, beginning three weeks from today, unless something is wrong. If you can't find us, go back to Gloria's. We'll get word to you there."

Lima. Colonel Jergen Schwartz looked up with a frown when he heard his office door open. Then he saw who it was and the reprimand died on his lips. "Good morning, Helmut," he said pleasantly. "You look like you're about to burst. What is it?"

"We've found him!" Rott said. When Schwartz pointed toward the hidden microphone, Rott nodded and spoke in a calm voice. "We've located that fellow we need to talk to. I'm on my way to see him in an hour."

"On an empty stomach?" Schwartz asked. "I was just about to have lunch. Why don't you join me? You can tell me about it while we eat."

Rott started to object, but nodded instead. "That would be kind of you, sir," he replied with an ironic smile.

Once they were outside the embassy, Schwartz dropped the façade. "Are you serious about leaving in an hour?" he asked. "Why don't we go into the church down the street? I doubt there's anyone around at this hour."

Rott nodded and nothing more was said until they were seated in a pew in the center of the nave. "No one should be able to hear us here," Shwartz said. "What do you have?"

"I heard from a source of mine down south. Haya and his party have been seen in Cuzco. They were traveling by car and were seen heading south on the road to Puno. That means it will be easy to get ahead of them and set up an ambush before they reach Puno."

"Are you sure they're headed to Puno and not to Puerto Maldonado?" he asked. It was one of the few times he took Rott by surprise. "Or didn't you think of that?" he asked, rubbing it in.

Rott glared at the colonel, but he held his tongue. "You are absolutely right, Jergen," he replied evenly. "I didn't consider that possibility. Thank you. It actually makes a lot more sense. Haya is not as well entrenched in Puerto Maldonado. For the last few months he's been consolidating his power in other places. Puno is not as important to him."

"It makes even more sense if Radford is after our coca leaf project," Schwartz replied. It gives us all the justification we need to kill him. Who are you taking with you, Dieter?"

"Yes, him and Chino, the guide we used before. He says he knows the country down there."

"Do you believe him?"

"It doesn't matter. What's important is that he speaks the native language. He also knows his way around in the jungle and he's a fairly good shot." He shrugged. "If he doesn't work out, there are lots of rivers to dump his body." He grinned and Schwartz felt a chill run up his spine. "Lots of crocodiles to help us out," Rott added.

"You think Dieter will go along with this?"

Rott's grin broadened. "Yes, I'm sure he will. Dieter knows the river's big enough for him, too."

Schwartz shook his head. "I don't know, Helmut. Going out with a drug addict and a drunk doesn't sound promising."

"That's why I've kept such a close watch on Dieter. He's not had a drink, much less a dose of cocaine, in several weeks now. I watch him like a hawk."

Shwartz shook his head. "Well, I'll have to take your word for it, Helmut. I hope you're right. Will you be taking the cocaine along with you?"

"Yes, but Dieter doesn't know that. It's locked up in a sealed document box. When we kill Radford, we'll leave some of it on his body. The rest will be in Herr Haya's suitcase. I may even hold out a little to give Dieter as a reward."

"I don't know, Helmut. It all sounds very risky."

"Desperate times call for desperate measures, Jergen, and we are not in favor at the moment. Berlin is pleased with success, so we need to give them one. No one gives a rat's ass how it's done."

Camino del Sur

13 Cuzco, Perú. The cantina was bright and cheerful, even though it was in a poorer area of the city. The interior was divided into two areas about the same size. One was a dining area with nine or ten square tables and a kitchen at the rear. The other had a bar running along one side with six or eight stools and a brass rail. A few tables were scattered around the rest of the room and there was a door at the back. This led out to an alley with a trench that served as an open-air pissoir. To one side of the trench was an outhouse for those whose business was more substantial.

It was clear to Jaques Paul that the cantina primarily served the neighborhood. Few customers came through the doors who did not live or work nearby, and the place had emptied for the siesta hour. The bartender had been surprised when they came in. He was napping on a cot in the storage room when the goat bell on the door jingled, and he reluctantly got up to see who it was.

Four men were seated at a table when the bartender came out of the back room, all of them strangers. When he first saw the men, he sensed they were dangerous. Even though they dressed alike, he knew only one of them was not a foreigner. Two of the other three looked European, and the last man looked like some kind of oriental.

The men ordered beer and the man who was clearly in charge asked if there was food. The bartender told them he had chili, potatoes, and fresh pork, along with bread baked that morning. The leader asked him to bring them four plates and bowls of everything he had.

When the bartender returned with their food, the men were deep in conversation. They stopped talking when he got close and didn't resume until he was out of earshot. While he was curious what they were saying, the bartender did not try to eavesdrop. He wanted no trouble with these men. "I'll be back there if you need anything," he said, nodding toward the back room door.

"So what did you find out?" Jacques Paul asked Marino when the bartender returned to his nap. The door to the storage room had been left open and he kept his voice low.

"Not a whole lot. Someone recognized Victor Haya. He was seen four days ago riding in a car with three other men. The man who saw him said they were headed south. They were on the road to Urcos. Someone else told me he thought they were headed for Puerto Maldonado."

"Three other men," Jacques murmured. "Was one of them Paul Radford?"

"I don't know, señor. I asked him if one of them was a *norteamericano* but he said they all looked like latinos. He did say his wife saw a *norteamericano* with a herd of horses on the same road the day before. He was headed south."

"That sounds like Radford, but what is he doing?" O'Leary asked. "Not many north Americans in this part of the world."

"Three of them are seated at this table," Jacques pointed out dryly. "You don't suppose he's returning the horses, do you? Victor has a hideout near Puno."

"You know him better than I," O'Leary replied. "Any idea where he got them in the first place?"

"Somewhere up north," Jacques answered. "They were seen riding south from La Oroya several months ago, long before they got to Puno. Or wherever they went." He shook his head. "Why else would he head south with horses from Urcos? All we know that's down there is Puno and the hideout. Victor seems to be headed for Puerto Maldonado."

Jacques turned to the guide and asked him something in Quechua. The guide answered in the same tongue. "Sir, could you stick to Spanish?" John Yellowhawk asked. "I couldn't quite follow that."

"Sorry, Sergeant. I was asking Marino what he thought."

"He's getting pretty good in Quechua, isn't he?" Marino asked Yellowhawk. "For an American." He smiled to take any offense out of his words.

"He's got a good teacher," the sergeant answered. Both he and the captain had been learning the native tongue from Marino, but Jaques Paul had a stronger gift for language. John Yellowhawk had to work at it.

"So what do you think, Marino?" Jacques asked, speaking Spanish.

"I think we need to head for Urcos to find out more," the guide told him. "Who do you need to follow most? Haya or Pablo?"

"Actually, both. So we need to split up. You and John need to head for Urcos and follow Pablo south. Take the train to Puno. That will save time. John knows what he looks like. More important, Pablo knows John. Mike and I will try to find a car and follow Victor and his men to Puerto Maldonado. We can meet up again in Cuzco."

"You don't suppose Pablo plans to join Victor in Puerto Maldonado, do you?" Michael O'Leary asked.

Jacques Paul nodded. "It could be. If that's the case, John, go ahead and follow him there. Or, even better, join up with him if you spot him. I'll give you a letter for him requesting that. You also need to brief him on what we're doing. Answer any questions he has."

"Requesting or ordering, sir?" John Yellowhawk asked.

"Requesting," the captain answered. What he didn't say was that Radford was Navy. Jaques wasn't sure he had the authority to order Paul Radford to do anything. Normally, that didn't stop him and he had the personal charisma to carry it off. Yet this was an usual situation. He was an Army captain on liaison to the Special Action Group and Radford actually held a slightly higher rank. Strictly speaking, Jaques Paul was not in the chain of command, even though he had oversight of Pablo's mission. No one in South America but Denis Blieu had command authority and, as a sergeant in the Marine Corps, John Yellowhawk certainly could not give orders to a Navy officer. That was not normally a problem in the flexible organization of SAG, but this was a highly unusual situation.

Lopez Ranch, Perú. The trip from Urcos to Gloria's ranch was uneventful. There were few other travelers on the back roads and none on the trails Paul followed once he left the main route from Cuzco to Peno. His main concerns were finding water and forage for the horses and avoiding military or police patrols. So he picked his campsites carefully and rarely made a fire in the places he chose.

On the fifth day after starting, Paul rode into the hacienda just as the sun was setting and Gloria ran out to greet him. "I'm so glad to see you, Pablo," she declared, giddy as a school girl, hugging him close. "I missed you so much!"

"I missed you, *mi alma*," he replied, kissing her with such passion she slumped against him. Even as he said this, he was surprised how much he meant it. Despite his feelings for Rosario. "We better move this inside before we embarrass your housekeeper," he whispered.

Gloria giggled. "Come, I'll help you get washed up from your ride," she murmured, taking his hand and leading him into the house. As they walked through the large living room, Rita, the housekeeper, and Alonzo, Rita's husband came out of the kitchen and Paul waved to them. They waved back, both smiling broadly. Marta, the cook, looked through the door and waved, too.

"They seem happy to see me, too," Paul observed as they moved down the hall.

"That's because you make me laugh," Gloria answered, shutting the bedroom door firmly behind them and locking it. "It's been a long time since I have." Then she began to tear off his clothes as he attacked the buttons of her blouse.

An hour later the two of them were seated at the dinner table, freshly bathed and dressed. "I am impressed," Paul said, surveying the feast laid out before them. "How in the world did Marta do all this so quickly?"

"Most of this is left over," Gloria answered, surprised. "We had a work crew in earlier this week and Marta and Rita had to feed them. So Alonzo and I helped. I did most of the baking."

"You are a lady of many talents," he murmured and Gloria blushed. "Maybe I should go to work for you."

Gloria gave him an odd look. "I already have a foreman, Pablo," she said. "Alonzo has been with me for years."

Paul returned her gaze, his eyes drinking her in. "I was actually thinking of something a little more...domestic."

"Don't tease me, Pablo," she said. "Not about that." She looked scared.

"I've given it a lot of thought," he told her. "From here to Lima and back. Are you telling me the thought has never crossed your mind?"

"I am very uncomfortable with this conversation, Pablo. I know what I said before and I meant it, but this feels too soon."

Paul nodded and reached for her hand. "Then we'll talk of other things, *querida*. For now. I think you know I love you. I also think those feelings...."

"Please, Pablo!" Gloria implored.

Paul didn't understand Gloria's response, especially in light of her earlier offer. Even so, he knew it was not the time to push. "Of course, *querida*," he answered, holding up his hands in surrender. "What would you like to do tomorrow?"

Gloria looked at him gratefully. "Why don't we take a picnic, if you're not too tired of riding? I don't think you've ever seen the Torre de Picotani. Or we could take the truck and go into Puno. I think you would like seeing the *chullpas* at Lake Umago."

"As long as I'm with you, *mi alma*," Paul shrugged. "What else matters?" Gloria smiled and that night as he was falling asleep, Paul thought he heard her whisper softly, "*Te amo, Pablo.*" I love you, Paul. The next morning he wondered if he was only dreaming. Yet, looking into her eyes over breakfast, he decided it didn't matter. It was true whether he dreamed it or not. Gloria loved him. Knowing that was enough.

Near Quince Mil. Even though it was late March and not yet the depth of the cold season, Jaques Paul and Michael O'Leary had to wear jackets as they crossed over the Andes. That quickly changed as they followed the growing river into the jungle. There it quickly became hot and muggy, and the flying insects soon found them. All that prevented it from being worse was the movement of the old truck they were driving. Yet the unpredictable ruts often meant they had to slow down enough for the bugs to catch up, and it was seldom they were able to go faster than fifty kilometers an hour.

There was little traffic on the road and very little relief from the monotony of the jungle and the rutted road. Nor were there many settlements along the way. "I understand why no one comes through here much," Jacques told O'Leary when they stopped the truck for a quick pit stop.

O'Leary nodded. "Between the heat and the bugs, I'd go mad if I had to live here. Not that I make any great claims on sanity. After all, look where I am now and what we're up to."

Jacques chuckled. "There is that." He slapped a particularly aggressive mosquito. "I'm sure the natives have a good way of dealing with these damned bugs. I wish I knew what they were."

O'Leary nodded and looked around. "You know, just about anywhere along this road would be a good place for an ambush."

Jaques nodded. "I've been thinking that, too. I think I'd wait for a river crossing. The cover along the road could work against you, too."

"I'd think you'd have to be pretty certain your victim was traveling this way," O'Leary added. "Otherwise, it would be an awful waste of time." He slapped a mosquito. "And blood. I'm glad I brought quinine."

They rode in silence a while before Michael spoke again. "I've been wondering something, captain. Why are we in such a hurry to find your man? You think my cousin sent more than one assassin?"

"I'm concerned about the Germans," Jacques replied. "My information is that they've been trying to find Paul. I'm sure they know he's traveling with Victor Haya and if we can find that out, I'm sure they can. They may be crack-pots but they're not witless. I'm not sure Paul is aware of the danger."

"Any idea why they're after your man? He must have done something to get them this annoyed. Or is there something else?"

The captain nodded. "He did, but I can't talk about it. Let's say that he was very instrumental in embarrassing the Reich a couple of years ago. I'm sure they haven't forgotten."

"Oh? He wouldn't have had anything to do with taking out that secret sub base off the southern coast, would he?"

"I can neither deny nor affirm that, Michael," Jaques told him, dodging a deep pothole. "I really can't say any more."

O'Leary nodded. "Well, if he did, I understand why they're so mad. Quite a fiasco, wasn't it? What I read in the papers was pretty bad. I imagine the true story was worse."

Jaques stopped the truck and got out to stretch. "We better keep moving or these blood suckers will bleed us dry. You take the wheel for a while."

As it turned out, the change of drivers worked to their advantage. They had not driven five kilometers farther when they rounded a bend in the road and came to a military checkpoint. "Let me do the talking," Jacques Paul told Michael. "What name is on the passport in your pocket?"

"Lynch, Simon Lynch," Michael answered. "My entry visa is about expired."

"Well, maybe we won't have to show it," Jacques Paul said. "Good afternoon, Sergeant," he greeted the NCO who approached the truck.

"Papers!" the sergeant demanded, holding out a hand.

Jacques Paul extended his passport. "I'm Jacques Paul. I have diplomatic status and this is my assistant, Mr. Lynch."

"I need his papers, too!" the sergeant insisted, looking at the captain's passport. He deftly palmed the fifty dollar bill folded inside.

O'Leary handed over the Simon Lynch passport and the sergeant inspected it. "Your visa is almost expired, senor," he said.

"I know. I hoped to get it extended in Puerto Maldonado."

"What is your business in Puerto Maldonado?" the sergeant demanded.

"Actually, I am a diplomat," Jacques replied. "I am here on official business. I believe that is all I need to tell you."

The sergeant looked at him suspiciously. "You don't look like a diplomat."

Jacques Paul shrugged. "Do you really want to take this up with your captain, sergeant?" he asked. "I don't think he would appreciate your wasting his time."

It hung in the balance for ten long seconds before the sergeant relented. The decisive factor was that he would have to share the bribe with his captain if it went that far. Nor was there any doubt the captain would get most of it. "Very well," he said, thrusting the passports back at them. "Be sure you get your visa renewed," he told O'Leary sternly.

"Thank you, Sergeant," O'Leary replied. "I'll do it right away."

"That was interesting," he observed as they drove past the road block. "We're lucky he didn't call your bluff."

"It wasn't a bluff," Jacques Paul told him. "Simon Lynch is an accredited part of the American delegation in Lima." He grinned. "So is Michael O'Leary."

"Pretty sure of yourself, weren't you?" Michael responded. "What if I had not accepted the job?"

Jacques smiled. "Then you would have been in a pickle. The ambassador would have withdrawn your credentials. He would have requested that the police pick O'Leary and Lynch so he could send them home for disciplinary action. Once you were back in Washington, you would have been turned over to the FBI."

O'Leary laughed. "You people have a warped sense of humor."

Jacques Paul shrugged and smiled. "There's a war on, Marine. Besides, it would have ruined your cousin's whole week."

Sillustani. Paul Radford stood quietly, looking at the tall tower made of smooth blocks of stone that reached forty feet above the ground. There was no opening in the smooth wall he faced, no door or window to relieve the sheer face of the circular wall. Only a smooth ring, perhaps a quarter of the way down from the top and about a meter wide, extended out a few a few centimeters. From where he stood, it looked like the top rose several feet above the ring, forming a dome made of stone blocks tapering toward the center.

"These are burial cairns?" he asked.

"Yes, but they are called *chullpas*," Gloria answered. "This one is from the Incas. The ones made of smaller stones are Tiwanaku."

"I think I saw the carving of a lizard in one of them," he told her. "Why a lizard?"

"The lizard represents life. When they lose their tails, they grow a new one. So it's a symbol of rebirth or regeneration."

Radford nodded. "I'm amazed how they managed to get those stones so precisely fitted and placed. Some of them are almost too big for the equipment we have now."

Gloria shrugged. "You've been to Machu Picchu, haven't you? There are much larger ones there."

"I know, and I can't see how they moved them."

"They say the Others taught the Inca how."

"The Others?"

"Yes," she said. "Those who came from the stars."

"That's one possibility. Whoever did it had much better technology than we have now. Either that, or better engineers. Or both." Radford shook his head. "It's amazing how tightly they're fitted."

"I personally think they used very strong pygmies from the Amazon," Gloria teased.

Radford chuckled. "Well, they'd have to be as strong as Superman."

"Superman? Who is that."

"A comic book character back home. He's supposed to be the strongest man in the world. He can leap over mountains in a single bound."

Gloria laughed. "That would be useful here in the Andes."

"He can fly, too, faster than a speeding bullet and he can stop trains with his bare hands."

"Goodness, I hope he's a good man."

"He's the best. When he's not doing good deeds, he hides who he is behind a facade. He pretends to be a wimp."

"A weemp? What's that?"

"A weak, ineffectual, mealy-mouthed person. I don't know the Spanish equivalent, at least, not the polite one."

"You mean a *cobarde*?"

"No, not exactly. Being a coward can be part of it, but it's more like a weakling. It's someone without much life force, not very manly. I don't know...." He paused in mid sentence, his eyes fixed over Gloria's shoulder.

When Gloria turned, she saw two men approaching them. One

of them was a Peruvian. The other looked oriental and moved like a tiger. Both men were wearing packs and carrying rifles. "Is it trouble, Pablo?" She asked, reaching into the large satchel she used for a purse.

"No, I'm just surprised. I know one of them pretty well. No need to draw your pistol." Seeing her look of surprise, he smiled. "I saw you put it in your purse before we left."

"Hello, Paul," the foreigner said, holding out a hand.

"Good to see you, John," Paul replied in Spanish. "Let's use local language. This is Gloria Lopez, a very special friend of mine. Gloria, this is John Yellowhawk, another friend."

Yellowhawk took Gloria's hand in his own and kissed it, bowing deeply. "I am pleased to meet you, m'am," he said in fluent Spanish. "How in the world did such a homely man as Pablo attract such a beautiful woman?"

"It's his beautiful soul," she laughed. "Actually, I find him quite good looking, too."

"This is Marino Delgado," John said, introducing the other man. He's our guide."

"We've met," Paul answered. "It's good to see you again, Marino," Paul said, offering the guide his hand." Turning to John, he asked, "Our guide? Who else is here?"

"Jock and a fellow named O'Leary," John answered. "We've been in country several weeks trying to find you. I have a letter from him for you. I'll brief you after you've read it."

"Does it have to be right this minute?"

"No," the sergeant replied. "It does need to be today."

Radford nodded. "Just so you know, Gloria's also a very good friend of Victor's, too," he added. Turning to Gloria, he said, "I'm sorry, *querida*, duty calls. I have to answer."

"Of course, you do," she answered. Turning to the sergeant Gloria asked, "Where are you staying?"

"Don't worry about us, m'am," he told her. "We'll find a place to camp."

"No, you come to my home," she said. When Yellowhawk tried to decline, she insisted. Marino, who was listening, just smiled. Later he told Paul that Gloria reminded him of his sister, sweet but bossy.

John looked at Paul, who grinned. "Sounds like an order, sergeant. Do I have to make it one?"

"No, sir," Yellowhawk replied, smiling. "A real bed would feel great. So would a bath and a hot water shave."

"Good. That's settled. It's much more comfortable at the ranch and much more secure. The food is great, too, and the hostess, very gracious."

That evening after supper, Paul suggested that John and Marino join him on the veranda. "We can talk there," he said. Turning to Gloria, he said, "I'm afraid it's government business, *querida*. My apologies."

"I understand, Pablo," she answered sweetly. "Take your time. I have some ranch business I need to tend."

Radford smiled. They both knew that she would hear every word said from her desk inside. It was the way the house had been designed by Gloria's late husband, who had built in a ventilation duct above the best place to sit on the veranda. The duct was attached to a strong fan and Gloria had warned Paul about it one evening when they were sitting beneath it. "The only place it works is in my husband's office."

"What if someone is listening to us now?" he asked.

"No one is. The sound both ways. If anyone was there, I'd hear them. The door squeaks and so does the floor. All I have to do to keep from being heard out here is turn on the fan." She pointed to a switch set low on the wall.

Once Paul had read the letter from Jacques, the briefing took very little time. Since the guide was present, Paul asked that it be in Spanish. "That bastard!" He growled after hearing that Hoover had sent O'Leary to kill Haya. "It would serve him right if someone put out a contract on him! How do we know this, John?"

Yellowhawk looked at Marino, who answered. "Simon told me about it after he decided not to do it," he said.

"Simon? Who is Simon, O'Leary?"

"Yes, sorry. Simon is the name he was going by when he hired me, Simon Lynch. His real name is Michael O'Leary."

"Did you believe him?"

172 JOEL B REED

"Yes, mostly because he didn't have to tell me at all. He said what he wanted most was to talk to you."

"Did he say why?"

"No, only that it was very important. Perhaps he wanted to warn you."

"Did he tell Jacques Paul all this?"

"Yes, I was there when he did. Jacques seemed to accept him at his word. He let him keep his weapons and doesn't seem suspicious."

"What's your take on all this, John?"

"I think Marino and O'Leary are both telling the truth."

Radford nodded. "I guess we better head out for Puerto Maldonado tomorrow morning."

Yellowhawk nodded. "Yeah. You know what time the train north leaves?"

"I can't go by train," Paul told him. "I'm still wanted in Perú for that surprise party we pulled west of here. Besides, we'd have to do too much backtracking. We'll head straight north until we hit the main road. Then we'll head east until we get there."

"You know the country?" John asked, clearly skeptical.

Paul smiled. "No, but I know someone who does."

Busqe El Gringo

14 Puerto Maldonado, Perú. The Bellanca Pacemaker bounced slightly on the runway before settling down to a bumpy ride to the hangar. After the pilot cut the power to the powerful engine, the passenger compartment seemed unnaturally quiet. The flight from Lima, almost a thousand kilometers, had been a bumpy one taking more than six hours and using three-quarters of their fuel. It had also been nonstop and by the time they reached Puerto Maldonado the four men were more than ready to set foot on solid ground.

"I don't know how long we're going to be here," Helmut Rott told the pilot. "I want to be able to leave at an hour's notice, so have the fuel tanks filled and keep me informed of where you are. I don't care if you're going to a restaurant or a whore house, keep me informed. I expect to be here at least three days but it may be as long as a week or two and I want you to guard the plane at night. During the day, you can rest in our rooms or wherever you please, but be ready to fly. You're limited to four beers a day and I want you rested. I also want you to stay away from coca leaves."

The pilot didn't like this, but nothing showed on his face. Chewing coca leaves was a national pass-time and they were easy to find in Puerto Maldonado. "Do you know where you're staying, señor?" he asked.

"I'll send a car to get you after we check in. Right now you need to refuel and do whatever else you need to do to fly. Be sure to lock up the whole plane when you're done."

Rott rode in the front seat with the cab driver on their way to the hotel, and Dieter and Chino in the back seat. Helmut took a photo out of his jacket pocket and showed it to the driver. "I need to find this man," he said. "His name is Pablo and he may be traveling with

Victor Haya. Fifty American dollars are yours if you can find him. He may have shaved off the beard."

"Señor Haya's in town, señor. I saw him riding in a big car."

"Do you know where he's staying?" The driver confessed he did not and Rott told him, "I'll give twenty-five dollars if you can discover where he's staying. If Pablo is with him, I'll give you the other twenty-five. Keep in mind I will have other men looking, too. The first to tell me where he's staying gets the money."

"May I ask why you're looking for him, señor?"

"He took something that belongs to me. I need to get it back. Do you drive for a taxi company or are you on your own?"

"I own my own cab, señor. I am available on a daily rate if you wish." The cab driver mentioned a price and Rott didn't haggle.

Dieter, sitting in the back seat with Chino, wondered if Rott would be as open handed with him if he was who first found Radford. He thought not. Then he looked at Chino and the guide shrugged. Dieter knew he had must have had the same question.

When they got to the hotel, Dieter was relieved to learn that he would be sharing the same room with Chino rather than with Rott. "We'll use my room for a headquarters and the pilot can sleep in your room during the day. This town has a rough reputation, so the two of you will take turns keeping watch on the plane during the day. So keep your pistols handy. There's a rifle in the plane, too, and an electric torch. The other man will be with me, canvassing the city for Haya and Radford. The cab will take one of you to the airport at eight in the morning and will bring the pilot here so he can sleep."

The next day the cab took Dieter to the air strip and Chino spent the day with Rott, getting familiar with the city. The pilot joined them late in the afternoon as they checked out local watering holes. Chino blended in quite well, as did the pilot, and Rott decided it would be better to have Dieter guard the plane from late afternoon through the night. "Be sure you are up and moving around during the night," Rott told the scullion. "The best way is to drink three large glasses of water before you go to sleep. Then take a look around when you get up to piss and drink three more glasses before you lie down again. You can catch a few more hours at the hotel in the morning."

Dieter didn't like this any more than the pilot had, but it would keep him out of sight and, hopefully, out of Rott's mind. He also decided chewing few coca leaves will keep him stay awake better than drinking so much water. So he slipped out of the hotel during siesta time and quickly found someone who was willing to sell him what he needed. While the leaves were not as effective as refined cocaine, they did the trick, leaving him in a good mood, and he was able to time his chewing so he could sleep through the morning. The only side effects he seemed to suffer were a hyper-vigilance that had him jumping at unusual sounds, and trouble waking up after sleeping at the hotel. Fortunately, Rott didn't realize his stupor was drug induced.

For the next three days the searchers scoured the city without turning up a trace of Victor or Paul. It was the cab driver was able to claim the reward for discovering where Haya was staying. Thinking that the statesman would be staying with one of his powerful friends, they had looked for him where the wealthy lived. Yet, Victor was a man of the people and had instructed Diego and Mateo to rent a place in a working class neighborhood. As it turned out, on his way home the evening of the third day, the cab driver spotted the touring car Haya was using. It was completely out of place in the neighborhood and the cab driver returned to the hotel right away to let Rott know.

Early the next morning, the driver dropped Chino and the pilot off at strategic corners where they could watch both the car and the house. Then he took Rott to the airfield to pick up Dieter. Then Rott guarded the plane until Dieter returned late that afternoon with word that Victor Haya and his men had been spotted coming out of the house. They'd been followed to a working man's cantina where they had a leisurely evening meal.

The cab took Rott directly to the cantina. When he got there, Haya was holding court among those coming in for a drink before going home. Rott, who had exchanged his black livery for common work clothes, slipped in unobtrusively and listened. He was wearing a dark felt cone shaped hat commonly worn by workers in the city, and he was careful to keep his Teutonic eyes out of sight below the brim. When a waiter came over to where he was sitting, Rott simply grunted and pointed to the beer the fellow beside him held. When it came he paid for it without ever looking up.

Keeping his hat brim low, Rott studied the people in the room while he was waiting for his beer. Victor Haya was easy to pick out, as was his driver. His bodyguards were not. They were dressed like most of the people in the room and only two things gave them away. One was the boredom Helmut could read in their faces. They had obviously heard what Haya had to say before many times before. Unlike the others in the room, they also watched the crowd rather than their boss. This was something Pablo had drilled into them, teaching them to read danger in the crowd.

Rott also noticed the two men were sitting where they could respond quickly to any threat, as was the driver. This, too, was something Pablo had taught them. Timo was seated at Victor's left hand where he could quickly move in front of Haya while cross-drawing his revolver from its shoulder holster. Diego and Mateo flanked the statesman in positions that allowed them to directly confront any attacker. Seeing this, Rott grudgingly approved. The bodyguards had been well trained. Not that this would save Victor Haya's life or theirs if Rott was the attacker. The pretty boy would die first, before he had a chance to move, and the statesman would be next. By the time the bodyguards had their weapons pulled, neither of them would have time to fire at him.

Rott's reflections were interrupted by a sudden silence. He looked around to see two uniformed policemen making their way through the crowd. One bore the insignia of a sergeant, and the other was a captain. Both were armed, though their pistols remained in their holsters. They were headed straight for Haya's table.

Helmut saw Haya say something to his men, and all four remained seated. When the policemen reached his table, Victor stood and smiled, extending his hand. Rott smiled at how well the captain pocketed whatever Haya handed him, most likely a bribe. The the captain took his seat and the sergeant walked over to the bar where he took a stool. From there he could keep an eye on the room.

The policemen didn't stay long. After a few minutes, the captain stood and shook hands again with Haya. Then he nodded to his sergeant, who walked across the room and joined him at the door.

Without a look back, the two disappeared into the night, shutting the door behind them.

Over the next two weeks, the day's events became the pattern as Rott and his two men watched. The only variation was where Haya chose to go to dine and hold forth. All three cantinas he visited were much alike and one thing Rott quickly noticed was that the longer Haya was in town, the more people who showed up to listen. They seemed to know where the great man would be and Rott wondered how they knew.

The other thing that changed took place ten days after they began to watch Haya. One day, not long before noon, Rott's driver came out of the house and walked to the market in the central part of town. He stayed there for a couple of hours, visiting various shops but never making a purchase. Then he invariably had something to eat at one of the food stands and walked back to the place they were staying.

This quickly became a routine, except that one of the bodyguards took the driver's place on a few occasions. When it was one of them keeping watch, one bodyguard spent a lot of time sitting at an outdoor table reading a newspaper. The other favored sitting in the shade nursing a bottle of beer and watching patrons of the market walk by. Yet both walked through the market three or four times before heading home.

Nor did it take Helmut Rott long to figure what the men were doing. "They're waiting for Pablo," he explained to Dieter. "They split up for some reason and he's supposed to join them here. The market is where he will come to find them around noon. So we need to keep careful watch. We don't know whether he will actually join them at the market or if he will simply follow the watcher home. That would be safer and Pablo's no fool."

As the days went by, keeping watch grew tedious. Chino accepted the task gratefully, glad to be paid for being in the shade rather than sweating and fending off bugs in the jungle. The pilot took a different view, grumbling about having to do boring work he considered beneath him. So it wasn't that hard for Dieter to persuade Rott to let him take a turn watching the market with Chino. Once there, he quickly took the opportunity to replenish his supply of coca leaves.

These were what helped him stay sane, or so he told himself, and for him the days flowed by in a pleasant haze.

By the end of the third week of surveillance, Rott was having a hard time justifying staying in Puerto Maldonado. Schwartz cabled him two or three times a week, demanding progress in the code language they used. Yet there was nothing to report. Nor did it help that the pilot threatened to fly back to Lima without them. Helmut had to threaten him with bodily harm before the man surrendered the keys to the aircraft.

Then, two days before Rott agreed to return to the capital, Paul Radford was sighted at the market. Timo was on duty that day and when he spotted Pablo, he scratched his neck. This was the signal that he was being followed and Pablo did not try to approach the young dandy. He held back, instead, and followed Timo at a discreet distance. Then, once he noted the house Timo entered, he walked on by, giving the signal that he would make contact later.

Even so, luck was with the Germans. Helmut Rott happened to be on market duty that day and spotted Pablo as he left the market. Once he had made sure that Radford was following Timo, Rott dropped back and headed for the telegraph office. He sent a coded message to Schwartz that reported the sighting. It went on to say that he would be sending the airplane back to it's owner soon and would cable again once their mission was completed.

A reply was waiting for Helmut when he returned to the hotel that evening. It acknowledged receipt of his earlier telegram and urged him to complete what he was doing as soon as possible. Buried in the code was the danger signal they had used for several years and the next line confirmed this. It said that Gunther Berg was waiting for Rott to return so he could talk to him.

Rott did not have to speculate about what kind of interview the Gestapo agent had in mind. There was no doubt in his mind that he would be arrested as soon as he set foot on the embassy grounds. The only question was whether he would be shot in Perú or returned to Berlin for extensive torture first.

Even so, Helmut Rott had prepared for this. There was a valid Argentine passport concealed in a waterproof pocket of his back pack along with ten thousand Swiss francs. There was also a half a kilo of gold in small bars, and he had the half kilo of cocaine he had planned to leave on Pablo's body. He could get rid of that quite easily in Puerto Maldonado. Then he could catch a river boat headed south down the Madre de Dios to the Amazon and the Atlantic Ocean. A ship would take him south to Buenos Aires where he could live out his days in anonymity. As for Jergen Schwartz, it was just too damned bad if the scholar got crucified by the Gestapo. It was time for Rott to cut his losses.

As tempting as it was to simply walk away that night, Rott had an old score to settle first. It would be easy enough to ambush Pablo on the road to Cuzco and then make his way back to Puerto Maldonado. He doubted that Berg would come after him while he was there. From what he'd seen of the Gestapo in Germany and Perú, it's agents were bullies who preyed on soft targets. Like all bullies, they'd shit their pants if they were met with resolve and a strong show of force. A treacherous ambush was more their style.

Having come to this decision, Rott felt as if a great weight had been lifted from his shoulders. A week from that day he would be on his way and if Radford was still in Puerto Maldonado the day before Helmut left, Rott would attack him there. He would probably have to take out all five men, but with good timing, a silenced pistol, and the element of surprise, it could be done. Unfortunately, Pablo have to be taken out first, and with a pistol. Rott would have preferred to save him for last, taking his time strangling him slowly with his bare hands or a garrote.

Puerto Maldonado. Paul Radford pulled back on the reins and looked around. There was not much to see in the growing darkness, but at some point they had left the countryside and were now in the outskirts of the city. They had passed a small village a few miles back, illuminated in the twilight by smoky wood fires burning between several of the houses. When he asked how far it was to Puerto Maldonado, one of the men sitting by a fire told him it was eight or ten kilometers. Yet his impression was that they had come much further than that.

"What do you think?" he asked. "Are we there yet?"

"Beats me," John Yellowhawk answered, but Marino nodded. "I think we are, Pablo. I don't remember anything being this far from the river but it's been many years since I was here."

"You know a place where we can spend the night?"

Marino pointed toward the dim outline of a large building behind a sheet tin hut. "That looks like a barn. We can probably stay there if we pay the farmer."

"See what you can do. I think John and I need to keep out of sight but be sure and tell him there are three of us. We need a place for the horses, too."

Marino was back in five minutes with an old man who led them into the large building. This turned out to be a warehouse, and Marino told them the tin building in front was the office and guard shack. The old man was the night watchman and he seemed glad to have their company. After he got them settled, he invited them to use the stove in the office to prepare their evening meal, and Paul accepted.

The old man was full of questions but he seemed to accept their vague answers at face value. When Marino asked what the warehouse was for, being so far from the river, the old man grinned. "Some foreigners own it," he told them. "The sacks you will be sleeping on are full of coca leaves. The locked room is full of pasta. They think it is safer here than in the city." He shrugged. "The police don't know about this place. The river's only two hundred meters that way." He pointed.

Paul didn't understand. "How could the police not know? It's right here on the main road."

The old man laughed. "They don't know officially. They turn the blind eye, but the path you followed here isn't the main road. You missed a turn five kilometers back but I don't understand how. Didn't you have to open a wire gate?"

"I didn't see a wire gate," Radford answered. "It was dark and I'm surprised we didn't run into it."

"Somebody must have left it open. We got a big shipment in this afternoon. I bet that stupid driver forgot. There's a big sign we put in front of it, too. It's got a big white arrow pointing the right direction. Ah, that stupid *penjedo*! He must have forgotten the sign, too. You want some coca leaves?" The old man pulled a pouch out of his shirt.

"No, but thank you for offering," Paul replied. He took a liter of whiskey out of his food sack. "Would you care for a drink?"

The old man laughed. "Does the river run downhill? Of course, I'd like a drink. The cheap whore's son who runs this place doesn't pay much. All I can afford is coca leaves and sometimes a beer. Cheap bastard foreigner!"

Paul handed him the bottle. "Not all foreigners are cheap," he said. "This is all for you." The old fellow twisted off the top and took a deep drink, sighing with pleasure after he swallowed.

"What kind of foreigner, old one?" John asked casually.

"Oh, one of those damned Germans," the old man told him. "He buys a lot of coca leaves but I don't know what he does with them. Maybe he makes cocaine. I don't know. He doesn't make it here. When they get enough leaves, he sends a big truck to pick them up. It always heads back toward Cuzco."

"I hope you don't get in trouble for putting us up," Paul told him.

"Who's going to know? I'm not going to tell him, the cheap whore-son. Nobody ever comes out here at night. They're scared of the snakes."

"So you have a lot of snakes around here?" John asked. He sounded like he was asking about the weather.

"Hell, no, but that's what he tells people, the owner. Now everybody in the city believes it. He does, too!" He laughed.

"That's better than a watch dog," Marino observed.

"Especially at night. The one they gave me wasn't worth much. All he did was crap right where people needed to walk. I was glad when he ran off,"

They visited with the old man a while longer until the bottle was about a quarter down from the top and the whiskey claimed him for he night. Paul helped the *viejo* onto a couch in a back room, turning him on his side in case he got sick. Then they headed for the warehouse and it wasn't long before Paul heard one of his companions snoring.

The sacks of leaves were comfortable enough to sleep on, but

Paul had a hard time switching off his mind. He found himself remembering his parting with Gloria, how sad she looked. She and Alonzo had led them cross country to the main road. It was about forty-five kilometers as the crow flies, but much longer by horseback. The trip took all day, and after twelve hours in the saddle, Paul was glad to get off his horse. Even with the padded saddle, he was sore.

The place they stopped was at a deserted house a kilometer or two from the Cuzco-Puerto Maldonado road. Even though it was deserted, it was clear that someone kept the place in good shape. The iron roof was not that old and the wooden shutters covering the windows were solid. There was also a well tended corral in back with a feed shed full of native hay. When Paul remarked on this, Gloria pointed to wisps of fleece caught in the poles that supported the roof. She told him the place was used as a shearing station for alpaca.

After supper, Paul and Gloria claimed the shed for themselves, leaving the main house for the three men. Even though the cold season was months ahead, it was cold at that elevation and they burrowed into the hay. "Don't you Americans have an expression about this?" she teased, snuggling close.

Paul chuckled. "Yes, we call it a roll in the hay," he told her. "I'd show you how it works but it's too cold."

"Then maybe we need to warm it up," she murmured, snuggling even closer.

The next morning when they awoke they lay close for a long while. "I'm going to miss you, Pablo," Gloria told him. There were tears in her eyes.

"I don't want to go," he assured her. "I'd rather stay at the ranch with you. You know that, don't you?" She nodded.

Nothing more was said between them until they were leaving. "Be careful, Pablo," Gloria told him.

"I will, *querida*," he told her. "I'll be back as soon as I can. I promise."

Thinking of this as he lay on the sacks of coca leaves, Paul wondered, not for the first time, what it would be like to spend the rest of his life raising llamas with Gloria. There was little that tied him to his native land except his parents. All the real friends he had were all in the frozen wastes of the Aleutians or here in Perú, as was his flesh and blood. It would be so very simple to just walk away, to disappear into the jungle and make his way back to the hacienda.

Even as this thought crossed his mind, he knew he could not do it. He had made promises he had to keep, not for the sake of the Republic, but for himself. He had to live with himself and he knew Robert Service was right. When one makes a promise, there is, indeed, a debt to be paid.

For an awful time the sadness of this thought overwhelmed him. Then he had a much happier thought. He had made a promise to Gloria, too, one he would take great delight in keeping for a long, long time.

Second Attack

15 Near Santa Rosa. Jacques Paul sat bolt upright in alarm, reaching for his pistol. When he did, his head swam and he almost fell out of bed. Strong hands prevented him from falling and he heard a male voice speaking calmly.

"Easy, there, Jaques. Everything's under control. Lie back and take it easy. You've been sick."

Jacques Paul did as he was told. There was really no choice. He felt as weak as a kitten and he couldn't get his thoughts together. Looking up he saw the underside of a sheet iron roof above him and looking left and right, he saw mud walls. He had no idea where he was or even what time it was. Weak light was coming in through a small, dingy window, but he couldn't see anything through the grime.

Then a man's face came into view. It was one he recognized though he couldn't put a name with it. It was a kindly face, full of concern, and he guessed it was a friend. The features were Celt and he guessed the man was Irish. There was also a lilt in the voice few Scots had. "Who are you?" he asked.

"Michael O'Leary at your service, Captain, late of the United States Marine Corps. I'm one of your merry men and a new recruit at that."

"Where am I?"

"The name of the place is Santa Rosa. It's just off the main road to Puerto Maldonado. That's where we were headed when you came down sick."

Jacques didn't know what the answers meant but he knew they were true. They were also important. "What's wrong with me, O'Leary?"

"I'm no doctor but I'd say Montezuma's Revenge. I'm pretty sure it's not malaria, though the symptoms are similar. We've been taking quinine."

"How long have I been sick?" Jaques felt a strong sense of urgency but he didn't know why.

"You've been down with it about six days now. Just after Quince Mil you started heaving your guts out. Diarrhea, too. I was able to keep you drinking fresh water, but it came right up again."

Jacques Paul nodded and started to ask another question. He felt a great wave of weariness roll over him and he couldn't seem to get his mind to focus. He found this distressing and fought to stay awake. Then, before he realized what was happening, he fell asleep.

"Nasty stuff," O'Leary murmured, hoping he didn't catch it, too.

When Jaques Paul woke again his mind had cleared somewhat. The room in which he was lying was dark, illuminated only by a coal-oil lamp. Turning his head he saw Michael O'Leary sitting on what looked like an animal carcass, his back against a mud wall and fast asleep. Then, as if he felt Jacques Paul gazing at him, his eyes came open. Seeing the captain was awake, the Irishman smiled.

"Good evening, Captain," O'Leary said. "You're back in the land of the living. Are things starting to make sense now?"

Jaques nodded. "It's still a little fuzzy. Where are we?"

"A tiny place called Santa Rosa. From what I can ascertain we're about seventy miles or so from Puerto Maldonado."

At the mention of their destination, Jacques Paul's eyes opened in alarm and he tried to get up. "We've got to get going!" he said. "They're after Paul!"

O'Leary shook his head. "Not tonight, or even tomorrow, for that matter. You are gravely ill, Captain. We didn't think you were going to make it. You're far too weak to travel, much less fight. You need to get well first."

"Then leave me and go!"

"Not for a bloody minute, sir. With all due respect. What if the frigging Germans found you here? There's a war on, sir, and they'd kill you for sure! Pablo can take care of himself. My job is to look after you."

Seeing the stubborn look on the Irishman's face, Jacques Paul knew nothing he could say would change the man's mind. Even so he had to try. "That's an order, Marine!" he declared.

"Yes, and you're out of your frigging mind, sir. Literally. How can you think any order you might give right now would be valid?" O'Leary grinned to take any enmity out of his words. "Tomorrow I'll make another assessment, Captain. You're a casualty of war, so focus on getting well. Now how about a drink of water or lemon soda? You're rather dehydrated."

Two days later they were on their way to Puerto Maldonado. O'Leary insisted on driving and Jacques Paul didn't argue the point. It was all he could do to stay seated upright, and he found himself fighting to keep his eyes open. He found himself glad for the lurching of the truck over uneven sections of road. It shook him awake whenever he dropped off.

They had driven about fifty miles when O'Leary suddenly slowed down and pulled off to one side of the road. He shut off the engine. "Did you hear that, Captain?" he asked Jaques Paul. The Irishman was frowning.

"Did I hear what?" the other asked. At that moment two shots rang out somewhere ahead of them.

"You stay here, sir," the Irishman ordered. "I'm going to slip through the jungle and see what's going on. I'll be back within an hour. If I'm not, you're on your own. Think you can drive into town?"

"I will if I have to," Jaques Paul said, drawing his weapon and laying it in his lap. Then he hid it with his broad brimmed hat. A minute later Michael was gone and, despite his best efforts to be alert, Jacques soon fell asleep.

O'Leary grabbed a rifle from a locker in the back of the truck and headed into the jungle beside the road. He soon found a game trail that led in the right direction and as he followed it, more shots rang out. Moving as carefully as he could, he made almost no sound and he soon reached the summit of a low hill. When he did, he spotted the shooters. There were two of them, a small man in black almost directly in front of him and another man fifty meters away on the far side of the road. Both had rifles and their target was a large touring car. The driver was slumped in the seat behind the wheel and it was obvious the car had run off the road. This was lucky for whoever else was in the car. It gave them shelter from the shooters. From the sound of the shots he'd heard, he guessed the victims were only armed with pistols. He was pretty sure this was Haya's party, too.

It was then that O'Leary saw the third man. He was dressed in dark clothes covered by a green poncho that blended in with the jungle. What gave him away was the movement of his dark felt hat, and the Irishman saw that he was circling around to flank the people behind the car. He was carrying a rifle and he didn't have far to go to have a clear shot.

Without conscious thought, a plan formed in O'Leary's mind. Taking out the silenced pistol he'd found in the gun locker, he slipped closer to the small man in black right before him. His intent was to knock the man out but his quarry sensed his presence and whirled around, attempting to bring his rifle to bear. Michael fired two quick shots. One struck the little man just under the rib cage, driving itself through the man's heart. The other, aimed at the same spot was a little high and struck the man under the larynx.

Slipping forward, O'Leary made sure the man was dead, then looked toward the third man. He saw there was no time to waste. The man had his rifle up and it looked like he was about to take a shot. Throwing his rifle to his shoulder, the Irishman took a quick shot toward the center of the largest mass, praying that the rifle was still zeroed in after all the jouncing from the truck. Working the bolt, he readied himself for a second shot. He could see the man was down, holding his middle. So the rifle was shooting a bit low.

Wounded as badly as he was, the man pulled out a pistol, trying to aim it at the car. O'Leary took another quick shot, this time aiming slightly higher. This time the shot stuck the man just in front of the ear, killing him instantly. He was thrown back into the brush and didn't move.

Turning to check the third man, O'Leary saw that he was aiming in O'Leary's direction and dropped to the ground. He heard the crack of a bullet passing right above his head just before he heard the sound of the rifle. Quickly he crabbed his way backward until he was hidden by the brush. Then he began his stalk.

When O'Leary looked through the brush again, he saw the third man approaching the spot where the man in black lay. From the way he approached, it was obvious to him that the fellow had no military training. Then, when he got to where the man in black lay, it was obvious that the fellow thought he had killed the little man. O'Leary was about to take the man down when there was a shot from the direction of the touring car. It knocked the hat off the third man's head and he dropped to the ground. Then he began to crawl backwards from the firing position, moving directly toward the Irishman.

When the third man started to turn around, O'Leary was right in front of him, aiming his silenced pistol right at the man's face. "Don't move!" Michael told him. "Twitch a muscle and you're dead."

Seeing that Dieter, the third man, had no intention of moving, O'Leary told him to put both hands in the small of his back. Once he had bound Dieter's hands and feet, Michael tied him around the elbows, too. "I'll be back," he told the frightened scullion. "Try to struggle and you'll only make the knots tighter. Now where are the other men?"

"There aren't any others," Dieter told him. "Just me, Rott, and Chino."

"There better not be, you scum!" another voice sounded from behind. O'Leary whirled around, his pistol ready, and stopped. Jaques Paul was standing there holding a rifle, barely able to stay on his feet. "You damned Marines," he said to O'Leary. "You hog all the fun."

"Well, if you want, Captain, you can stroll down there and convince the lads we're on their side."

"No need of that," another voice spoke from behind them. When they looked around they saw Sergeant John Yellowhawk looking at them with a wry grin. He was carrying a silenced pistol. "You white men just can't stalk," he said.

An hour and a half later they were on their way. The touring car was pulled back onto the road, no worse for wear other than a couple of bullet holes in the coach work and one through the windshield.

Once it was ready to go, Victor and his two bodyguards left with Mateo driving. Diego Montoyo rode in the back seat with Victor. It was decided to take the body of Timeo to Gloria's ranch, where it could be buried until it could be returned to his family in Argentina. The bodies of Rott and Chino were stripped of anything that could identify them and left to rot where they lay. Were they found, their deaths would be attributed to bandits. The Puerto Maldonado area was known for that kind of thing.

It was Jacques who put this in perspective. "They brought it on themselves," he pointed out. "The scavengers need to eat, too."

"Yes, sir," John Yellowhawk responded. "I just hope it doesn't poison them."

While all this was being done, Pablo, who had been seriously injured in the first volley from their attackers, was treated as best they could. Then he was laid in the bed of the truck. "He needs a hospital, sir," Michael O'Leary pointed out to Jaques Paul.

"Yes, but we can't risk that," Jaques answered. "He is in this country illegally. He could be arrested as a spy and shot."

"Would they really do that?"

The captain nodded. "He really upset some of the powerful people in Perú . These people are very sympathetic to the Nazis. One of these days, I'll tell you about it. It's classified top secret."

"So where do we take him? Moving him far in the truck could kill him."

"We take him to Peno. The ranch lady will know a doctor we can use. Or we can take him to a hospital in Bolivia."

"You could fly him there, sir." Dieter was sitting nearby, still tied up. "I know where the plane we flew in is hidden. Herr Rott has the keys."

"That's the little man in black," Jacques said. "I emptied his pockets." He reached into a satchel and pulled out a set of keys. He also pulled out something about the size of a brick and wrapped in waxed paper. When he opened a corner, a small mound of white powder formed in his hand. Gingerly smelling the substance, he said, "Cocaine. I wonder why Rott had it?"

Then Jaques sniffed hard and shuddered. "Quick energy," he

explained to the group. Dieter's eyes were glued to the brick. "I think Braun might like a sniff, too," he added. Dieter nodded but Jaques replaced the wax paper and tucked the brick away.

"We could fly Paul directly to Bolivia," O'Leary suggested. "La Paz is a big place."

"That would involve a lot of explanations," Jaques replied. "I don't want the police involved."

"I saw an airstrip near the...place he was staying," John Yellowhawk told them. "It looked like it could take anything up to a Skytrain."

"All right," Jaques said. "That's what we'll do. Go steal us a plane." He was very thin but there was no sign of fatigue. The cocaine had worked. For how long was anyone's guess.

"It beats hauling a corpse around in the back of the truck," O'Leary replied. "Particularly with police patrols on the road. What do we do with this sack of pig shite?" Dieter's eyes grew wide with fear.

"Depends on how much he helps us," Jaques Paul replied. "He is embassy staff, so I'm reluctant to shoot him out of hand. We could just let him go. What do you want us to with you, Braun?"

Dieter had given this some thought. "Could you report me dead, sir? That way I can take a boat from Puerto Maldonado and get away to Brazil. If you send me back to the embassy, I could get shot or sent to Germany."

"Let him go, Jock." It was Paul Radford speaking. He had been given a shot of morphine and had pulled himself up against the side of the truck bed. "There's been enough killing. Take all his papers and let him go. I don't think he's going to cause trouble. It's a long walk to town."

"What about Haya's driver?" Marino asked. "Someone's got to pay for that."

"Someone has," Pablo replied. "It was Rott who fired the first shot and killed Timo. I think it was the guide who shot me. It was an act of war, not personal."

"All right, Braun," Jaques said. "You take us to the plane and I'll let you go when we take off. So where is it?"

"There's a landing strip in the jungle about a kilometer back. It's on the south side of the road."

"Very good. Yellowhawk, you and O'Leary find the plane. Take Dieter with you but keep him out of sight. I don't want the pilot seeing him at all. And if he makes one false move, shoot him. We'll follow in ten minutes."

The aircraft was captured without incident. Dieter led them right to it, and Yellowhawk and O'Leary captured the pilot before he was aware they were there. O'Leary was able to park the truck close enough to transfer Paul easily and Jaques Paul managed to get the Pacemaker into the air. Since the plane was fitted with dual controls, he showed O'Leary how to keep the aircraft level and on course and leaned back against the cushion. He could feel the initial effect of the cocaine wearing off. "Holler at the first sign of trouble," he told the Irishman. "Now try a slight left turn and bring us back on course."

Satisfied with Michael's performance, Jacques took the controls again and took them up to ten thousand feet. Then he surrendered the stick to O'Leary. "Head for that peak way up there. Wake me when we get close to the foothills. That will be in about forty-five minutes. Thirty seconds later he was asleep.

The rest of the flight went well. When O'Leary woke Jaques Paul, the captain took the controls and headed for a wide river valley leading into the mountains. Luck was with them and the river lead them to a low pass over the mountains. Once they made it to the other side, they could see Lake Titicaca in the distance. "See if you can get Radford up here," Jacques Paul told O'Leary. "I don't know where this place is."

Pablo spotted the hacienda right away. Jaques Paul followed his directions and circled the ranch headquarters twice. The second time around, people came out of the house and Jaques Paul headed for the landing strip he saw close by. Glancing at his watch, he was surprised to see that only two hours had passed since they had taken off. By truck it would have been a hard day's drive.

By the time they had taxied back to a spot close to the house, the ranch truck was there waiting. Jaques opened the door and asked, "Is this the Lopez Ranch?"

Yet Gloria had already seen Paul and was waving. "We need some help getting him out," Jaques added. "He's been hurt."

Jaques Paul spent two days at the ranch recuperating. Gloria's doctor had been fetched from Puno to tend Pablo's wounds and he had done what he could. "He needs a good surgeon," he told Gloria. "There's a lot of damage to his left shoulder and he will not recover much use of his arm without it. He's lucky the bullet went high didn't deflect into his the heart or lungs."

"It wasn't luck, doctor," Paul replied from the bed. "Only the good die young and I apparently don't qualify."

"Or maybe God looks out for fools and drunkards!" Gloria riposted. Then she burst into tears and rushed from the room,

"I'll check on you in a few days," the doctor said dryly. "I gather it would be best if the police don't get word of this."

"Thank you," Paul told him. "That would be embarrassing for all concerned. That's why I cannot go to Lima for surgery."

"Oh," the doctor said, smiling. "The fellow I was going to recommend is across the border in La Paz. That's less than three hundred kilometers from here. The sooner you see him, the better."

"Excuse me, doctor," said Jaques Paul. "I am the lieutenant's commander. Are you saying this makes him unfit for military service?"

The doctor shrugged. "It certainly would in Perú , but we're not at war. I don't know about your country."

"Your word is sufficient, thank you." Turning to Pablo, he said, "Well, Lieutenant, it looks like you're on convalescent leave. I'll get a statement from the doctor here and I'll submit it to the powers that be. Don't be surprised if you get a medical discharge."

"What about the...project I was on?"

"A bum arm wouldn't slow you down there. Maybe you can continue as a civil contractor. Working for the embassy. But all that still needs to be worked out. You need to get your surgery and get well first."

Once they were out of the room, Jaques pulled the doctor aside. "Please let your colleague in La Paz know that cost is no object. The lieutenant is to get the very best care. You will be well compensated, too."

The doctor looked at him gravely. "Thank you, Captain. You

need to know that he would get it, anyway. Señora Lopez is a good friend, as was her husband."

The day Jacques Paul and O'Leary flew to Cuzco, the captain stopped in to say goodbye to Paul. He laid a black satchel on the table next to the door. "That's to pay for whatever you need, Pablo. There's quite a bit there, so you might want to secure it. Señora Lopez can help you get the Swiss francs changed for sols."

"Thanks, Jock," Radford replied. "I appreciate it." Jaques knew he was in pain, but Pablo seemed more relaxed than he'd ever seen him.

"By the way, you don't happen to know what happened with that brick of cocaine Rott had, do you?"

Radford smiled and chuckled. "As a matter of fact I do. I saw Dieter slipping it out of your backpack while you were trying to get me into the plane."

"Why didn't you say something?"

Pablo thought a moment. "I don't know. I guess because he looked like a little kid stealing from the cookie jar." He shrugged. "We didn't leave him with much else, Jock. He needed something to get a new start."

"As a drug dealer?"

"You have my apology, if that helps," Pablo told him. "I was kind of out of it at the time. It just struck me as funny. Do you think he'll actually sell it? Unless I read him wrong, most of it will go up his own nose."

"I'll have to take your word for that," the captain said. "Oh, there's one other thing. I got a wire from Blieu. I don't know the details, but that last Silver Star you earned, the one for saving the battery?"

"Yeah. I didn't think I really deserved it but the general told me to shut up and take it."

"Well, the Senator got pissed off about it when he read your file. To put it in a nutshell, it's been changed into a Medal of Honor."

To Jaques' surprise, Radford began to laugh, almost hysterical. "Thanks, Jock," he said, wiping tears from his eyes. "That's the best one I've heard in a long time."

"I'm not kidding, Paul. It's true."

"You don't understand, Jock," Paul replied, still laughing. "That's what makes it so frigging funny."

A Time to Heal

16 Lopez Ranch. A week after Paul arrived at the ranch, Gloria and Alonzo carried him to Puno in the ranch truck and hired him flown to La Paz. There her husband's powerful contacts ensured no police involvement. Gloria told the doctor that Pablo, her guest, had been injured in a freak hunting accident and her story was accepted. "He's lucky they were using military ammunition," the surgeon observed dryly. "A soft nosed bullet would have completely destroyed his shoulder."

"That's all we have," Gloria told him truthfully. "Civilian ammunition is very hard to get these days."

The surgery went quite well but the surgeon insisted that Paul remain in La Paz for convalescent care. "We have a fellow here who is very good at rehabilitation. It's a bit expensive, but I think you'll find it well worth the cost. He can probably get Pablo back to as much as fifty, and maybe seventy-five percent normal use of his arm."

The day after Paul's surgery Gloria found herself an apartment in La Paz. "It's our little love nest, Pablo," she told him. "I think you'll love it. We can stay here as long as you wish."

"It might be smart," Paul agreed. "Maybe some of Victor's friends can help me get things straightened out in Perú ."

"Maybe some of my friends can, too," Gloria told him. That evening she wrote a letter to one of the most powerful men in the country, asking to see him at his earliest convenience. A letter came back to La Paz ten days later inviting her to visit and the next day she flew to Lima.

"He's no lover of the Nazis," she told Paul when she arrived back. "He was very upset when the German bases were discovered, and when I told him you were the one who discovered them, he wanted to shake your hand. He said it would take some time to get things straightened out, but he promised to get it done."

Paul smiled. "Thank you, *querida*. That would make life a lot simpler.

"He's also a close friend of Victor. He doesn't agree with everything Victor says but he's grateful to you for saving his life."

"I know you're trying to help, but you probably shouldn't have told him that."

"I didn't," Gloria replied, smiling. "Victor did." Seeing the look on Paul's face, she asked, "What's wrong, Pablo. Did I do something wrong?"

"No, *querida*, not at all. I told you about Rosario and Lou. It's just that every time I think there will be a wonderful future, something happens. I don't dare hope it will be much different this time."

"It will, Pablo. You've got to believe that. You're due some good luck. Don't give up hope. I've told God it's time for that now!"

Radford chuckled. "I think meeting you is one of the luckiest things that ever happened to me," he said. "Will you marry me, Gloria?"

She looked at him gravely. "When it's time, Pablo, yes. When you know me better and we've been together a while, yes. Don't ask me just when that will be because I don't know. I will tell you the moment I do."

Paul nodded and kissed her. "Then I won't pester you about it." He kissed her again. "You know, my shoulder's in a cast, but maybe if we're careful...?"

Gloria laughed. "How did you know what I was thinking?"

Two months later, Paul moved back to the ranch. The cast was off and he had to wear a brace for another month, but he had already regained half the use of his left arm. The deep lines around his mouth had softened and he'd gained a lot of the weight he'd lost.

It was about two months after he returned to the ranch that a light plane circled the hacienda twice one morning and landed on the runway. Fortunately, the wind had cleared the snow and when the plane taxied up to the waiting truck, Paul saw that the pilot was Jaques Paul. "I wonder what the hell he wants?" he muttered to

Gloria. There was no response and he looked her way. Her face was stricken. "Don't worry, *querida*, I'm not going anywhere. Let's see what he wants."

When they were settled around the dining room table, Gloria started to leave, but Paul stopped her. "This is your business, too, Gloria," he said. "Please stay." He glared at Jaques Paul, daring him to disagree.

The captain smiled. "Please, señora," he said to Gloria. "I'm sure this affects you, too." He pulled a large craft envelope out of his briefcase and gave it to Paul.

Paul opened the envelope. He noticed his hands were trembling. "It's a side effect of my wounds," he told Jaques Paul, lying through his teeth.

"I'm sorry to hear that," the captain replied, not fooled a bit. "I hope it clears up with time. The first item there is a medical discharge from the Navy. It comes with fifty per-cent disability pay. It's not all the money in the world, but it will give you a little walking around cash."

Paul nodded absently and laid aside the discharge. He took the second piece of paper out of the envelope and was shocked at what he saw. "You weren't kidding, were you?" he said.

"That's a certificate for the Congressional Medal of Honor," Jaques explained to Gloria. "It's the highest military honor the United States gives. Paul earned it for his service in Alaska. That's about all either of us can tell you. Stand up, Paul."

Paul complied and Jacques took another item out of his briefcase. "It is the President who normally does this but he's very ill. He wanted you to have it right away, and I'm honored to stand in for him. It comes with an invitation to lunch at the White House at your mutual convenience." Jaques hung a wide blue ribbon around Paul's neck. A golden eagle hung from the ribbon and a gold five-pointed star was suspended below it. Jacques stepped back and gave Paul a regulation military salute. A moment later, Paul returned the salute.

"Let's sit back down," Jaques suggested. He reached into his jacket pocket and pulled out another item. "This has the greatest practical value," he said handing the small booklet to Paul. "It's a diplomatic passport. You have been appointed to the embassy of Perú as a roving cultural affairs officer. Your credentials have been accepted by the government of Perú, thanks to this gracious lady here." He smiled at Gloria.

Jaques continued. "The appointment comes with a salary of one dollar per year, and your duties are whatever you see fit. Your assignment is to promote friendship between Perú and the United States and to study indigenous cultures. You are asked to check in with the embassy whenever you are in Lima. The biggest thing is that you are free to come and go as you wish. Your diplomatic credentials have also been accepted by Bolivia."

Pablo shook his head. "All this is a lot to take in at once, Jock. What's the fly in the ointment? "

The captain shrugged. "We may ask you to check on something for us from time to time, but that will be minimal. You are free to decline. You are also free to refuse the appointment and stay here as long as you like as a private citizen."

"How long do I have to decide? I'm still recuperating."

"Hang onto the diplomatic passport for now. You can turn it in any time you wish. I take it you're planning to stay here?"

"As long as I'm welcome," Pablo answered, looking at Gloria. "There's a chance it may become permanent." Gloria looked down.

Jacques smiled. "Well, I don't want to intrude into your private life."

"Horse hockey!" Paul declared. "When did that ever stop you before?"

Jaques shrugged, mostly for Gloria's benefit, and glanced at his watch. "I need to get going. I'm due back in Lima tonight."

"Surely you're staying for lunch," Gloria declared. It was clear she would not take no for an answer.

While they were eating, Jaques gave them news of the war. The biggest thing was that Rome had fallen and there had been a solid beachhead established on the Normandy coast. "We've been pushing the Germans back since we invaded North Africa," he told them. "Now we're headed for Berlin. It won't be easy, but we'll make it."

"Anything from the Aleutians?" Pablo asked.

"Not since you were there," Jaques answered. "We're on the move in the Pacific. Once we get Saipan nailed down, we'll be in bomber range of Tokyo."

The talk turned to other things and Gloria seemed to enjoy Jaques' company. Yet she surprised Paul when they took him back to the landing strip. "I'm glad he's gone," she said, watching the aircraft disappear into the blue. "He's very charming, but I don't really trust him."

Paul nodded. "He's always kept his word with me, but I think you're right. With Jock, I'm never sure what he's after. He doesn't seem to be a team player unless he's calling the shots. Even so, I'd have to say he's an honorable man. He's always treated me right. I think the medical discharge was his doing, as was the diplomatic passport. Of course, if I use it, that means I've agreed to his terms."

"That's what I meant," she told him. "I think he came here to recruit you. Not as an officer, but as one of his personal spies."

Six months passed with no further word from Jaques Paul or anyone else from the Special Action Group. Paul continue to heal and by the time Christmas was only a week away, he had regained most of the use of his left arm. The shoulder still gave him trouble when the weather was about to change, or when he tried to push himself too far. Yet, most of the time he was able to forget about it and to lead a normal life as a rancher and companion to Gloria.

The two of them also took advantage of Pablo's new freedom and traveled to Argentina and Brazil. Paul was taken by the charm of Rio de Janeiro but it was the beach he loved best. They spent two weeks exploring the city, but their lazy tours of the city were punctuated by long days on the bright sand. "It's not the beach you like best," Gloria teased him one day when a covey of lovely ladies walked by, claiming his admiration. "It's the wildlife."

"The wilder the better," he murmured, nuzzling her neck.

"You just wait!" she purred. "I'll show you wild."

Argentina was altogether different. Pablo had always wanted to see the Pampas he'd read about growing up. "I really liked the gauchos when I was a kid," he told Gloria. "I thought those flat brimmed hats with the little balls dangling from them were the living end. I also liked the way they roped with bolos and the long knives they carry. They made American cowboys look tame."

"You know what those little dangling balls are for, don't you?" she answered.

Pablo nodded. "That's to keep the flies out of their faces." Then he frowned. "I never thought of it but that means the flies must get pretty bad. Maybe we need to stick to the beach."

As the days passed, the war became more and more remote from their life at the ranch. Every week the paper came in the mail, but neither of them paid much attention to it. Alonzo dutifully kept them informed about the major events of the war reported in the paper and in the shortwave broadcasts he listened to every evening. Late in August, they learned of the liberation of Paris and, ten days later, of the liberation of Brussels. Not much later they heard news of action by the Brazilian Expeditionary Force in Italy. Then in late October Aachen fell, the first city in Germany captured by the Allies.

One news story that interested Pablo was the election of Franklin Roosevelt for his fourth term. Then in April came the sad news of Roosevelt's death just months into his last term. Very little was known about his successor, Harry S. Truman and Paul speculated whether the invitation to lunch at the White House would be honored by the little man from Missouri. "Not that I'd ask," he added.

Yet it was the death of Adolph Hitler and the unconditional surrender of Germany that affected Paul most. "I don't believe it," he told Gloria. "This God awful war will finally be over." There were tears in his eyes as he said this. "So the Nazis are finally done. Thank God."

"There is still Japan," Gloria reminded him.

"That's going to be a blood-bath," Radford told her. "I know how hard the Japs fought for a God forsaken chunk of frozen rock in Alaska. Imagine how much harder they'll fight for their homeland."

"I'm just glad you're not in it," Gloria answered. As she did, she wondered if he felt the same.

As if he read her mind, Pablo said, "I am, too, *corazón*. Yet, part of me wishes I could be there doing my part. But don't worry. That's a very small part of me. I've paid my dues in blood, sweat, and tears."

"Thank you, Mr. Churchhill," Gloria teased.

Victor Haya came to visit before after Christmas and spent several weeks with them, writing every day and using Pablo as a sounding board in the evenings. This time he sent his bodyguards home to be with their families and celebrated the holiday with Gloria and Pablo. It turned out to be one of the very best Paul had ever known, and he felt sad when it ended and they put away the simple creche and candles used to decorate the living room.

Victor was delighted to hear of Pablo's vindication. He laughed when Pablo told him about his new status as a diplomat and teased him by addressing Pablo as "Excellency."

"Right," Pablo said dryly. "All I need is a monkey suit and an attitude to go with it."

As much as they enjoyed Victor's company, Gloria and Pablo were glad when his bodyguards come back to get Haya in late January. It was the end of the warm season and there was much to do on the ranch, so their days were busy. Paul liked the work and he liked spending the quiet evenings alone with Gloria. They talked about everything under the sun except two things. One was the war and the other was the subject of marriage. Pablo wondered why Gloria was reluctant to move ahead with their plans, but he held his tongue. Then there came a time he was glad for her restraint,

It was in August that two things happened that touched Paul deeply. The first came early in the month when two atomic bombs were dropped and Japan surrendered. "Good God!" he declared. "Can you believe it? One bomb carried by a single airplane can destroy a major city. A quarter of a million people were killed in two explosions! I know it may have saved a lot of lives in the invasion, Japanese and Americans both. But two cities wiped out by two bombs? Think what will happen if this gets into the wrong hands! No one will be safe."

Yet, it was the second thing that shook Paul Radford to the core and turned his world inside out. It came in the form of a letter from Juan Calderón. The old padre was brief and to the point.

My dearest Pablo,

Thank you so much for your letters over the last months. They have

brought a world of grace to this old man's heart. It is good to hear your recovery goes well and I know that the presence of the lovely Gloria has played a large part in this. I know she has been a real gift of grace to you, just as you have to me.

I write to give you news you must have. I do so in fear and trembling, for I know you will find it troubling. Nor do I know how to counsel you. I am at a loss to know what to say.

To grasp the nettle firmly, Rosario's husband, Sergeant Juan Gomez was shot and killed two weeks ago in a police raid on smugglers near Pisco. His captain, Carlos Molina, was also gravely wounded, but he is recovering. I have traveled to Lima to visit him in the hospital and we share the same concern. What is to become of Rosario and her children? Or, to put it more personally, what is to become of Azúl, your daughter?

I am not sure how things stand between you and Gloria, Pablo. Nor do I want to add to your burdens. Would you be willing to support Rosario and her children, to give them enough money that they can live a decent life? I know little Juanito is not your child, but he is Azúl's brother. Juan was the one who supported his large family and I know that they cannot afford to feed three more mouths. God only know what they will do now that Juan is no longer there to help. So I ask in the name of the One whom I hold most dear. Can you help, Pablo? Please let me know soon.

With all the love I have for you,
Juan Calderón

When Paul finished the letter, he sat there, stunned by the news. Gloria, who had been looking through the rest of the mail, sensed something and looked up. "Pablo!" she cried. "What's happened?"

Dumbly, Paul handed her the letter. Gloria read it through quickly, then read it through again. "You can afford to help them, Pablo. You have plenty of money and if you don't, I do."

"Money is not the problem," he replied softly. "There's plenty of money."

"Then what's...." Gloria began. "Oh."

Paul sighed and looked at her. "That's right. The problem is Azúl. The problem is that I am her father. I want to be part of her life."

"I don't think Azúl is the problem," Gloria replied with tears in her eyes. "We could take a place in Lima and you could be a large part of her life. There is plenty of money for that, too. The problem is Rosario, isn't it? You still love her."

Paul sighed again. "The problem is that I love you, too, Gloria. The problem is that I always thought of Rosario as my wife, even though she married Juan Gomez. I was angry at the choice she had to make, but not at her, and I never stopped loving her."

"Then you need to go to her. You need to be with her. I know how it is to be widowed. Thank God my children were almost grown and I had Rita and Alonzo to help. But that is where you belong, Pablo, with your wife and child. It cuts my heart to say it, but that's the truth."

When Paul tried to argue, Gloria laid a gently hand on his lips. "No, Pablo. I'm right and you know it. We have had a wonderful affair, but that's what it was, a love affair. Now it's over."

"Please, Gloria, I don't want to get ahead of ourselves. Rosario may not want me in their lives. Juan's family may not, either."

Gloria looked at him with tears in her eyes. "Do you really believe that, Pablo?" Seeing the answer in his eyes, she nodded. "You place is with your family."

"I don't want to leave you, Gloria. I love you. I want you in my life, to spend whatever time I have left with you."

"So you're going to make me kick you out?" There was steel in her voice. "I can, you know. Even loving you the way I do."

"Please, Gloria. I need time to think this over."

"I think you already have. You were very sad the last time you came back from Lima. You saw Rosario and Azúl, didn't you?"

"I said goodbye to her, too. I knew Azúl might seek me out later, but I said goodbye to Rosario. I intended never to go back. That's why I was sad. How could I not be?"

Gloria nodded and sighed. "Well, beloved, I think you're wrong but you need to discover that for yourself. You need to think this through and you need to go to Lima and see your family. I mean that. Right now you need to write Father Juan and tell him you will help with the money."

Tears were streaming down Gloria's face as she said this and

Pablo took her in his arms. Then he led her to the room they shared and made love with her, gently and quietly. When they were resting, Gloria looked at him and said, "You will always be welcome in my home and in my bed, Pablo. It doesn't matter what you decide. You will always be welcome." Then she gave him a stern look. "Now go write that letter. Send it with a bank draft."

Ten days later Father Juan Calderón was startled to see Pablo standing on the stoop when he went to answer the rectory door. He was even more startled at the size of the two bank drafts Pablo showed him. One was for Rosario and her children, and the other was for Juan Gomez's extended family. When Alicia came to see who was calling, she greeted Pablo warmly but was reluctant to take the thick envelope he held out to her. "This is for you and Father Juan," Paul told her. "I would give it to him, but he forgets to wind the clock." Two days later, Pablo left for Lima.

Down the Years

17 Like human lives, a story has a beginning, a middle, and an end. Yet human lives are like stones dropped in a still pond. Ripples move out from the point of impact, and the decisions people make set other things in motion.

Two months after he received Father Juan's letter, Paul Radford married Rosario. He began living with his new family in Lima, where he bought a large home. His natural daughter, Azúl never called him Papa. She called him El Parejo, the bird, and this was quickly shortened to Parejo. Her brother Juanito, Juan Gomez's child, never knew any father but Pablo. Yet he, too, called his dad Parejo, even though he referred to him as his father. Rosario tried to correct this but Pablo discouraged her. "We will have lots of other things to be concerned with, *dulce*," he told her.

To keep himself from going stale, Pablo presented his credentials to the local university and was given a position as a guest lecturer in geology. There was no one in the country who knew more about the geology of the Andes and he was a popular teacher, often taking groups of students into the mountains to learn their country first hand. It was not long before the university offered him a permanent position with a small stipend and he repaid them with numerous articles in scientific journals in both Spanish and English.

A year after he moved to Lima, Father Juan suffered a stroke that left him unable to continue as a priest. At Pablo's insistence, he and Alicia moved into the house, and Pico was a frequent visitor. There was a large fenced back yard where the two women grew an abundant garden of herbs and ornamentals, and they shared both the housework and the care of Juan Calderón. When he died a year later, Paul insisted that Alicia remain as a member of the family and Pico moved in with her.

A third child was born to Pablo and Rosario a few months after the padre died and Rosario insisted he be named after his father. Pablo's mother and father flew down from Texas for the first time, and they were embraced and overwhelmed by Pablo's extended family. As he thought she would be, his mother was delighted with all her grandchildren. Although she didn't quite understand the timing, she accepted things as they were and would have been happy to stay longer.

Paul's father took him aside at one point to ask if he ever intended to return to the United States. "There's nothing for me there, Dad," Paul answered. "Perú has become my home and I wouldn't really fit in there. I won't inflict Texas on my children."

"This is a foreign country," the senior Radford tried to protest, but Paul shook his head.

"I'm well known here," Paul said. "I'm politically connected with the movers and shakers and exciting things are happening here."

What Pablo didn't add was that he had also become known as the best authority on the indigenous people of the jungle. Every year he took a trip over the Andes and into the jungle with a fat young burro, and every year he came back without it. While he was there, normally for several weeks, he continued the work of Juan Calderón, baptizing the children and giving his personal blessing over the native marriages.

Once a year, normally in the cold season, Pablo also visited Gloria at her ranch near Puno for a couple of weeks. When he did, he took his family along, and Gloria and Rosario became close friends. Pablo didn't understand exactly how this could be, but he was wise enough not to fix what worked.

The biggest surprise came on their very first visit when Rosario sent him to Gloria's room on the third night they were there. "She needs you," Rosario told him quite simply. "She is expecting you." Then she smiled. "Be good for her."

Captain Carlos Molina retired from police work and married a wealthy woman from Lima a few years after Paul moved there. Her first husband was much older than she and had died of a lingering cancer. Oddly enough, he and Molina's father had been good friends growing up and the captain had visited him often during his illness.

Colonel Jergen Schwartz was able to avoid being sent back to Berlin. He did this by pulling in every political marker he had in return for a posting to Buenos Aires. He was able to make himself useful to the Nazis fleeing to Argentina during the fall of the Third Reich and became a prominent member of the German expatriate community there. Like many of his contemporaries, he died of old age, having successfully published his memoirs.

Dieter Braun ended up in Argentina, too. Unknown to him, Brazil had declared war against the Axis in 1942 and he was almost shot as a spy. Through an unlikely set of circumstances, he was able to escape not only with his life but also with three kilos of pure cocaine. Landing in Buenos Airies without papers, he identified himself as a Nazi party member to a sympathetic immigration official and was put in touch with the Nazi community there. He became a popular supplier of drugs for that community and there was poetic justice in his death in a car crash three years later. The driver of the car that struck Dieter was one of his best customers and was stoned on Dieter's product when he killed him.

Michael O'Leary served the Special Action Group well during the remainder of the war. He became quite close with Jaques Paul, and when the Agency was chartered by Congress in 1946, he became Jacque's first executive officer. He also was the first instructor in the Agency's agent training program and served in that capacity until his death in a light plane crash in 1964.

Jacques Paul became a frequent guest of Gloria Lopez after Pablo moved to Lima. At the end of the war he was instrumental in the evolution of the Special Action Group into what became known as the Agency and successfully lobbied for a Congressional charter in 1946. Through his efforts, the Agency was able to remain independent from other intelligence agencies including the NSA and the CIA. He remained the head of the Agency until his death from cancer not long after 9/11.

Paul Radford never returned to the United States after the war except to bury his parents after they both died in a car crash in 1955. He was surprised to learn that he was the heir to a substantial fortune and the executor of their estates. This he turned over to an attorney and returned to Peru.

Like Jaques Paul, Pablo lived to be a very old man who was active until shortly before he died at his home in Lima, surrounded by his children and grandchildren. He was preceded in death by his beloved Rosario. He never remarried.